SEPARATION ANXIETY

SEPARATION ANXIETY

LAURA ZIGMAN

THORNDIKE PRESS
A part of Gale, a Cengage Company

LIBRARY OF CONGRESS CIP DATA ON FILE.
CATALOGUING IN PUBLICATION FOR THIS BOOK
IS AVAILABLE FROM THE LIBRARY OF CONGRESS

ISBN-13: 978-1-4328-8045-3 (hardcover alk. paper)

Published in 2020 by arrangement with Ecco, an imprint of
HarperCollins Publishers

Printed in Mexico
Print Number: 01   Print Year: 2020

*For my family: Brendan, Ben, and Lady.
And for Lisa Bonchek Adams, who really
should still be here.*

There may be situations, depending on your circumstances and the nature of the disaster, when it's simply best to stay where you are and avoid any uncertainty outside by "sheltering in place."

— U.S. Department of
Homeland Security website

If it was once a stigma when you divorced, today the new shame is choosing to stay when you can leave.

— Esther Perel,
Where Should We Begin?

CONTENTS

■ ■ ■ ■

Part One:
Sheltering
in Place

■ ■ ■ ■

THE SLING

I start wearing the family dog, a mini-sheltie, a little Lassie, in an unbleached cotton baby sling across the front of my body like a messenger bag, a few weeks shy of fall. Until I slip the sling over my head and feel a strange surge of relief run through me, a liquid narcotic from an unknown source, there's nothing special about the day. It's no one's birthday, it's not the anniversary of someone's death or a reminder of an ancient career milestone, long gone and unsurpassed. Nothing in particular is reminding me more than usual of life's quick passage of random moments, some good, some not so good, some very very bad, disappearing like train cars into the vanishing point of a distant horizon. It's just an opaque Thursday in late August, a month before New England is ready to give up the thick haze of summer, a day I randomly pick to try to radically de-clutter the basement using a book everyone is swearing by. The ruthless purging of possessions to the point of self-erasure is what I'm after. I already feel invisible; why not go all the way?

I'm fifty when I head down to the basement. My son is thirteen. He no longer wears matching pajamas or explains the virtues of Buttermilk Eggo waffles compared to Homestyle, or holds my hand when we cross the street or walk through a supermarket. He no longer begs for LEGOs, pulling me into the store at the mall, pointing at all the boxes, jewels on the shelves, gifts waiting to be given.

It's hard for me to believe those moments ever happened; that I was ever in the middle of all that love, and time, and possibility, and that now I'm not. Life eventually takes away everyone and everything we love and leaves us bereft. Is that its sad lesson? That's the only explanation I have for why I now wear the dog; my version of magical thinking: little tiny cracks are forming inside me every day and only the dog is keeping me from coming apart completely.

Like most of the mistakes I've made — wearing a three-piece brown corduroy "suit" (jacket, vest, and skirt) for my bat mitzvah instead of a dress; refusing to take remedial

SAT classes after repeatedly failing to crack 500 on either the verbal or math sections; telling people I don't like carrots and squash and other orange vegetables instead of just lying like a normal person and saying I'm allergic to them; marrying Gary instead of someone else or maybe not getting married at all — to name only a few — there are so many — I consider wearing the dog to be something that happens "by accident."

I don't go down to the basement that day with the intention of looking for the sling a vegetarian friend gave me years ago when Teddy was born that I'd mocked but never used. Back then, I couldn't imagine "wearing" my newborn all day across my chest in what looked like a giant diaper. Teddy had been ten pounds at birth. Hadn't I "worn" him long enough? The front carrier, a BabyBjörn, another gift, was too complicated — so many straps; so many clasps — but the sling seemed even worse. Uncomfortable and unfashionable. Ridiculous, even. I'd taken it out of its eco-friendly burlap sack long enough to roll my eyes at it before repacking it and shoving it into the back of a drawer. Eventually it ended up in one of the big plastic containers from Teddy's babyhood marked SAVE in extra thick black Sharpie on a jagged piece of

15

masking tape. All caps, in case there was ever any question.

The day I descend the stairs I have the de-cluttering book's central question in my head — whether the objects in my basement give me joy or not — to determine whether they should be kept or thrown away. So little gives me joy now that I'm afraid I'll get rid of every single thing I've ever owned and end up with nothing. Which isn't necessarily a bad thing. Feeling empty only makes me want to be emptier. But within minutes of pawing through the first big plastic box, full of Teddy's old clothes, I find neatly folded pajamas and jerseys and pants, all impossibly tiny, all heartbreakingly meaningful: the French-striped newborn-onesie we'd brought him home in; the tiger shirt he vomited all over at four months but that I managed to wash in time so it didn't stain; his first pair of dinosaur pajamas from when he was three; his last pair of Batman underwear from when he was five. Each item I unfold and refold crushes me. Each time that I ask myself the book's central question, my answer is always the same: these used to give me joy but don't anymore, because they only remind me of what isn't anymore.

I'm into semantics now, but I don't have

the book itself — I was too cheap to buy it and couldn't square the internal conflict between acquiring a possession (the book) for the express purpose of clearing away possessions — to clarify whether, based on the past/present issue, I should keep or purge the things that once gave me joy but now only make me want to stab my eyes out. I blink at the sea of plastic containers, at all the buried treasure — all the best years — babyhood, toddlerhood, the preschool and elementary school years — everything before middle school — forever gone. I drop to my knees then, onto the damp musty cement floor, my hands still touching the clothes, and weep — a messy untidy unjoyful kind of weeping. I wish I could purge myself of my self.

At some point I dig around in one of the boxes for an old burp cloth to wipe my nose with. And that's when I pull out the burlap sack with the unused sling in it. Like I said, it happens by accident.

The sight of the sling now doesn't make me think about women in Birkenstocks and hemp pants floating through organic produce aisles with their newborns. This time, the sight of that empty sling gives me joy. It makes me want to pick it up, and hug it, and marry it. And fill it. With something.

■ ■ ■ ■

And so, it starts slowly. One minute I'm hugging and wiping my nose with the old baby sling; the next minute I'm slipping the sling over my head, marveling at the economy of its simple design: no straps, no clasps, no ties or buckles. How many of life's paths are forged this way — one small unplanned step toward, and away from, something else unknown? At some point I stand up. The sling hangs down below my hips. I feel like Björk at the Oscars wearing that swan.

I take a step, then another step, wondering the whole time why I so stupidly never used the sling when I'd had the chance. All that missed opportunity for human closeness. I snap the lids back onto the big plastic boxes of Teddy's childhood and head upstairs, the fabric swinging back and forth across my abdomen as I go. It's annoying but not a deal breaker. I know I'll get used to it.

Once upstairs, it doesn't take long before I wonder what it would feel like to carry something in the sling. Something soft but heavy. Something baby-like. It's been so long.

I scan the kitchen; consider first a clean and folded bath towel at the top of the laundry basket that could be molded into a baby-like rectangle; then a red cabbage on the counter waiting to be sliced and braised with chicken for dinner that could be the baby-head; then a few cans of tomatoes from the pantry that could be thrown in for some baby-weight. But none of these things feels right; none has the right heft; none gives me the feeling I crave of having something next to my body that is alive and childlike, something that wants to be cradled constantly and carried everywhere. Or could be convinced to want that.

So maybe that's when the dog walks into the kitchen. Or maybe it's later, when the dog is sleeping on the floor next to the couch, her paws twitching every few seconds and her face, in repose, looking so peaceful and calm — a rare thing for a sheltie, whose mission in life is to herd, to boss, to control — that it first occurs to me. I can't remember. Does it matter? At some point, as the baby-simulating items go in and out of the sling, I raise an eyebrow and think: *What about the dog?* And then: *What* <u>about</u> *the dog?*

Desire blinds me. I get down on the floor and tug on her collar. And just like that, as her reluctant paws slide along the floor like a Tom and Jerry cartoon sequence, everything changes.

At first, I only wear the dog inside the house, when no one else is home. It seems harmless enough. An improvised self-care remedy that instantly works better than any psycho-pharmaceutical or baked good ever has. When school starts again right after Labor Day, I drive Teddy in the morning, then come home and pace, avoiding the stacks of bills and my work. But I can't ignore the dog. I eye her, asleep peacefully on the floor — and try to resist — really, I do — I have a second cup of coffee, check my email and Facebook and Twitter and Instagram accounts twenty more times, knock out a few rounds of Words with Friends, try to block out the awful things the government is now doing daily. But I always give in, defeated. There is no fighting the need to take comfort in whatever form is available. I walk slowly across the house to the bedroom, kneel down in front of the white IKEA bureau that had caused Gary and me to fight so bitterly years earlier while putting it together — Gary had actually accused me of "withholding directions" to its assembly, as if I wouldn't have done anything to cut our agony by even a nanosecond if I could have, not prolong it — and open the drawer that had once been just for sweaters I never wear anymore. The mere act of reaching blindly for the sling behind all my moth-eaten cashmere always brings instant relief.

Sure, I feel like a perv when I slip the sling over my head and stalk the dog around the room — catching her in a position where she can be picked up quickly and smoothly, like a weight lifter's clean-and-jerk lift, before rolling over on her back, thinking it's some kind of bonus playtime, is always a challenge. Especially when it takes three or four times before I can grab her in a surprise attack and maneuver her inside, always getting dog hair in my mouth and enduring a moment when I fear I might drop her or fall over before finding the sweet spot of the heavy sling on my lower stomach and hip.

Charlotte isn't light — twenty pounds on a good day — and she is unwieldy sometimes, like when she wants to get out for no reason other than the fact that she's a normal dog who just wants to be free and her paws scratch against the fabric, even though I always make sure she can see and breathe just fine in there. I usually throw in one of those disgusting dried bull penises sold in pet stores as a chew snack — a bully stick — as a bribe. I know it's not fair for the dog to endure my obsession without there being something in it for her, too, so I always have plenty of treats on hand to get her in the sling and keep things fun.

It doesn't take long for the dog to like it. To look forward to it. I know that might sound like wishful thinking or projection on my part, but who's to say that even if I *am* projecting that the dog *doesn't* actually like it in there? The two ideas aren't necessarily mutually exclusive. I might be floridly demented in thinking the dog likes being carried around in a giant diaper, but the dog might really like it in there. Because seriously, what's not to like? It's warm, there are snacks, and for a few hours every day she doesn't have to walk or sniff or chase or make any decisions of her own. It's like a vacation, a stress-free state of suspended animation that I sometimes wish I could replicate for myself.

Those hours when the dog is in the sling are restorative for me. Like a new drug, it's helping me taper off an old one, overlapping and masking the side effects of withdrawal. By which I mean, wearing Charlotte is helping me get through the end of Teddy's childhood. By which I mean, instead of turning to my husband with that over-whelming sadness and longing, I've turned to our dog.

No wonder we're separated.

WELL/ER

I wear the dog around the house while I do my "content-generating" work, writing short engagingly shallow online posts for Well/er, a health and happiness website run by a small local startup with national aspirations whose management team has a median dude-age of twenty-four. Well/er believes in tiny incremental gains in physical and emotional wellness (hence *Well/er,* not *Well*), instead of big ambitious ones: DOING JUST ENOUGH IS ENOUGH TO CHANGE YOUR LIFE is the website's actual tagline. As a fundamentally lazy person myself, I can't say I disagree: sometimes less *is* more.

There's a bank of article ideas and suggested due dates on the content-management system (CMS), as well as an updated list of timely topics that I can pick from every morning — maintained and sent out by Eden, the content manager who is based in Atlanta and whose avatar is a blue female Avatar from the movie *Avatar,* even though people refer to Eden with male pronouns in email chains. Whatever. We're occasionally supposed to "meet" via Google Chat or Skype, depending on which platform has working sound or video, but since I started a year ago our team Skype calls have mostly been without video. Which is fine with me — I'd rather not remind people of how old I am if I don't have to, which is the unfortunate effect that staring at my turkey neck on a Skype or Google Chat call — and the occasional and deeply humiliating interruption of my AOL *"You've got mail!"* alert — has on people. I'm certain that the second the call is over all the twenty-year-olds whisper sweetly among themselves about how I remind them of their moms. I'm certain because that actually happened once before we all got disconnected.

As a contractor paid by the piece, I'm expected to submit three to four "articles" a day, each one no more than three hundred to four hundred words, written in short paragraphs and in a snappy style, nothing too taxing for our attention-span-challenged readers, but always including links to "scientific" "studies" that back up whatever dubious point I'm supposed to be making, even if the research sounds made up to me. People love neuroscience now, how it can support almost every single bad habit and instinct we have, whether it's for spending too much money (money buys happiness if you spend it on experiences instead of things) or earning less money than you need to (income has a positive impact on happiness, but anything over $75,000 is only mood gravy), or inherent laziness (tiny changes in habits are better and easier to maintain than big changes). I'm not sure any of this is true. In the years when I earned a fair amount of money, it made me quite happy actually, no matter what I spent it on.

But that was a long time ago, when a picture book I wrote, *There's a Bird on Your Head,* an embrace-your-weirdness manifesto, became a surprise cult classic and then an animated PBS television series. I'd never imagined, as an art history major in college and then in the early part of my career when I was working for Black Bear Books, the children's book division of a big New York publisher, that I would ever earn that much. During those good years, everyone told me I would go from success to success, that money and opportunity would keep rolling in. But they didn't. Life is like that. It's a series of advancements and regressions, the same tide, coming and going, giving and taking away. A secret part of me still believes the current will come back in after all these dry years. But the bigger part wakes up in the middle of the night wondering what will become of the four of us — Gary, Teddy, Charlotte, and me — if it doesn't.

"Content-generation," the work I do now, feels like another regression, another failure, but Gary and I aren't getting any younger and there are bills to pay, so I pursue it with nothing short of desperation. *Doing just enough is enough,* I tell myself when I pick a topic, knock out a few glib paragraphs, search for the perfect gauzy stock photo of a piece of avocado toast or the silhouette of a silver-haired forty-year-old doing yoga on a wood deck at sunset, then pause to come up with a suggested click-bait headline before hitting "send" and starting another. Magic is everywhere, even in content-generation, like when fabric clogs on a foot model make the perfect visual point for your *"Does working at home make you less attractive?"* post. Maybe this new career will magically lead me somewhere, to the next step in my proverbial journey, to a pot of gold at the end of a nonexistent rainbow.

It's the fantasy of being saved that keeps me going.

The question of where to put my laptop since my lap is now occupied by the dog is an adjustment at first, until I realize that I don't actually have to have the dog *on* my lap — Charlotte can be half on my hip and half on the bed. This isn't an Olympic sport, after all. There are no rules, no mandatory movements or positions, no points taken off for bad form. I can make it up as I go along, just like I do with my work. *"Are dogs the ultimate antidepressant?" "Can dogs ease empty-nester heartache?"* Anything is possible with a well-placed question mark and an endless supply of dubious functional MRI conclusions available from a simple Google search. Any thought, question, or half-baked idea of mine can become a Well/er piece.

About an hour before it's time to pick Teddy up from school and before Gary gets home from work, I take Charlotte off, hide the sling in the middle drawer, and bring her out to do all the things a normal dog should be allowed to do in the course of a normal dog-day — including a long walk — slingless, on and off the leash, in the neighborhood or around the reservoir that we drive to, where she gets to play and socialize with other dogs. Once home, she finds a place to nap on the floor or on the bed or on the couch before I leave. The afternoons and evenings pass easily, usually — laundry, cooking, a little more content-generation distracting me from missing the weight around my neck, against my hip, balancing my laptop next to that warm cotton sack of dog fur.

Eventually, though, the hours in between sling-time drag, and I find myself wanting, then needing, to wear the dog like a baby all the time. Who wouldn't? But need leads to impulsivity, and impulsivity is how accidents happen.

It doesn't take long for my secret to get discovered. A few weeks after I start wearing the dog, right after school starts, I get sloppy and lose track of time. I forget that every third Tuesday Gary leaves work as a part-time snackologist at a large communal work space near MIT — managing the infinite selection of organic non-GMO snacks and beverages for the hordes of startup teams and independent contractors half our age paying for daily shared office space — and races home, eager to do a few one-hits out the upstairs bathroom window hours before Teddy gets back from school and while I am usually still out running errands. That September afternoon, as I lumber from refrigerator to sink with the sling, fixing myself and the dog a little snack — cheddar cheese cubes and a few stale Fritos, our favorite — Gary suddenly appears in the kitchen. Tall and rangy and fit, he is wearing his mandatory company black fleece zip-up vest with the WORK IT TOGETHER (WIT) logo over the left breast, black jeans, and black T-shirt, a uniform he hates. With his still-full head of longish salt-and-pepper hair and rimless round Lennon glasses, he looks like an architect or designer, not an underemployed former musician trying to fit into a new corporate culture to help make ends meet.

When I see him I stop short. How will I explain why our dog's slender pointy-snouted head is poking out of a diaper across my chest? I look down at the sling as if I'm as surprised as Gary to find it hanging there. "I was just cleaning out the basement," I say, implying the basement cleaning was today, not almost a month earlier. I reach into the bag for another handful of corn chips but don't eat them. I hadn't planned on being discovered. I don't have my story down yet. But as freaked out as I am, I'm actually relieved. It's time. I'm tired of having a secret, of having to pretend that everything's fine. This is who I am now in middle age — lost and confused and shifting constantly between my own world and the real world. If the dog is helping me survive these dark days, then good for me. I shouldn't be ashamed. In fact, I should be applauded for finding a harmless, nonalcoholic, nonnarcotic, noncannabinoid solution to my pain. (Right?)

Gary leans forward an inch or two, waiting for the rest of my explanation, which is not forthcoming. "*And . . .* the sling just jumped out and demanded to be worn?" He looks at me like I could not possibly be weirder, like I have a bird on my head.

I slip a corn chip into the sling, then nod at him above the sound of the dog's crunching, a sound I love almost as much as I love the sound of Teddy crunching Cheez-Its or Goldfish. "Actually, that's pretty much exactly what happened."

His eyes dart over to the freezer. "You didn't eat any cookies, did you?"

"*Pot* cookies?" Sensing an opening, an opportunity to divert attention from my sling-problem to his pot-smoking problem, which started innocently enough a few years ago as a medically prescribed solution for extreme anxiety but has, in the past few months, gotten completely out of hand, I shake my head slowly. "Seriously. You can't keep pot cookies around: we have an actual teenager in the house."

He opens the freezer, finds what he's looking for — a small tinfoil square in a nondescript Ziploc bag marked DOGGIE SNACKS — then leans back against the counter. He looks at the dog and then at me, his relief at finding his stash safe already turning to disappointment: If pot cookies aren't the reason for my bizarre behavior, then what is?

"So, how long have you been carrying her around like a baby?"

I'm about to lie but again, we're so beyond that now that I can't come up with a reason why I should bother. We're separated. Sort of. Technically. None of this is his business. I have nothing to lose. In fact, the more estranged we are, the easier it will be when we can afford to actually split up.

"A few days. A week. Maybe more. Does it matter?"

"Wow," he says, then shakes his head. "That's sad."

I straighten, feel my chin jut out and up. I might be an increasingly strange, increasingly invisible middle-aged woman, hiding an ever-expanding perimenopausal body in boxy sweaters and boyfriend jeans, but clearly I'm not the only one who is struggling. "Said the dude who vapes one-hits out the window and eats pot cookies."

"They're called *edibles* now," he says, patting the dog's head inside the sling and then, with affection, mine, too, on his way to the basement.

Wearing the dog is ridiculous. An act of desperation. I know this. I know that the strain of a twenty-pound animal hanging around my neck in a cloth sling, no matter how well constructed or convincingly it guarantees to "distribute weight and swing evenly on the shoulder, back, and hip," isn't good for me, physically or mentally; I know that it will become a bad habit I'll come to love and then have to give up, like cigarettes, like falling for a married man. *No good will ever come from this; this will never end well.* Going in, I know I'm doomed.

But there is the loneliness. The aloneness. How I startle awake in the dark, panicked, full of dread, floating on the night sea on a tiny raft surrounded by all that vast blackness. I see myself from above. The light from the moon guides me nowhere. I'm connected to nothing and no one, lost, and certain only that I'm destined to die broke and alone from one of the swift lethal cancers that took my parents in their later years, without getting another chance to turn things around. Even before Gary starts sleeping in the snoring room, when the marriage already feels like a suffocation, his florid debilitating anxiety disorder having turned my desire into maternal concern years ago, I wake like that, worried about the short run, the now, the present: *How will I get from this moment to that moment? Where is the vine that will swing me to the other side?*

My vine, as it happens, has appeared in the form of a sling. All I can do is hope that it is strong enough to hold me.

DRIVING TEDDY

It's six minutes to morning meeting and the tapping of the peace gong, and of course we're late. I hustle Teddy — almost taller than me, a bedhead of brown curls, and giant sneakers still untied — into the car on this sharply bright October morning, then tear down the street, looking like a Jules Feiffer sketch of modern frantic parenthood with my giant hair and furrowed worrybrow behind the wheel. I'm going to have to explain and apologize to Mr. Noah and his aggressively annoying Montessori man bun that it's my fault, not Teddy's, for being tardy on this day, especially on this day. The school seemed perfect for Teddy when he'd started in second grade after a few disastrous years at the nearby public school, but a month into seventh grade — in their newly formed middle school, only in its second year with none of the kinks worked out — it doesn't seem to be the best place for him now.

Even though we're late, I can't help indulging in my daily habit on the drive to school: the Inventory of Other Houses, when I ogle all the well-maintained homes along our route that belong to other people. Ours, the one that the *Bird* book and series bought but can barely maintain, with its peeling shingles and broken gutters, is becoming the shabbiest on the block.

Five minutes to morning meeting and the tapping of the peace gong.

When Gary and I first moved to Cambridge, still in our late thirties with Teddy about to be born, full of stupid youthful optimism, fantasies of block parties and progressive dinners and neighborhood yard sales played in my head. I wanted community, and connection, and a sense of belonging. I wanted to carve pumpkins and drink eggnog and complain about shoveling snow, then extol the virtues of the miraculous New England spring — daffodils and tulips and those tiny blue flowers I'd always loved but had never known the name of pushing up through the barely thawed earth — with everyone. Not anymore. That openness is long gone. I've moved from outgoing young mother and children's book writer to invisible middle-aged content-generator and dog-wearer. An irreversible trajectory, I'm sure of it. If only I could have squeezed out another book before writer's block set in, Gary and I would have enough money to separate like normal couples instead of having to live in the same house and pretend for Teddy's sake.

Four minutes to morning meeting and the tapping of the peace gong.

I look at Teddy sitting next to me in the front passenger seat — because he is old enough to sit there now — I can't remember the last time he sat in the back — and wonder again as I so often have since the transparency of childhood and boyhood gave way to this — this brutal teenage opacity — what he is thinking. I don't ask anymore and he never tells me. My eyes leave the road for a second or two to search the flat surface of his profile, but it's like a stone skimming water. He gives up nothing. Every day I try to square the fact that I don't know, can't know, will never again know everything crossing his mind the minute it crosses it the way I used to because he used to tell me — *trains, dinosaurs, baseball, LEGOs, skateboards, chicken, pizza, chips* — but doesn't anymore. Sometimes even the dog isn't enough to keep those molecules from coming apart.

37

Three minutes to morning meeting and the tapping of the peace gong.

Steering around parked cars and oncoming traffic, the inventory continues: I compare shingles and shutters and lawns and fences to our disintegrating ones. That morning I'm especially tweaked by an ever-expanding three-story addition going up in the back of an already massive turreted single-family Victorian. I brake and lift my sunglasses in an exaggerated slow-motion drive-by of shock and awe, watching the workmen come in and out of their parked trucks with windows and casings and boxes of tiles and long planks of lumber. So much wood; so many trees sacrificed for state-of-the-art kitchens and mudrooms and laundry rooms and separate marital snoring rooms. If we weren't so late already, I would probably lean out the window and take a photo, then post it with a snarky caption on one or all of my social media accounts. I'm sure that the people moving in, whoever they are, still sleep in the same room, in the same bed; still earn livings and have savings; still plan for the future the way normal people do, though I know that my childish presumptions could be wrong: you never know what peoples' lives are really like.

Two minutes to morning meeting and the

tapping of the peace gong.

I force myself to stop the inventory and focus instead on our destination: I tell myself that it's just middle school, just seventh grade, taught by a leftover hippie dude full of childlike wonder who spends too much time sculpting his facial hair. But it's the day I'm scheduled to talk to Teddy's class about writing, answering some of Mr. Noah's questions about what it's like to make books (fun to write and draw them; less fun to publish and promote them): how cool it was to have an animated series based on one of my books (extremely cool); how old I was when I first started writing any-thing (sixth grade); what my favorite color, food, and animal is (black, coffee, dogs).

One minute to morning meeting and the tapping of the peace gong.

I know Teddy had hoped I'd cancel, that something else would come up at the very last second the way it used to when he was small — the calls from my mother when she was out of pain medication; from my father when he mixed up night and day again; when it was time for hospice for both of them. He'd gotten used to plans changing suddenly; from the bottom dropping out; from occasionally being picked up by some-one else's parents and eating at another

39

family's dinner table. He'd always looked so pained when I'd had to leave him, which wasn't actually that often, since I took him almost everywhere with me, like I do now with the dog — and since working from home allowed us to spend a lot of time together. Then at some point he came to like it: being somewhere else. The relief of it. I think of all that he'd seen those years before he was even ten: the hospital beds, the infusion rooms, the home nurses coming and going from my parents' house while I tried to distract him with bigger and bigger LEGO sets — and I wish again that we could get a do-over for that whole phase of his life. I barely remember going to the children's museum or the science museum with him those years, but I can remember every hospital cafeteria and which one had the best chicken nuggets or chicken patty sandwiches as if it were yesterday. It hardly seems fair, so much precious time lost.

One minute past morning meeting and the tapping of the peace gong.

"I know. You're dying that I'm coming in today," I say, elbowing him. I keep my eyes on the road, desperate for the laugh track from the old days of his boyhood, but as always now there is just silence, then a protracted sigh with a word at the end:

"Mommmmm."

I push past the awkwardness, even though I know that trying too hard and showing my desperation to stay relevant will only make things worse. "But that's the deal with your school: parents help out." His eye-roll doesn't stop me. "It's a *cooperative independent school*" — I say the words slowly, because I can't take my hands off the wheel to pump my usual air quotes — "so when a teacher asks you to come in and teach their class for them because they're too lazy to," I add, unable to stop myself from editorializing, "you're not supposed to say no."

"Mr. Noah isn't too lazy to teach."

I forget how loyal he is, how kind and generous to others he's always been. He's never had a mean bone in his body, and Gary and I have always marveled at how much better and more evolved a person he is than we are; how different he is from us. Was it the luck of genetics and biology? More engaged parenting than we'd had? Conscious differentiation on his part? Gary always says that we could learn from him, but we never do, instead just blurting things out without thinking. Like now.

"You're right. It's not laziness. He just needs extra time to manscape his goatee."

"Mom. *Stop.*" He looks at me finally. He

is all Gary, with his perfect ears and straight nose and blue eyes, though I know the lips and chin and, sadly, the crowded teeth, which will need straightening, are mine. "You don't have to come, you know. Jackson's mom and Gavin's mom and Robert's mom couldn't come. I can just say you're too busy. It's no big deal." He looks out the window again, away from me to somewhere else.

I blink and feel the sudden sting of tears. "But I *want* to come." The sentence is a repentant whisper that leaves me confused: Why, when I miss my little boy so much, am I pushing away what's left of him? "Dude. I was just kidding." I'm begging now. Like plate tectonics, something inside me is finally cracking and shifting. Melting. "I want to come. I really do."

He shrugs. "Are you bringing the dog?"

"I have to," I say, as if I'm explaining why I have to drag an oxygen machine in with me, that my survival depends on it. "It'll be worse if I don't bring her." I look down at my lap, in the space between my body and the steering wheel and the harness strap of the seat belt, and see the top of the dog's head inside the sling. It's then that I notice all the dog hair on my black sweater and wish I'd thought to run a lint brush over myself before leaving the house on such an important morning.

"It's worse for me if you do."

"I know. I'm sorry. But I can't help it right now."

He shrugs again — *whatever* — and just like that we're finally at the school, pulling into the no-parking zone and leaving the car in front of the MORNINGSIDE MONTESSORI: WHERE PEACE RULES mosaic sign, the one we helped make one chilly late-October afternoon during the school's annual Harvest Day, when Teddy still sat in the backseat and had long drummer hair and wore Led Zeppelin T-shirts and kissed me hello and goodbye without restraint or shame.

And then, as if we aren't three minutes late for morning meeting and the tapping of the peace gong, I take my hands off the wheel and touch his head, the one without a bird on it, and then his hair, pretending to fix it. To my astonishment he lets me and doesn't pull away, and for a brief moment before we leave the car and race into the school where I know I will embarrass him terribly, we are who we used to be, before the world as we knew it changed.

MORNING MEETING

In the school's multipurpose multiage room, Mr. Noah's voice, very community-theater-director, rises above the low roar of the hundred or so K-6 children burning through the unrefined-sugar highs of their organic breakfasts. As head of school, in layers of flowy cotton and wool and his man bun affixed to the top of his head with a single black lacquered chopstick, he moves through the crowd, which includes the handful of middle-schoolers — fewer than fifteen teens who have decided to stay for the school's brand-new seventh and eighth grades instead of switching to a different private school or going back into the public school system. Passing them, he stops to play Kissinger to two boys from the lower school, probably seven years old, or eight, who are fighting over a fuzzy mallet in front of a big bronze disc suspended from the ceiling from what looks like macramé pul-

44

leys. There is pushing, shoving, and fierce fleece-hoodie pulling.

"Boys! Boys! You can't fight over the peace gong! It defeats the whole purpose! *We share here!*" Mr. Noah separates the boys and then, after some whispered diplomacy and with all hands on the mallet, brings them back in. They tap the gong together.

I turn to roll my eyes at Teddy but he is no longer next to me, or right behind me, or wherever he was when we'd rushed from the car into the school. I scan the sea of small heads and hooded jackets, hoping to find him in a group of boys, yelling and laughing and doing something completely idiotic and annoying and un-Montessori-like, but by now I know better. He's become a solitary child — neither academic nor athletic; neither popular nor universally loathed; no longer a tween, but barely a teen. It is an existential purgatory, not knowing who you are and who you will become. Even though I can't see him I know that he is waiting somewhere on the periphery of the faux gymnasium for the unspeakable torture of Bring-Your-Parent-to-School Day to begin: alone, without a friend to confide in or roll his eyes to. My heart balls up like a fist in my chest. No wonder people day-drink.

We'd moved him here to this small private school from public school for second grade, when the fact that he'd entered kindergarten without knowing his letters had reached such a fevered pitch of concern on the school's part that they practically forced us into medicating him for depression. Gary and I would have been happy to agree to that if he'd indeed been depressed, but we both knew what being a sad child looked and felt like, and Teddy wasn't a sad child. Except when he was in school. When he wasn't in school he was full of energy and glee, playing with the boys down the street all day outside and becoming a tiny monster-guitarist at the nearby music school that was run by one of Gary's old friends. But no matter what we told the team of special educators who came together every few months to review Teddy's individualized education program (IEP), and no matter how much I tried to convince them that Gary and I weren't against medication at all — in fact, we were extremely pro-meds ("Between the two of us, we keep most of the big psycho-pharmaceutical companies in business!" I'd joke, until they looked at me like I had a bird on my head) — it never did any good. My explanations sounded like excuses, the kind every middle-aged mother made when she was desperately clinging to her own distorted version of reality. The fact that Teddy might have a minor learning delay and some processing issues — what was now called *executive functioning* — not depression — was never discussed until we applied to Morningside Montessori and an informal diagnosis was made based on the assessments and school progress reports we submitted for admission.

Just as I start to back away from the crowd to look for Teddy in earnest, Mr. Noah begins the school's daily briefing. He claps his hands close to his chest, then mimes for everyone to sit down. "Time for morning meeting, Peace Pals."

In seconds, peace prevails, and there is the soft thud of a room full of little and medium-size bodies dropping to sit on the wooden floor. My eyes fill the way they often do now, at the tiniest moments of grace or beauty, always without warning. I find a wall to lean against, then wipe my nose on the back of my hand, then take a deep cleansing breath to signal to my body and brain that it is time to focus on the News of the Day.

"Our annual intensive all-school deep-dive Autumn Inhabitancy begins soon, which we're very excited about," Mr. Noah says, holding a large photo above his head of a group of people in animal costumes. From where I'm sitting, I think I can make out a cow, a horse, and maybe a moose. "This year, for something new and very different, the People Puppet Theater is coming all the way from Vermont. They'll need room and board for a few weeks, so ask your parents if you can be a host family." He stops to gasp. "I mean, how fun would that be? To have real live People Puppets in your house? Puppets-in-residence! It reminds me of college!" He stops to sigh wistfully. I squint, and though I can't be certain, I think one of the layers of clothing he's wearing — T-shirt, oxford cloth button-down, light-weight quilted down vest, cotton neck-smock — is some kind of bib. "But this morning we're very excited to have Teddy Vogel's mom visiting us for Bring-Your-Parent-or-Grandparent-or-Beloved-Guardian-to-School Day."

Even though I still can't see him, I know that Teddy is horrified at the mention of his name, which is not even really his name, since Vogel is my last name, and Teddy's last name is Flynn, Gary's last name, but the school, irrepressibly progressive, insists on allowing teachers to call children by the mother's surname instead of the father's, even if the names aren't hyphenated, whenever they want to. I can feel myself start to bristle — a school should call a child by their given name, not a politically correct interpretation of what their name could be, right? — when I realize Mr. Noah is coming to the end of his brief parent-intro and that in seconds it will be time for me to get up and speak. I pull out my old dog-eared copy of *Bird* from my bag, the one I used to read from when I still did readings, and pick a few pieces of stray dog hair from my sweater.

". . . so here's Judy Vogel to tell us all about writing children's books!"

I hug the sling as Mr. Noah waves at me to come forward, out of the shadows. When I'm standing next to him, I realize that he is indeed wearing a bib — made from terry cloth, with a little lamb on it. Maybe he wears one first thing in the morning with the preschoolers? He points at the sling.

"Teddy didn't mention there was a new baby!"

"There isn't." I finally find Teddy in the crowd, and as soon as I do I almost wish I hadn't. His face has crumpled into misery. "It's a dog," I whisper.

"A dog-baby! How a*dork*able is that?" he coos, and just as I'm about to start nervous-talking about the dog and how much I love wearing her and how she's helped get me through a difficult time, I watch Teddy sink into the crowd and disappear, like he's fallen backward into a dark lake that has swallowed him up whole. I want more than anything to find him and apologize for embarrassing him, but instead I pull something else out of my bag: a *Bird on Your Head* knit Peruvian-style hat that was part of the official promotional merchandise for the book and animated television series. I take a deep breath and put the hat on over my hair, tucking the long strands behind my ears and letting the multicolor yarn ties fall straight along the sides of my face. Then I step forward to start my presentation.

That's when the doors to the all-purpose room fling open and a teacher runs into the crowd. Her hands form a frantic T — for *time-out.* "We need you upstairs right away, Mr. Noah!" she yells in a panicked screech. "It happened again!"

Mr. Noah turns and stares at her across the sea of student bodies. His mouth drops open into a horrified O. *"Again??"* he says, before chasing her through the crowd and out the doors toward the middle school, his crepe-soled shoes squeaking on the polished wood floor as he flees.

■ ■ ■ ■

The interruption of my "talk" before it even starts proves to be a total buzzkill to the crowd, and to me, and I can't help feeling annoyed that what I assume is nothing more than a clogged toilet or maybe a mouse in one of the middle school classrooms couldn't have waited until I finished. Rattled by the teacher's dramatic entrance and Mr. Noah's even more dramatic departure, I stand there for a few silent seconds with the stupid Peruvian bird hat on my head, staring out at all the children, who are looking at me expectantly. My presentation, if you can even call it that, lasts no more than five minutes — just long enough for me to explain that my book was essentially a "weirdness manifesto" about "embracing difference," and that I'd written it because my mother always used to look at me like I was the strangest person on earth — "like I had a bird on my head." When it's clear they have no idea what I'm talking about, I try reading from a page tagged with an ancient Post-it note:

"Why are you wearing orange tights with a purple skirt?

Why not a girl's blouse instead of a boy's shirt?

Why don't you color instead of playing with dirt?" my mother always said,

Looking at me like I had a bird on my head.

"There's a bird on my head! A bird on my head! But I love my bird!" is what I said.

Crickets. I don't understand the logic of having a parent or grandparent or beloved guardian speak to an audience having such a large spread of ages — how could you possibly appeal to everyone? What might be mildly interesting to thirteen-year-olds will be excruciatingly dull to eleven-year-olds and incomprehensible to six-year-olds. I might just as well be speaking in tongues.

Once I'm done, and once I open it up to questions — and get none, which surprises me, since all they ever told us when we started at the school was how curious and inquisitive Montessori kids are — I'm instantly overcome by a strange combination of humiliation and relief. Just the way I was when I did painfully underattended bookstore events for my second and third books — *Stop Doing That!* and *Why Don't You Like Me Anymore?* — all I wanted to do was leave.

This morning I speed-walk with my arm under the sling through the school's hallways, which are festooned with student artwork (*Who I Am: A Self-Portrait Project* is clearly the current unit, which I have mixed feelings about — isn't this generation self-referential enough?) and fake-talk into my phone past the library to preemptively avoid real-talk with anyone who might try to engage me in conversation. I pass a TUITION DUE! sign on the window of the main office and ignore Grace, the combination business manager, Spanish teacher, and after-school program director, who'd summoned Mr. Noah and interrupted my presentation earlier and who is now practically falling over herself waving at me through the glass, trying to get my attention.

I put my phone away, give a mom walking toward me a big aggressively smiley "Hi!" because she's staring at the sling, and then at me, like I have a bird on my head, and am about to storm through a side door onto the playground. Just when I think I'm safe, I feel the poking: first on the arm, then on the shoulder. I close my eyes and try to collect myself before turning around to face Grace, who has somehow managed to catch up to me.

"Boy, you're *fast*!" I say, hoping that opening with an aggressive compliment will help me stall for time. "And you're not even winded!"

"I run." Grace shrugs matter-of-factly. "Marathons."

"Seriously? That's impressive." She is wearing a fleece zip-up with the Morningside Montessori logo and a nylon knapsack loaded with hot and cold reusable beverage containers in both side mesh compartments.

Another shrug. "Not really. I used to have an eating disorder but now I run. Which means I just traded one obsession for another."

I blink, then smile, trying my best to lean into the awkwardness.

"I'm sorry," Grace says. "TMI."

I laugh out loud. "Are you kidding? You're talking to *someone wearing her dog in public.* I'm the embodiment of TMI. Which means *I'm* the one who should be slinking away in shame." But instead I'll just stand here and endure my shame, hoping you take the dog-bait and forget to ask about our overdue tuition.

"And I'm sorry about the interruption this morning."

"Yeah, what was that all about?"

"I can't say."

"Really?"

"No. I can't. Privacy issues."

"Like HIPAA?" I ask, and Grace nods. "You can tell me anything — I don't talk to anyone. And even if I did, I'd probably forget what you told me anyway." I tap the side of my head with my finger. "Senior moments on a daily basis." That's when I realize I'm still wearing my *Bird* hat. I pull it off as fast as I can and stuff it into the sling.

Grace smiles nervously, then looks down at the dog. "*Such* a cutie!" she coos, pointing to Charlotte's head poking out of the off-white cotton opening. The sling-dog distraction appears to be working. Grace is being super friendly. She couldn't possibly be any nicer. There's no way she'll bring up money now. "And you take it everywhere with you like that? Despite it being disabled?"

Confused and slightly offended, I take a step back from her. "The dog isn't disabled."

"I'm sorry. Differently-abled. Or walking-challenged."

"Wait, what? The dog is fine."

"So why don't you just walk it? — I'm sorry. I don't know what gender your dog identifies as so I keep calling it 'it.' "

"Girl. Female. Charlotte."

"Then she's a therapy dog. Without an official vest."

"Nope! Not a therapy dog!"

"Then why do you carry her?"

I shrug and sigh. "It just kind of happened. And now we can't stop. It's just what we do."

Grace nods vigorously. "I know what that's like. And I also know that sometimes life is too painful without a little buddy to help you feel safe."

I hug the sling. "Exactly! I'm her little buddy!"

Another head-tilt. "Oh. I thought *she* was *your* little buddy."

I make a big face. "Then *I* would need the vest!"

We both laugh again until Grace clears her throat. Here it comes. "This is, like, *so* awkward." She cringes, lowering her voice to a whisper. "But you guys are really *really* behind on tuition."

"I *know*!" I cringe and whisper, too. "I'm so sorry!"

"I'm sorry, too!" Grace looks truly pained. "So many people are struggling right now. It's such a bad time in the world."

Relief washes through me. I grab her arm, a little too hard, I realize a little too late. "So it's not just us? We're not the only ones barely staying afloat? No matter what I do I can't seem to get ahead." My voice trails off the way it does when I forget I'm with a person and not just talking to myself and I almost tell her about how truly awful the last few years have been — in detail — but something — her awkward smile, the half step back she takes — stops me. Because I realize suddenly that she probably can't wait to get away from me. Who could blame her?

"I'd just hate for Teddy not to be able to come back next year," Grace whispers. "Everybody loves him."

"Really?" I blurt. "I just mean — he's gotten so quiet. Sometimes I worry that people mistake that for unfriendliness or hostility."

Grace shakes her head. "Oh no. It's just a phase."

"You think?"

"He's a teenager. They all get like that."

"You mean that awkward phase of adolescence when they seem like sociopaths?" I joke. I think of him on the fringes of the multipurpose room that morning, of how quiet the house has become; how he barely ever picks up his guitar or talks to me in the morning before school or while I'm cooking dinner the way he used to and wonder if every mother of a teenager is walking around like a cored apple, completely hollowed out inside.

"Teddy's always been so special," Grace says, smiling. "I still remember the first day he came to Morningside. He had that long rocker-hair that covered half his face and purple skinny jeans. He was wearing a Frank Zappa T-shirt. He was so shy at first, but everyone thought he was incredibly cool. Including all the teachers."

I hug the dog and bite my lip, but still the tears come.

"It'll work out." Grace takes a step toward me now, rubbing my arm and reaching into the sling to pet the dog. "He'll come back. Boys always do."

"Do they really?" I'm crying now, and so, I see, is Grace.

"Of course they do. They're just scared. Underneath it all, they're just little children in big bodies. They still need us."

Grace hands me a tissue and keeps one for herself. We blow our noses, and as we do I look at her face, her skin, trying to get a sense of how old she is. Younger than me, I'm sure — everyone is now — but beyond that, I'm not sure.

"I just realized I'm standing here crying with you and I don't know anything about you. Your life. What you do when you're not here. Do you have kids?"

Grace looks away, wipes her nose. "It's

complicated."

"I'm sorry."

"Don't be. It's no one's fault but my own."

I have no idea what that means and no idea what to say next — I've never understood people who don't like to talk about themselves — so I put the tissue in the sling for the dog to play with. Then I stand up as straight as I can, which, given the weight and position of the dog, makes me overcompensate by sticking my stomach out the way I did when I was pregnant.

"So how much time do I have?"

Grace sighs, looks up and away. "Another year or two. In my experience, by sixteen things start to turn around."

"I meant for the payment."

We both laugh at the misunderstanding, but I feel like all the molecules in my body have suddenly rearranged themselves into a snowflake of hope. There's a clock on my heartache, and I've just started running it out.

"November fifteenth. That's the drop-dead date for what's overdue and the next payment. And," she says, an idea suddenly occurring to her, "if you're interested in housing some People Puppets, that could definitely reduce your payment."

"*Def*initely. I'll talk to my husband."

"Great."

"November fifteenth," I repeat.

"Six weeks."

"Six weeks," I repeat again.

Grace gives me a quick hug. "It'll work out."

"Okay."

"Hang in there."

"Okay." And then I add: "You, too!"

Grace turns and smiles, and when she does I reach into the sling and take Charlotte's paw and wave it at Grace even after her back is turned and she is halfway down the hallway.

THE SNORING ROOM

The snoring room is in the basement off the laundry area, a guest room/playroom that Teddy never actually used when he was little enough to need it because it felt too far away and separate from the rest of the house, which he didn't like. As an only child, he had learned at a young age to entertain himself for hours, but he always wanted to know that he wasn't actually alone. That there were other people in the house — even if those other people weren't siblings — which is what he wanted more than anything in the world. (That's why, when he was eight and I was, well, older than that, we got the dog.) There's a bright orange modern sofa that converts into a bed without even folding out; a guest chair; two floor lamps; bookshelves, side tables, and Teddy's old train table, which now functions as a coffee table.

It's been a few days since my conversation

with Grace about our tuition issue when I stand in the doorway and watch Gary pull from a giant purple bong. I used to come down here late at night to throw in a load or two of laundry, but after a few times of catching the muted but unmistakable moan and groan of online porn coming from behind the makeshift curtain room divider, it seemed safer and less awkward to use the machine during the day. With the curtain open now, the gurgling of the bong is deafening. Usually he uses a sleek little black vaping inhaler, but every now and then, when he comes home early enough, he likes to go old-school with smoke and dirty water and bubbles. He finally notices me, covering my ears melodramatically with my hands, and grins.

"Want some?" he croak-talks without exhaling, angling the bong in my direction.

"No thanks." Gary smokes entirely too much pot these days, even though it's the medically prescribed kind, formulated especially for his kind of debilitating anxiety, with all the THC removed — something I'd even managed to work into a few of my top-read Well/er posts. (*"Is the 'new pot' for you?"* *"Why cannabis beats Klonopin for anxiety."* *"If just seeing the word* cannabis *makes you anxious, keep reading."* *"Yes, pot sommelier is a thing, and you need one."*) But, as usual, I don't say anything. Why open myself up to the conversation that would certainly follow — the one that would surely include my role in the fact that our marriage is essentially over even if we can't afford to live separately like normal people? Why would I want to go there when I can just pretend to ignore the fact that he is smoking himself into oblivion? Isn't that what marriage is all about? Avoiding terrible arguments and self-examination that could expose your own complicity in the breakdown of your union?

But there has always been Teddy to consider, his happiness, the preservation and protection of what's left of his childhood, and so we came up with a practical afford-able solution that seems to be working for us: an in-house separation masquerading as separate sleeping arrangements due to intense snoring. Separated but still living together. And every six months or so we assuage our guilt for failing each other by going through the motions of seeing a new couples therapist on the off chance that we can change or, at the very least, improve on our imperfect solution. It's also fun. We get to tweak an unsuspecting therapist who has no idea that we know we're beyond help. It is performance art, cheaper and more fun than a dinner-and-movie date night.

I watch the smoke pour out of his mouth — so much smoke that I quickly close the sling over the dog's head so she won't get a contact high. "Every time you ask me I say no. So why do you keep asking?"

"Because maybe one day you'll say yes." Gary closes his eyes, throws his head back. *" 'Hope' is the thing with feathers / That perches in the soul / And sings the tune without the words / And never stops — at all."*

I sit down in the guest chair. *The Collected Poems of Emily Dickinson* is in the middle of the train table, an elastic band around it. I pick it up and run my fingers over the title. "You gave this to me after our first date. Remember?"

"Of course I remember," he says, with a slow shake of his head. "God, how pretentious."

"It wasn't pretentious. It was sweet." I touch the elastic band until it makes a sad twang. "We'd left that bookstore reading early. Of course."

"Because it was so insufferable."

"And because we love leaving early." Especially when we feel justified in leaving early. That night: an independent bookstore on the Upper West Side when we still lived in New York, a few months after we'd started dating. A pompous windbag-author was reading from a biography of Henry James, my favorite writer in college — I'd loved how seemingly tiny moments were often his character's biggest turning points — droning from a makeshift podium amid folding chairs full of tweedy types with corduroy pants and public television tote bags.

Stuck in a middle row, holding hands, we'd exchanged glances during his insufferable presentation — *Ready. Set. Go.* — then, without words, we'd fled, like shoplifters. Outside on the sidewalk, excited by our tiny theft of time and freedom, we'd kissed, long and hard, then finished with a faux-theatrical dip. We were That Couple, full of passion and snark and the private loathing of others.

"I'm so glad we left," he'd whispered into my hair. It was summer, late evening, all the light still left in the sky turning pink and purple and orange as dusk fell.

"Me, too."

"I hate readings."

"Me, too."

"Let's never go to another one again."

I'd nodded. How fun it was to make rules — future rules — rules about what we would and wouldn't do — together. After spending most of my life feeling utterly alone in the world, surviving the cycle of dating and heartbreak that repeated itself over and over again throughout my twenties and early thirties, I now felt part of a secret world: all it took was this one person for us to create a whole new parallel universe. I never wanted to leave it.

"Unless it's a reading for your book," he said. "Then I'll go."

"How do you know there will be a book?" I said. I was still waiting to hear from Glenn, my older editor-colleague-friend at Black Bear Books, who had recently been transferred to our publisher's flagship office in Boston when we went through a sudden company-wide downsizing. Things were slower there than in New York, she had told me, but I was still convinced that in the end the news I'd get would be bad.

"Because of course there will be a book," he'd said without a trace of doubt. "Glenn will love it."

"How do you know?"

"Because I know Glenn." Gary had been an office temp, on and off, at Black Bear for years after college while he was still trying to get his music career off the ground. "She loves you and she's going to love your book. It'll all work out."

I didn't understand his faith in the future, his relentless hopefulness. It didn't make sense to me: how people believed in the positive when the negative was so much more likely. My family had never uttered that phrase — that things would work out — because, quite simply, they didn't believe it. They knew from almost direct experience in fact — my parents' parents were all Holocaust survivors — that often things didn't work out and that sometimes the worst happened instead. Faith in the future was not part of my DNA, and trusting Gary felt like telling myself to stare at the horizon while on choppy water: if I kept my eyes trained on him, maybe it would all be okay.

I'd smiled and let him pull me toward him again. "See, that's what I love about you," he said. "How hope-challenged you are."

I remember that moment, staring at him, frozen. It was the first time he'd used the word *love,* and I wasn't sure whether to acknowledge it, to ask if he meant love-love or if he simply uttered it in the gleeful afterglow of having been released from inexorable boredom. Like so many other times, before and after, I would let a moment pass without asking an important question. *Better not to know than to get the wrong answer.* Instead I just asked this:

"Is that a hardcover book in your pants or are you just glad to see me?"

He'd laughed, then reached into his jacket and handed me a book of poems. "I was so bored I forgot to give it to you."

As I looked at the book jacket and the pages in disbelief I was thirty-five years old and no man had ever given me a book of poetry until that night — he touched a wisp of hair that had come loose from my ponytail. "And just so you know, when it's your reading, I'll go *and* I'll stay through the whole thing."

"Well, you'll have to. Because I'll have to stay. Because I'll be the one reading."

"That's true. Besides: leaving early alone isn't nearly as fun as leaving early together."

I'd looked at the book again and then leaned into him, putting my forehead, then my ear, on his chest. I remember hearing his heart beating underneath his T-shirt, a sound I was still getting used to, a language I only partially understood. There may or may not have been tears in my eyes when I'd whispered, "Someone's getting lucky tonight."

But I was the one who'd gotten lucky: I'd gotten an answer without having to actually ask a question. And I'd gotten someone loyal and loving beyond measure.

That was a lifetime ago. Now, a few hours before our teenager will be home from school, the book is a relic, a souvenir of a time and place I sometimes don't believe actually existed. I flick the elastic a few times with my finger and wince at its flat tuneless sound. "What's with the rubber band?" I say, looking at the book's spine to see if it has somehow split and would explain the need for something to keep it together.

"Some of the pages came loose. Because I read it so much." He takes the book from me, puts it on his lap, pets it. A little too lovingly, I think, until he throws his head back and sighs loudly. "God, what happened to us? We had such promise. Now we can't even afford to separate like normal people." He stares somewhere off into the middle distance. "Maybe I should just go back to law school already."

I look at the book in his lap, then at the dog in the sling in my lap. Our marriage, our finances, our life are in ruins. I sigh. "It's time."

Gary sits up. "I'm not quitting pot. I can't. I'm not ready. Nothing, not even Klonopin, touches the anxiety like weed."

"I know. That's not what I'm talking about."

It takes him a second or two to understand, but when he does he shakes his head. "Oh, no. Not again."

"We have to. We have to find another therapist."

"Do we?"

"Don't we?" I, too, would rather die than go back into couples counseling, but if we're going to continue this separated-but-living-together-under-the-same-roof arrangement, we're going to have to be able to talk about things like Gary's pot smoking, my wearing the dog, how to deal with seeing other people — not that I can imagine having any interest whatsoever in ever dating again — I haven't had a normal libido since before Teddy was born — but he does.

"We went through three therapists last year," Gary says. "With all the money we wasted on them I could have moved out already."

The thought of dredging everything up again makes me want to slide off the chair onto the floor and stay there. But then we'd still be here, in this same place, this awful purgatory, and I'd feel even deader than I do now.

And then there's Teddy. Whether what we're doing and how we're doing it is having an effect on him.

I stare at the train table, lean forward to touch my fingers to the scratches and grooves where he used to run his trains back and forth on the wood, before he learned how to snap the tracks together and build loops with curves and straightaways and tunnels and bridges. "Remember when he would stand and play at this table for hours?"

Gary looks at me, then at the lighter in his hand, then at the table. Of course he remembers. It's as if Teddy is right there in front of us, with his tiny pants and minihoodie-sweatshirt, clutching a train car in each hand and pointing at us to watch.

COUPLES THERAPIST
NUMBER FOUR

We sit on a long couch facing Deirdre Nussbaum, MSW, whose name we got using a new therapist-rating-and-locator app I'd written about for Well/er (*"If Open Table and Yelp and Headspace had a baby, 50Minutes would be it"*). Sporting boxy cotton separates and giant wearable-art earrings, she smiles and takes our new patient clipboards from us, leans in as she scans them, then looks up at us soulfully.

"How can I help?"

I clear my throat, wait for words to come, but none do. They never do. For all my alleged ease with them, I am more often than not at a total loss for coherent sentences, stammering out half syllables, especially in stressful situations like this. I scan the walls, then the bookshelves, tilting my head slightly to read the titles: *The Dance of Anger. Un-Coupling. Children of Divorce. There's a Bird on Your Head . . .*

"Judy?"

My lips finally move, but the words don't feel like mine. "We're trying to negotiate our separation. In terms of our son."

Deirdre kicks off her boiled-wool clogs to sit crisscross-applesauce in her midcentury leather shrink-chair. Then she points to the sling. "Is that your son?"

I laugh, too loudly at first, flattered to be considered young enough to be wearing a baby, then uncomfortably at the weirdness of the truth. "No! No. That's the dog."

Gary sighs. "She has anxiety issues."

"Wait," Deirdre says, looking at us over red half-glasses. "Who has anxiety issues: Judy or the dog?"

Gary, the one with *the actual* anxiety problem, sits up a little straighter, raises an eyebrow at me. *Maybe this won't be so bad after all,* the eyebrow says. He's wanted to discuss Sling-Dog Millionaire for a while, but until now the time has never been right.

"She was a rescue," I lie, the way I always do, too ashamed to admit that we got the dog from an actual pet store, which I like to think means we actually did rescue her, and which conveniently makes it less of a lie. "She needs constant reassurance that she's safe and loved."

"Judy was also a rescue," Gary adds until

I shoot him an annoyed look. "Just kidding. Judy doesn't need reassurance. She knows she isn't safe or loved. Nothing you can tell her can convince her otherwise." He shrugs. "It's how she was raised. Literally without hope." He then mentions my grandparents.

Deirdre shifts in her chair. "We can come back to the dog, and to Judy's childhood, but let's focus first on what brought you here." She looks down at our clipboards but can't seem to make sense of much of what we've written. Except for one phrase that I wrote in block letters, which Number Four now points to and reads out loud:

"It says *'Separation anxiety.'* "

Even though it isn't funny, why we're there, we smirk at the joke. The pun of my inability to separate from the dog and our inability to separate from the marriage — and Gary's actual acute clinical anxiety — is suddenly extremely funny. Every time we see a new therapist, our effort is a spectacular failure. We've never found one with a sense of humor, and Deirdre's obvious lack of one now on the clipboard test proves that today will be no exception.

We will leave early.

"So you need to work out custody and visitation?" she asks.

"Not exactly," I say. "We're having some

financial challenges, so we're still living in the same house. In separate rooms."

Deirdre nods, scribbling furiously. "Kind of like double-nesting — when divorced parents each get an apartment and come back and forth to the family home instead of uprooting the kids."

"What Judy isn't explicitly saying is that we're broke so we can't afford to split up. What Judy also isn't saying is that one of the reasons we separated is because we never had sex anymore."

I roll my eyes. "I wouldn't say 'never.' I'd say rarely."

He rolls his eyes. "I'd say extremely rarely." He looks at Deirdre for help. "Judy used to be really into it, but then she wasn't anymore. It's like one day that part of her just shut down."

He isn't wrong. Even the Chinese acupuncturist I started seeing when I still thought it was a temporary shutdown lingered ominously after taking my pulses. "You closed for business down there," she had said, slicing her hand through the air with absolute certainty. "Closed. For. Business." But the needles didn't help.

"I'm just stressed-out! And exhausted!"

"Everyone's stressed-out and exhausted!"

I think about the past decade, see myself

trapped in a snow globe's bubble with Gary's debilitating anxiety, which has radically curtailed his social life, and ours; the death of both my parents within two years of each other; the intense pressure of being the primary breadwinner — all of it falling down, in a silent snow, around me. The strains on our marriage turned our relationship into a friendship — or, more precisely, a family: full of closeness and kindness and deep love while short-circuiting the sexual connection. Didn't Freud write about this? And how many articles have I read that say this is the new normal, not to mention my own anecdotal research over the years proving that almost every woman I have ever known since Teddy's preschool days confessed to me the same lack of interest, the same toll of stress and petty grievances and the cruel diminishing of hormones. Aren't I just one in a long line of hourglasses turned over, on the other side of time? Aren't I kind of normal?

"Sadly, this is actually quite common for many many couples, Gary, for a whole host of reasons," Deirdre slips in soothingly before Gary makes clear in a loud voice that he doesn't care about other couples right now.

I hug the dog and scan the office for a

white noise machine, the mainstay in every therapist's office, hoping no one in any of the neighboring offices will overhear us. But Deirdre's machine is especially small and ancient-looking, huffing and puffing and working overtime in a corner; we need one the size of a basement dehumidifier here to drown us out. "Now that we're officially technically separated," I tell Deirdre, "I've told him he's free to do what he wants." I turn to Gary and fling my hands out over the sling. "Go have sex!"

"But I wanted to have it with you!"

"But it just didn't work out that way!"

"But why not? I still don't understand!"

Deirdre leans forward. "Yes, why not, Judy?"

I stare down at the dog, listen to the hum of the white noise machine. I have no other answer except for this: "Because I'm dead inside. And I don't know if I'll ever feel not dead."

"Well then, Gary," Deirdre offers, "let's think about your options."

"How am I supposed to have options when we still live together?" Gary yells. "If I meet someone, where would I bring her? Home to my family? To my — 'crowded nest'?" He shakes his head. "What good is an open marriage if all the doors and windows are locked?"

Deirdre looks up from her pad, eager to clarify. "So this is an 'open marriage' as opposed to a separation?"

He waves her away. "I don't care what you call it. Judy should help me find someone. If the roles were reversed, I would do it for her."

"You would help her find a boyfriend." Deirdre shoots me a little side-eye.

"Absolutely." He sits back, crosses his arms over his chest, then turns to me. "You know it's true."

I shrug. "It *is* true. He *would* help me. That's the thing about Gary. He would do anything for me. Even that."

Deirdre hugs her mug of tea with both hands, folds her feet up under her long flowing skirt. She's getting comfortable for the rest of the story. "Tell me about that, Judy."

I shrug, then force myself to speak. "The whole thing is just really embarrassing, for both of us," I whisper. "Our arrangement. Not having enough money to be able to get divorced like normal people."

"It sounds like you feel that there's shame in staying. Shame in not leaving."

I blink in disbelief. That's exactly how I feel.

"Lots of couples can't afford to split up

right now in this economy," she says. "Lots of couples with children either stay together, like you, until they figure it out, or they get divorced and double-nest. There's no single right answer. And this kind of child-centered parenting can buy you some time while you figure things out and everyone adjusts."

"But we're not being child centered. Not really. Gary started sleeping downstairs in the guest room two years ago. Teddy was eleven then, and we told him it was because Gary's snoring was out of control, which is just a big lie."

Gary nods. "Judy's the one who snores like a barn animal, but she'll never admit it."

I ignore him. "Do you think Teddy knows what's really going on?" I ask Deirdre.

"Kids always know."

"Do you think we've damaged him?"

"Children are resilient," she says with a gentleness I'm grateful for, then exhales the way they do in yoga classes to signal a redirection. "I want to come back to Teddy but I need to get a bit more of the big picture. Tell me what kind of work you both do."

Gary shifts in his chair. He hates this topic as much as I hate the no-sex topic, but he's learned to just plow right into his shame.

79

"After I dropped out of law school because of my anxiety, I've done SAT and LSAT tutoring; dog walking; worked in a special-needs after-school program. Now I stock snacks in a coworking space for startups. Which is ironic, since I barely know how to use my phone and I hate technology."

"What's the source of your anxiety, Gary?"

He shrugs, pretending his family résumé is no big deal. "Middle child. Raging alcoholic father. Long-suffering divorced mother. You know, the usual."

"It doesn't sound like 'the usual,' " Deirdre says. And it isn't. Both of Gary's sisters have struggled with drinking over the years (he got sober before we met), and all three of them were estranged from their father, now dead, after the divorce when they were teenagers. But during the years when all our kids were small and we still got together for holidays and birthdays and summer vacations, before Gary had to limit how much time he could spend around his family because it made him too anxious, they were fun: they were loud and angry and volatile, but they were also affectionate and hilarious and inclusive. I was the odd one out — the only child, the lone Jew in a room full of Irish Catholics — always being pulled into a conversation about sports I knew nothing about, or to listen to, and sometimes mediate, a story about some terrible childhood misadventure — near-fatal riptides, sunburns, bouts of food poisoning — that almost felled them all. I loved every minute of it.

When it's my turn I tell her that I used to write but don't anymore.

"*Real*ly, Judy. What did you write before you stopped writing?"

I feel Gary bristle the way he always does when we get to this part: when the therapist finds out I'm a writer. Or was one. I point to her bookshelf. "*There's a Bird on Your Head.* It's about —"

Deirdre's eyes get huge and her voice is full of exclamation points. "Ohmygod! Judy Vogel! *The* Judy Vogel!" She fans her face with her hands the way women of a certain age do when they're having a hot flash. "I know it's highly unprofessional but I'm a little starstruck! You'll have to sign my book before you leave!"

Gary shakes his head. "Here we go."

Deirdre ignores him. "So what happened after *Bird* that would make you stop writing? Can you trace the source of your writer's block?"

I shrug. "After the PBS series, I wrote two more books, but they both sank without a trace. So I guess I figured I should just stop." My mind flashes back to an empty chain bookstore: I'm sitting next to a giant sign promoting a signing for my second book, then my third book, somewhere, in another city not my own, fondling a cup full of black Sharpies and staring into space as people walk by without stopping. I'm alone but for the bird on my head.

Gary shrugs. "I told her to do a sequel."

"And I told him to keep playing gigs."

"You're a musician, Gary?" She checks her notes, as if she's missed something.

"I *was* a musician. A bass player. Before and after I tried law school."

"His band opened for Aerosmith. Right after college. Before I knew him."

"Once. And it was all downhill from there."

I ignore him. "He's really talented."

Deirdre looks up, impressed. "Really! So why did you stop, Gary?"

He folds his arms across his chest. "The venues we played were terrible."

I sigh. "They weren't all terrible."

"I'd say The Barking Crab and The Lobster Claw were terrible. Although they had great clam rolls." He turns to Deirdre. "I like a grilled bun."

"Maybe if you'd agreed to leave the state

once in a while you might have found some venues you didn't hate."

"I didn't want to abandon Teddy."

"Working isn't abandonment!"

It's when we start fighting about money that Deirdre makes the hand gesture for a time-out. Then she leans forward and clasps her hands together solemnly. She's either going to tell us our time is up or ask us to leave and never come back.

"Lots of couples fail in their careers, but it doesn't mean the marriage has to fail, too."

Gary and I look straight at each other and then back at Deirdre. She's now the one with a giant bird on her head.

"Wow. Okay," Gary says, trying to collect himself.

Deirdre looks at him and then at me. "Did I say something wrong?"

"Kind of." He's vibrating as if he's stuck his finger in an electrical socket. "I wouldn't exactly say Judy 'failed' in her career. No one works harder than she does, and she's had some bad breaks. And I'd hardly say three books is something to be ashamed of."

Now I'm nodding. "And Gary didn't 'fail' in his career, either. It's not his fault he has these mental health challenges, and despite them he couldn't be a more supportive spouse or better father."

Deirdre tries to apologize but Gary shrugs her off. "We're used to it. Everybody says the same thing. *'What happened to Judy's career?!' 'You should have just finished law school!'* There are no guarantees. Life doesn't owe you anything. That's why 'failure' is such a big topic for us."

"Very big," I confirm.

"It's kind of our hot button."

"Very hot."

"We could explore that," Deirdre says, with equal parts hope and desperation, glancing at the secret clock partially hidden behind the box of tissues. "We still have twenty minutes left."

We nod politely, but when we look at each other again a spark jumps between us. My hands are already underneath the dog sling and Gary is already reaching for his jacket.

Out on the street, on a stretch of Harvard Square where, when I was growing up, there had once been three record stores, two bookstores, four coffeehouses, and a revival house movie theater but where now there's just a big stupid CVS and yet another bank chain I've never heard of, we walk toward the car. There is an unmistakable bounce in our step, which wasn't there an hour ago.

Escaping someplace we don't want to be has always given us joy. It's the happiest we've been in a long time. It's almost unseemly how elated we are.

"I'm so glad we left early," Gary says.

"I know, right?"

"I mean, why stay? She wasn't going to help us. She's no Marriage Whisperer."

"Is there even such a thing?"

We make big smug faces now, like we've just cut our losses by leaving a shitty restaurant without ordering dessert. Which doesn't make sense: If we're so in sync about leaving things we hate, how bad can our marriage actually be? Wouldn't we both have already left if it were really that bad?

We step off a curb and a silent Toyota Prius comes out of nowhere and almost runs us over. Gary pushes me out of the way just in time. "Stupid Priuses with your stupid silent battery-engines!" he yells out after the car. "Why don't you make any fucking noise?"

The driver rolls down his window, sticks his head out as far as it will go. "The plural of Prius is *Prii,* asshole!"

Gary runs into the street after the car, giving the Prius the finger. Breathless, he walks back toward me. "Massachusetts drivers.

85

They almost kill you and then correct your Latin."

Inside the car, I pull the harness strap of the seat belt gently around the dog and me until it clicks while Gary yanks on his seat belt and flips up the visor. In the short time inside Deirdre's office, the sun had moved, coming in sharply now between two gorgeous maples and bathing us in an orangey-red light. "Not to mention the bad shoes," Gary adds, an endnote to his rant. "Another fifty minutes we won't get back. Or, actually —" He looks at his phone screen. "Twenty-four minutes. A new record."

As Gary starts the car and slowly pulls into traffic, I stare out the window, hugging the dog like a big stuffed animal. Autumn, my favorite season, has always made me sad — the brightness of the sky and trees, the promise of hope and renewal always feels like a trick, an invitation for disappointment, instead of a gift. Now I feel the creep of regret. Maybe we made a mistake leaving early. Maybe, this time, we should have stayed. I think of Deirdre's fuzzy clogs and remember the similar pair I bought my mother when she first got sick, when everything became about comfort and softness and compassion. There was so much pain, so quickly; even the skin on her feet hurt.

The Bird on My Head

For most of my life, I had trouble describing the signature look my mother gave me. Which was strange, given that my unofficial hobbies were recreational psychoanalyzing, conspiracy theorizing, and watching serial killer documentaries. In short: human behavior. Every child's first science project is mapping and analyzing their parents' emotional DNA, and while the official Human Genome Project took thirteen years to complete, figuring out your mother — or trying to — is a never-ending farce. It requires decades of data collection, the patience of Margaret Mead, and the skills of an FBI profiler. All I did was whine and complain and make mental notes. No wonder I failed to crack her code.

Proof of my efforts exist, though: there's an anthropological field guide the size of the old New York City phone book inside my head, filled with all the "faces" and "looks" she made over the course of my lifetime, and hers: dog-eared, with Talmudic-length interpretations and annotations scrawled in the margins, it's the homemade version of Darwin's *The Expression of the Emotions in Man and Animals.* Like the real one, my collection of deconstructed facial-muscle contractions and gestures had expressions universal enough to make labeling easy — especially the negative ones: the "majoring-in-art-history-won't-get-you-a-job-with-benefits-but-a-teaching-certificate-will" face; the "what-will-become-of-you?" face; the "I-don't-understand-why-you're-still-not-married" face; and the "I-don't-like-your-husband" face, to name only a few. But while monkeys and humans use the same muscles to laugh and show rage, I'd bet my door-stopper-size tome that monkey-mothers are physically incapable of the faces human mothers make when their daughters' lives don't go according to plan. Expressions of maternal disappointment are luxuries of domestication, not the wild, and their variations are infinite. There isn't a book — real or fake — big enough to contain them all.

For years, I opened mine to the same page and pointed to the one unidentified, uncaptioned look I could never get past: my mother, head tilted, brow furrowed, facial muscles a patchwork of bemusement, confusion, and disapproval. Sometimes she just gave me the look; other times she added a verbal component: "You're so weird!" But whatever the delivery, I always got the message: no matter what I said, no matter what I did, my mother didn't "get" me. Anyone who reads or watches the news these days knows that there are far worse things to overcome than not being completely adored by your mother, but being told you're weird at a young age almost certainly guarantees you'll feel weird as an adult. Some children grow stronger in the broken places, like bones; others grow sadder. I did both.

One day, when I still lived in New York and worked for Black Bear, after a meeting with a boss who didn't get me and couldn't stand me, Glenn followed me back to my office and poked me.

"Did you see that?"

"See what?"

"The way she looked at you!"

I shrugged. The boss had looked at me like I was incredibly weird. So what else was new?

"She looked at you like you had a bird on your head!"

I looked at Glenn like she had a bird on

her head. Because I finally had a caption —
the "there's-a-bird-on-your-head" face.

No longer would I strain to describe the
look to therapists — the people I paid never
to look at me like I had a bird on my head.
No longer would I think feeling like I had a
bird on my head was all in my head: my
mother had looked at me that way my whole
life. And who, frankly, could blame her? At
four, I'd admitted to a fear of clouds; at
seven, to a fear of carbonated beverages.
Her face worked overtime during my teenage years: at fifteen, I'd convinced my
parents to let me spend a semester at a
friend's high school — in Holland; at
seventeen, I was still taking — and trying to
get gym credit for — weekly pantomime
classes. By the time I reached adulthood
she could have used a face-making double:
Gary and I got married two years after having Teddy instead of before he was born; I
waited until my children's books were out
of print before finally getting an author
website and blog to promote myself. Nothing I did made sense to her, which never
made sense to me.

To be fair, sometimes nothing I did made
sense to me, either. Like when Gary and I
moved back to Boston, where I'd grown up,

and where my parents still lived before they both got sick. Though it was initially Glenn's idea because of her transfer there, and though Gary had agreed — he'd loved Boston when he went to Berklee and always wanted to return to New England eventually — the secret fantasy of living close to people who didn't get me was wholly mine. Sure, it would be great to move someplace where a friend was already waiting, but it was more than that. Facing your demons was what emotionally secure people did, and in a strange case of mistaken self-identity, I thought I was one of those people: I'd survived a lifetime of my mother's "what-will-become-of-you?" looks and somehow managed to couple and procreate; I'd earned a living without the teaching certificate she'd always urged me to get as an insurance policy against failure; an animated PBS series had been based on my first book. Hadn't I earned the right to take my L-shaped fingers off my forehead? Freud said there are no accidents, and my move home proved him right: for all my weirdness, for all my insistence on doing things my way, it turned out that I was completely normal at my core:

I wanted to make the bird on my head disappear. I wanted my mother to like me.

THE FOREHEAD

I've been friends with Sari Epstein, a creativity-life-coach-guru with a national following, for less than a year. And by "friends" I mean only on the Internet. But it's been an important friendship to me — and by "friendship" I mean me following Sari Epstein on social media — reading every word of her creativity-life-coach-guru updates, taking screenshots of every one of her creativity-life-coach-guru photos so that I can creep on them for extra details you just can't get without the creeping. My feed on each social media platform is full of active creative-types, constantly and shamelessly self-promoting themselves, posting about their daily output: their word counts, their book deals, their bookstore appearances, their downward facing dogs and yoga handstands. I would be doing this, too, if I had any creative output, or could do yoga, but nothing ever happens when I open a new notebook and uncap a pen. Whether it's in the morning, or the afternoon, or at night before bed; whether I'm home alone with a few minutes in between Well/er pieces, or out at a coffee shop, happily eavesdropping and people watching for inspiration; the same paralysis sets in. My mind goes blank. It seems I am closed for business up there, too.

Maybe that's why I become secretly obsessed with Sari Epstein: her workshops and weekend retreats promise those who attend will magically rediscover their creative spark. Could this be my answer? I'm still not sure.

What I am sure about is that something is off with Sari Epstein's appearance. I've known this for a while, but it isn't until I show a certain picture of her to Glenn — who knows everything about everything — that the mystery is finally solved and it all falls into place. We're at our favorite restaurant, Shepherd, in Harvard Square, sitting near the windows, when I show her Sari Epstein's luminous Ali MacGraw–like head shot on my phone. Glenn puts her hand over her eyes and squints like we're on a beach at high noon.

"Oh my God," she rasps. "The glare off that forehead!"

I laugh slyly and sip my double decaf latte with whole milk slowly, trying to make it last. I have absolutely no business ordering a $5.25 drink with so little income, let alone the full-fat version, but I would rather die than drink coffee with skim or low-fat milk, and I can't order nothing. Ordering nothing makes people uncomfortable. Why should Glenn have to breathe in the fumes of my failure when all she wants to do is distract herself with some cheap laughs about someone's too-big forehead?

"Seriously! *Look* at it!" Glenn pokes the phone screen with her finger. "I need sunglasses!"

I bite my lip with fake guilt. "We're terrible."

"No! *She's* terrible! For inflicting that giant over-Botoxed moon face on everyone."

She takes a tiny sip from her wineglass — Glenn always orders prosecco, even in the early afternoon, which it is, and even though she isn't supposed to drink now, which she does anyway. *How am I supposed to get through this without alcohol?* she always says. But now I think that Glenn just pretends to drink to create a sense of normalcy or for the taste of alcohol on her lips: the level of her glass today, I realize, hasn't gone down. In all the months we've come, I wonder suddenly if it's ever gone down. Not knowing the answer to that question, not noticing something so obvious, is part of my denial. I don't want to know. I don't want to see. I have been here before and I don't want to be here now. I especially don't want to be here with Glenn. She not only published *Bird* at Black Bear Books but, after that encounter with that boss, it was also her idea all those years ago — a short, illustrated, kids-oriented story about being yourself, a modern version of *Free to Be . . . You and Me.* At first I'd ignored her — children's books were just what I did for work, fiction was what I wanted to write — but eventually, after playing around with some very simple pen-and-ink drawings, the story rushed out of me in rhymed verse. I'd tried and failed for years to write a novel, but *Bird* came together instantly and painlessly, as if it had been inside of me my whole life, just waiting for a way out.

"You don't wear your hair parted in the middle when you have a giant forehead like that!" Glenn goes on. She grabs my phone again, then creeps on the face, pinching with her thumb and forefinger, to make it larger. "You get some bangs like a normal person, or you part your hair on the side, and you cover that shit up. And you don't talk about adult coloring books like they're going to change the world and solve everyone's problems. I mean, seriously, *coloring* books? To solve *writer's block*? What are we, children?"

I love Glenn. "You could have your own show."

"What kind of show? A yelling-about-annoying-people show?"

The group at the next table — tweedy ancient Harvard-types — stare at her, then turn back to their conversation. Or try to.

"Oh look," she says, loudly enough for them to hear, which is her intention. "I've offended them with my honesty and my brutal truth-telling." They try even harder to ignore her, but once activated, Glenn will not be ignored. "I know what you're thinking," she says, directly to them now, with a pitch-perfect Boston accent. "Who am I to make fun of someone's giant forehead and how they do or do not wear their hair, when I myself have *no hayyy-ah.*" She pulls the hand-knit cap off her head in one quick tug to reveal her bald chemo-head, a sight I'm not used to, no matter how many times I've seen it over the years during her illness.

The group is in motion now, trying desperately to gather their things — their books and papers and briefcases, their cardigan sweaters and light jackets — it is October and chilly, of course, in New England, which can't make anything easy for anyone, ever — so they can make their escape. "Oh no. I've scared them!" Glenn rolls her eyes at me, full of disgust. But as the people flee and the space between Glenn and me is suddenly empty and quiet, her eyes fill with tears. "I'm sorry," she whispers.

"Don't be."

"I'm such an asshole." She turns quickly to look at the group she scared away, visible now through the glass windows at the front of the shop, whispering and walking close together on the sidewalk. "They didn't do anything to deserve that." She puts her hat back on and blows her nose into a napkin. "I just get so angry sometimes. I can't control it." She turns around again, trying to gauge if she can possibly catch up to them, to apologize, or maybe to just explain the reason for her rudeness, but even if she were healthy and quick the way she used to be, it would be too late. They are already gone.

"Don't worry about it," I say, but Glenn is slumped in her seat. She makes circles around the top of her glass with her finger.

"Tell me something right now, right this second, that will take my mind off the fact that I'm dying and that I scared off some incredibly uptight but completely innocent people who just happened to be in the wrong place at the wrong time."

I still can't believe that Glenn's breast cancer — which was diagnosed right after my third book, and second dud, *Why Don't You Like Me Anymore?* came out — returned a year and a half ago with such a vengeance, to her bones and her liver, the way she always feared it would. Before that, her nonstop cancer-talk annoyed me, as if illness was her identity and she couldn't let it go; she'd been healthy for over five years, and it seemed ridiculous to keep worrying about recurrence. *She. Was. Fine. She should get over it already.* I'm embarrassed to say that I actually thought that. Then came the news that changed everything: it was back, and it was bad. I'd just lost both my parents and Teddy both his grandparents: How would we all survive this now?

Glenn was told she might have three years, or ten years. But only a year of chemo and radiation and two clinical trials later her cells are dividing and redividing faster than ever. In fact, if I'm honest with myself, which I hate to be — I much prefer the fog of dissociation and denial — she looks worse today than she did two weeks ago.

I'm worried that she's on a downward trajectory that can't be stopped.

"Shit. Now I've traumatized you, too," she says. "I shouldn't have used the d-word, but everyone's dying. We're all dying. All the time. You know that more than almost anyone else."

I nod, and suddenly we're both crying — then laughing, then wiping our noses and eyes and sipping from our drinks, which don't even taste good anymore.

"Please," Glenn whispers, trying to sit up straight and wincing, though to anyone watching it would have looked like she was just recovering from the kind of breathlessness that comes from laughing too hard at some great girl talk. "Distract me. I don't want to think."

I tell her about Mr. Noah and his new man bun and his bib; about how tall Teddy is getting and how every day I miss him even though he's still right here, sort of; about Gary and I leaving our most recent couples therapy appointment early; about being behind in tuition and about wondering what will become of us if I can't find a better paying job than Well/er or if I can't ever write another book. And then I tell her about my disastrous school presentation, how it was interrupted before it even began, and how the school is bringing in People Puppets from Vermont for Inhabitancy this year.

"People Puppets?" Suddenly she's paying attention.

I describe the photo Mr. Noah showed of adults wearing animal costumes, taken outside, on a farm, near bales of hay. "The school is looking for host families," I explain. "They'll even give you a credit toward tuition if you host them."

She is sitting up now. "Host them."

"Are you kidding? You know that Gary is phobic about anything in costume, and Teddy would die: at his age, all he wants to be is invisible. The last thing he'd want is a bunch of weird people living in our house." I can't help remembering the younger version of Teddy, who would have begged me to let them come and stay, how he loved anything and everything that involved filling our house with friends, with voices and energy, with life.

Glenn lifts her glass to sip from it but puts it back down without drinking from it. "You're at a moment when everything has stopped, right before it starts again. Like T. S. Eliot's poem: *At the still point of the turning world. / Neither flesh nor fleshless; / Neither from nor towards.* This will be like pushing the reset button. Gary will deal. He's a brave bear."

She is the only person who knows him well enough to say that, and for me to believe it — how sometimes if you push back against his anxiety and challenge it, he can rise to the occasion. Like the time at work all those years ago when we only had two hours to put up our booth at a major trade show because all the boxes had been shipped to the wrong place and how Gary, sputtering comically on the verge of panic, was somehow calmed and spurred on by Glenn's pushy encouragement. *Deep breaths, Gary. You can do it. You're a brave bear.* A mantra he repeated constantly as he worked tirelessly to get the job done.

Or when we dragged him with us and Teddy to Story Land in New Hampshire — a small adventure park for toddlers where he had initially refused to go because it was full of people in costume, but he didn't want to miss out on it for Teddy's sake. While I went on the tiny rides with Teddy — sitting in the rotating teacups and in the flying Dutch shoes and on the little pirate sailboat — Glenn took Gary by the hand to each area that had storybook characters physically built into them, her own version of tough-love exposure therapy. They sat on either side of a creepy clown on a white wooden bench and next to a giant Humpty Dumpty on a fake stone wall, even pressing the button to make it talk, though apparently Gary drew the line at allowing a traveling pack of Barney characters to hug him. I'd had to drive home that night — Gary was too drowsy from all the extra Klonopin he'd taken — but every time Glenn smacked him affectionately on the head from the backseat and called him a "brave bear" for what he had accomplished that day, he'd beamed. *I'm a brave bear,* he'd whispered. *I'm a very brave bear.*

Glenn reaches over and sticks her hand inside the sling to pet the dog. "Now, take me home." Her face is pale, but there's a spark in her eyes that wasn't there a minute ago: the promise of future entertainment that she knows will come in the form of texted photos with descriptive captions of a farce about to unfold, fun — possibly disastrous — at our expense. "I'm exhausted and nauseated and I miss my Lucy."

Later that night, much later, my phone will ring. It will be Glenn, and at first I'll assume she's checking in about my visit tomorrow — I always do a weekly grocery shop and Gary always helps with the heavy things — the water and ginger ale and dog food — but instead she'll ask me if I ever think about being in the wrong place at the wrong time, the way those Harvard types had been that afternoon at Shepherd when she'd chased them away.

"Because that's all I think about," she'll say. "My body. All my cells. Everything in the wrong place at the wrong time. Is that what life comes down to? Luck?"

I won't know what to say, so I won't say anything.

"If I had kids I would just die," she'll whisper. "I know you don't want to hear that because you have one, but if I had one and if I knew I was dying like this, I wouldn't be able to stand it. I couldn't take the heartbreak." She'll sigh, but now that she's started she won't be able to stop talking. "Parents get sick and die all the time. How do they stand it? Knowing they're leaving too soon and not being able to fix it?" There'll be a long pause and then the words that come next will be thin and full of air. "As it is, I can hardly bear the idea of leaving Lucy." Her little corgi, her constant companion.

"Lucy will be fine."

"But what will happen when I'm gone? Who will take her when I'm gone?" She'll cry then, and the sound of it will be so crushing that I'll wish I could throw the phone across the room to make it stop. It's excruciating to watch someone disappear, slowly at first, and then quickly. Having done it twice, I can't fathom having to do it again.

"I will," I'll say. "I'll take her."

"You'd do that for me?"

"Of course I will."

"But how could you handle another dog? You can't wear two slings."

"Maybe by then I'll be better," I say, thinking of a day in the future that neither of us believes will actually come, "and I won't be wearing any slings."

■ ■ ■ ■

PART TWO: CABIN FEVER

HOST FAMILY

In the kitchen, with the autumn sun going down fast and a sharp chill in the air, since like all self-respecting long-suffering New Englanders we refuse to turn the heat on until well into October, Gary and I make dinner. I've been tempted over the years to try one of those meal-box delivery services, to spare us the hassle of figuring out what to cook and then doing all the shopping and chopping — and mostly to collect those colorful laminated recipe cards that, according to all the social media ads and posts, you get to keep — but Gary won't do it. He feels sorry for people who get those boxes, like the young couple next door, a doctor and a professor, who, in my opinion, are legitimately too busy to shop and chop. He's embarrassed for them and their infantilized style of noncooking, and he hates that he knows something so intimate about them — that every week they open a big box with wonder and excitement and play at cooking like oversize children. He wishes he could unsee it on their stoop every week, full of tiny wasteful little plastic baggies of ingredients they should already have — one garlic clove, a teaspoon of cumin, two wedges of lemon — that they will use to re-create the meal pictured on the laminated card.

More than anything, he's annoyed by the box itself, which often sits for days after they've emptied its contents, waiting, with all its recyclable packing innards, for a return pickup by the company. It makes him anxious seeing it day after day, waiting in the rain or chilly wind to be rescued. Once, on a particularly cold and snowy February day, he put a small fleece doggie blanket over the box, hoping they'd get the message that we all see the poor eyesore of a box, freezing its ass off on the bench in front of their house, but instead they were moved by what they interpreted as compassion. With the returned blanket came a bottle of wine and a thank-you note — which included the news that they'd signed us up for a free-trial box from the meal-box company, too. *Thanks for being such a thoughtful neighbor!* If they only knew. When our box came, Gary opened it in the kitchen but as expected was too overwhelmed by the sheer volume of items in the box and too annoyed by all the wasteful packaging to actually consider using it to cook the meals. Instead, he dropped it off at Morningside Montessori's after-school program so they could use it as a teaching tool: this is how to cook using premeasured ingredients, and this is what stupid wasteful packaging looks like.

Tonight Gary has already started the salad when I take out salmon and broccoli from the refrigerator, which, when finished, will look nothing like the perfectly plated dishes on the meal-box-delivery cards that I've seen on Instagram. "So remember when I did that Bring-Your-Parent-or-Grandparent-or-Beloved-Guardian-to-School Day recently?" I wait for him to nod before I tell him the rest. "Well, Mr. Noah announced that they've invited some People Puppets from Vermont for this year's Autumn Inhabitancy who are going to need housing."

Gary stares at the cucumber in his hand and his face goes slack. "I don't even know where to start with that sentence."

"I know, but the important part is that host families will get a tuition credit, which we could really use," I say, without getting too specific — I keep most of the details of our financial distress from Gary, since they only make him more anxious, which makes me more anxious. Then I close the refrigerator door slowly so I don't accidentally whack the dog sling with it, and move over to the cutting board with my onion, garlic, and lemon.

"Um, what exactly are People Puppets?"

"What I got from the photo that Mr. Noah held up," I say, pointing with my knife, "is that they're some kind of life-size costumed characters."

"Like Disney World and Chuck E. Cheese?"

"More handmade, and crafty. With bedsheets for bodies and papier-mâché heads." I wipe my onion tears on my sleeve. "I think."

Having to comprehend and categorize a new life-size puppet hybrid is clearly making him anxious: he puts the knife down and reaches into his front pocket for a Klonopin, then bites off half. "So they're not hand puppets."

"No, they are most definitely not hand puppets."

"And they're not large marionette-type puppets with strings?"

"No. They did not appear to have strings. Nor did they appear to be sock puppets. Or Muppets. I think I saw a cow and a horse

110

and maybe a moose, but I wasn't wearing my glasses, so who knows what was actually in the picture."

Gary paces with the still-unpeeled cucumber in his hand, waiting for his pill to take effect. "I can't believe we're talking about puppets."

"Yeah, well, this is what we signed on for when we left public school: puppets, and 'Inhabitancies' " — I hand him the peeler — "which in regular school are just called special 'units.' "

He stares absently at the cucumber and then at the peeler. "Maybe we should pull him out of there."

I ignore him. Knowing that we're behind in tuition — *really really behind,"* to quote Grace — and realizing that leaving early might actually be forced on us, and on Teddy, makes me not even want to joke about it. Leaving early is only fun when it's a choice. And when it doesn't involve the school that your child likes, even though he won't admit to liking anything anymore.

"Not to mention an aggressive fluidity with normative surnames," I add, then explain that when Mr. Noah introduced me to talk about writing, he referred to Teddy as "Teddy Vogel."

"God." Annoyed, he starts to loudly chop

the cucumber even though it's just supposed to be sliced. "So did you at least make
everyone wear bird merch?" he says, changing the subject.

I tell him that I wore my hat but didn't
bring any T-shirts from the endless stash of
giant cardboard boxes in the basement.
Then I shrug like I don't care, even though
I care more than I thought I would, more
than I want to admit. "Which was a good
thing, since there was some kind of emergency in the middle school building and
someone came running in to get Mr. Noah
at the exact moment I was supposed to start
talking."

"Someone replenished the soy milk but
forgot the almond milk?"

I try to laugh, then change the subject to
an even tougher one. "I saw Glenn today."

Despite my halfhearted attempt to sound
upbeat, Gary stares at me. "Is she okay?"

"Not really."

"I thought the chemo was working."

"I don't think it is. She looks worse. She
looks worse every time I see her."

He puts the knife and the cucumber
down. "I feel like we've had this conversation before."

We have: five years ago with my mother,
then three years ago with my father. Each

112

time we'd try to find signs of improvement
— however minor, however incremental —
that didn't exist — until the end, which was,
sadly, the only improvement.

"Does she know?"

"Of course she knows." I tell him about
our coffee date: the people she scared off,
how badly she felt afterward, the way she
begged for distraction. Then I tell him about
her request that we host the People Puppets. Which feels like a final request. Gary
walks over to me, buries both hands inside
the sling in the dog's thick fur, the closest
we get now to hugging or touching. "We
can't say no," I say.

"Of course we can't. Which she knows.
God, she's such an asshole," he whispers,
because if he didn't he would start to cry.
And I haven't even told him the part about
agreeing to take Lucy. He shakes his head.
"I still can't believe this is happening."

I paw at the dog now, too. I can't believe
it either.

"How long?" he asks.

I lean my back against the counter and
put my hands on my hips, feeling the flesh
folding over the top of my jeans, beyond the
sling. Normally I'd grab it and curse it, but
thinking of Glenn in her bed right now, with
all her rapidly dividing cells and her not-

long-for-this world eyes, I feel lucky to have it. "Three months — maybe six?" But I'm lying. I'm actually thinking a month, two if we're lucky. I remember my parents, how they compared at those time markers — their weight, their stamina, their appetite, their will to live — and I sense that she is further along than we think — but I don't want to upset Gary, so I backtrack: "I'm probably overreacting. She was probably just tired."

He takes a deep breath, holds it, lets it out slowly — one of the calming exercises he's learned to control some of the physical symptoms of his anxiety. When he reaches into the sling one last time to pat the dog on the head, he reaches out to pet me on the head, too. Which, like most things about our relationship, is totally weird but somehow not weird at all. It's at that moment that I notice Teddy lurking just outside the kitchen — he has an uncanny ability to pick up on when we're having an important conversation; to sense when we're trying to keep something from him.

"What's wrong with Glennie?" he asks me, moving into the kitchen from the shadows and staring at the vegetables we're chopping, knowing he won't eat them. Glenn is the fun aunt he never officially had,

114

the one who gave him extravagant gifts —
huge stuffed animals, paints and easels, giant LEGO sets — and, after my parents
were gone, went to every school performance and concert at Morningside Montessori, including the African drumming and
improv Inhabitancies, and even the little
pre-Thanksgiving and pre-Solstice classroom celebrations.

"She's sick. But you know that."

"So why were you talking about her?"

"Because I just saw her. We met for coffee
today and I was telling her about going to
your school the other day, how my presentation got interrupted, and how they're looking for families to host People Puppets. She
thinks it would be fun for us to host them.
Like we'd get some good stories out of it
that would be fun for her to hear." I smile
broadly, desperately. "If Daddy agrees."

"Of course I agree. I'm a brave bear,"
Gary says, nodding, taking another deep
breath, convincing himself. "And so is
Glenn. She's a very very brave bear."

"Would she come over and visit if they
were here?"

I shrug. "I hope so!" I shrug again. "She'll
probably feel a little better next week. Or
the week after. We'll just have to see!" My
voice cracks but I cough over it, then wipe

my eyes with the back of my hand. "Stupid onion!"

Teddy is still looking at me like I'm telling him there is a Santa Claus: like he wants to believe but knows he shouldn't.

"Is she gonna die, too?"

Long before the sling, during the fall before my mother got sick, when the universe of our tiny immediate family was still in perfect alignment and I was the sun of Teddy's world, we got into a new routine: once a week or so, after school pickup, I'd take him to Costco for a snack: a churro or a slice of pizza or some ridiculous thing they called a chicken bake (chicken, cheese, bacon bits, all wrapped up in a cheese-covered crust). Costco was right off the highway that connected school to home, and it seemed as good a place as any to kill that strange and slightly sad gap in time between after-school and going-home, especially as the fall would wear on and it got colder and darker earlier and earlier.

We didn't go to Costco every day: most pre-sling days I'd take the dog for a walk; some days Teddy would have a playdate or stay a few hours at the after-school program, building forts in the woods behind the school or shooting baskets in the all-purpose room that's kind of a gym but isn't really or playing made-up card games with the younger kids, imagining that they were all his siblings. Other days we'd just come home and he'd play outside if the kids on the street were there or he'd watch TV and I'd make him a snack — a little frozen pizza or some macaroni and cheese from a box or a bowl of ramen noodles, torn from the plastic package, the bowl on a saucer with a napkin underneath to catch the spills. But for a few months we'd gone to Costco on a pretty regular basis, and while it wasn't something I bragged about on social media, since his churro or slice of pizza or chicken bake didn't come with a side of organic broccoli or a soccer practice or a French horn lesson, it was something he liked to do — with me — and so, we'd do it.

I loved taking Teddy to Costco and sitting and eating and talking at a white indoor picnic bench with a red plastic umbrella under all that unnatural artificial turkey-neck-revealing fluorescent light. It was my guilty pleasure, what I looked forward to most every week. Because even then, years before it happened, I knew that there would come a time when I'd be begging him to do things like that. Being a child's primary focus is temporary, fleeting; I knew that the aperture was closing, that the light on me would eventually dim and I'd be replaced with friends.

Once he'd decide what to order, I'd pay for it, then he'd find a table and get the napkins while I waited for the food and got the little cups for free water. Life is made up of tiny rituals, and those were ours, the ones I loved most, especially the part when I would find him and set the food on the table and sit down across from him. While I watched him eat, we'd talk about his day, my day, his friends, my friends; we'd talk about which we liked better, plain pizza or pepperoni, churros or fried dough, the Stones or the Beatles; and while the questions and answers would vary, the feel of our Costco trips was always the same: it was special time. Joy is joy, no matter where you find it or what you're doing, and those afternoons at Costco, sitting together under all that harsh light, was our version of special time.

As my mother began dying that winter, we even made a friend there: a big white-haired old man who always wore an L.L.Bean field coat and wide-wale corduroys, and who would often appear in the snack area at the same time we did. He cut such an unusual figure and had such an otherworldly presence when we'd talk that I started to wonder if Virgilius — that was actually his name — was real or if he was instead some sort of apparition, a phantom, a ghost, sent to teach me something I didn't know I needed to learn. Natural or supernatural, by early spring as my mother continued her decline, we stopped seeing Virgilius at the snack bar. The emptiness I felt at the unexplained absence of a virtual stranger made me almost wish we'd never met him. There was only so much loss I could brace for.

Teddy would finish his churro or his slice, or both, and then we'd do a fake-shop: I'd use my expired membership card to enter the warehouse area and walk around without buying anything. We were trying to save money, and not renewing our old membership seemed like a smart thing, as did walking up and down the aisles and looking at all the shiny stuff we knew we weren't going to buy: flat-screen TVs and video game systems, keyboards and guitars, toaster ovens and vacuum cleaners, giant slabs of meat and huge boxes of cereal. Not even a weirdly packaged DVD of the first season of *There's a Bird on Your Head* that Teddy once found and held up to his face until I took his picture with my old BlackBerry, back

119

when he would still let me do things like that. After a complete circuit through the store we'd leave, slipping out through an empty register aisle, past the snack area where we'd started, toward the automatic sliding doors into the cold and out to the car, looking one last time for Virgilius.

Sometimes Teddy would ask me if I thought we didn't see him anymore because he was sick and dying, too, and unlike some of the other questions he'd ask me then — *What kind of cancer does Bubbie have? Why does she sleep all the time now? How come she isn't fat anymore? Is she going to die?* — I didn't have an answer for him. All I knew was that his absence was proof that people stayed with you for the rest of your life no matter when you stopped seeing them or when their body disappeared from your world.

Just as we'd go through the sliding doors and my face would hit the rush of cold air, just when I'd feel myself slipping away into the familiar comfort of that dissociative state, away from remembering that my mother was dying, Teddy would take my hand on the way to the car, and bring me back. We were buddies on a field trip, going somewhere on the other side of the glass together.

THE SECRET POOPER

On the way to school the next morning, I plan on telling Grace that we want to be a People Puppets host family. I'm leaning out the window, staring at an addition to a house that seems to have sprouted up overnight, which is when Teddy pokes me on the arm.

"Someone's been pooping at school."

"Well, I should hope so," I say, distracted by a monstrous three-story turret-like-silo jutting out of the left side of a blue-black Gorey-esque Victorian. "That's what bathrooms are for. And it's bad to hold it in every day, by the way, if that's what you're still doing. There's no shame in doing your business at school if you have to. Everybody poops." I wonder if I'll ever pass up an opportunity to bore him with a teaching moment.

"No, Mom. They didn't poop *in* the bathroom. They pooped in the hallway *in front* of the bathroom. Like on the floor."

I turn to him. *"On the floor?"* He nods. I'm certain that I've missed something. "Start again."

He does — and this time he describes, in a fair amount of detail, how the first incident started when Ms. Grace, as the students call her, ran into the classroom, wild-eyed and almost in tears and yelping in a high-pitched squeal to Mr. Noah: "Oh my God! There's something you need to see right away!"

The middle-schoolers — all ten or eleven of them, gangly and awkward and barely coordinated — somehow rushed into the hallway before Mr. Noah could get in front of the troubling tableau and block their view of it: "it" being a perfect pile of poop, much like the ubiquitous cartoonish emoji: tiered, piled high, deep brown. Grace squealed in horror again, as did Mr. Noah, before they managed to corral the students back to the classroom and call the janitor, Ms. JoJo, to remove the mess. The teachers — rattled, whispering in the corner — could then be overheard assessing the possibility that the excrement had been produced by a dog that had somehow entered the building, done its business, and then let itself out — all without being seen or heard. But the "dog theory" was debunked as quickly as it had been suggested, since both teachers, who had several dogs between them, knew, as did their pet-owning students, that there was a clear difference between animal poop and human poop. No one who had ever picked up after the family dog in the backyard or on a walk in the woods would mistake what they'd seen on the buffed wood floor of the second-floor school hallway for anything other than what it was: people poop.

The second time was the morning of my presentation. The students and Mr. Noah were already in the multipurpose room when Grace, who had lagged behind the others to prepare a handout for a pre-Inhabitancy PowerPoint presentation — "Puppetry Through the Ages" — came upon the pile of feces in a slightly different spot — this time, on the floor *inside* the unisex bathroom: outside the stalls and in front of the row of sinks. Later that day, the students were questioned, one by one, in the science lab adjoining the main middle school classroom, by the teachers who tag-teamed, continually checking the hallway for another pile of poop.

"What do you mean you were questioned?"

"They asked each of us if we were the

Pooper."

"Flat out. Like, straight out. As in, 'Are you the one who pooped on the floor on purpose?' " Teddy nods. "And when you said no, what happened?"

"They asked us if we had seen anything weird, if we had any idea who was doing it."

"And had you seen anything weird?"

"No."

"So as far as you know, some kid has somehow managed to drop their pants," I say, mindfully using a gender-neutral pronoun, "and poop instantaneously — and very very quickly — leaving the scene before anyone sees them."

When he shrugs, I shake my head. "I'm sorry, but I don't buy it."

"You don't believe me?"

"Of course I believe *you.* I'm just not sure I believe that it's happening the way it seems." Instead of explaining what I mean — I'm not even sure I know what I mean beyond having a nagging suspicion that something about this story isn't making sense. How does someone, outside a full classroom the first time, and down the hall from an entire schoolful of people gathered for an assembly the second time, poop on the floor that quickly — on command, essentially — without being seen? I focus on

124

the fact that this secret pooper has been on the loose at the school for almost a week and no one has notified the parents. Which is maddening and strange, since the school usually finds any and every excuse to communicate operational minutiae to parents via email and voicemail (*"Please note: the refrigerator in the teachers' room is being replaced this week with one that has a bigger capacity but a much higher energy-efficiency rating!" "New entrance mats for foot-wiping have now been installed! Children from homes that still use commercial salt and sand mixtures [and who should really switch to environmentally friendly nontoxic compounds . . .] please wipe well before entering the school!"*) So why the sudden radio silence, now that one of the middle-schoolers is a probable sociopath?

"The bottom line is that the school should have told the parents."

"But *I* told you."

"But you're a kid."

"But now you know. Isn't that what matters?"

"Yes, but what also matters is that the adults do the right thing." Finally past the giant addition, weaving around the usual mess of tow trucks and backhoes and pool diggers — *Pool diggers? In Cambridge?* —

125

but there's no time for house ogling today. "They're the grown-ups. They're supposed to tell us about any kind of dangerous situation."

"Dangerous? It's just poop."

I can see a flash of fear in Teddy's eyes, even under the hair that crosses his nose, how he starts to fidget with the zipper on his hooded sweatshirt. Great. I've leaked my fear and distrust of life and sparked his, just like my parents did to me. Have I learned nothing about how to pretend I have faith and hope in humanity so that I don't incite and escalate my child's imagination about all the dormant evil lurking in the world? "You're right," I say, trying for a calming clinical tone. "I'm being ridiculous. It is just poop." And then, of course, because I can't help myself, I add: "But sometimes disturbing behavior is a symptom of something else."

"Like what?"

"Sadness. Loneliness. Being deeply troubled." I look down at the sling and realize that I should probably either use myself as an example of the connection between feelings and behavior manifesting in some kind of outward sign or metaphor — *I'm sad, therefore I wear my dog* — or stop talking so he doesn't make the damning connection

126

himself. "Sometimes the things we do are clues to how we're really feeling. So, like, if someone poops like this, on the floor, at school, it probably means they're unhappy. Or angry. Or maybe they're unhappy *and* angry at school, since that's where they're doing the pooping." I pause to think. "Unless they're also pooping on the floor at home, which would mean they're unhappy there, too."

Teddy is now running the zipper of his sweatshirt up and down in short frantic spurts. "Maybe it's not a kid who's doing it."

I pull into the school lot, push the gearshift into park, and turn to him. It hadn't occurred to me that it wasn't. But now that he's mentioned it: maybe he's right. Maybe it's a grown-up, a pissed off teacher, a disgruntled employee. "When the poop was discovered, were both teachers in the classroom?"

He thinks for a minute. "The first time, Mr. Noah was teaching and Ms. Grace was on her way into the classroom. And the second time was when we were all downstairs for your thing."

"So Ms. Grace found the poop both times." That's like finding a body. Once is possible; but twice? Isn't that too much of a coincidence? Or maybe it is entirely a co-incidence. Teachers probably get their anger out in different, less creepy ways — refusing to give extra help after school when asked for it; grading down; being shitty to kids they don't like. Little power-grabs and shame-fests. Could it be that Morningside Montessori is harboring a teacher with a serious grudge against the school? Doubt-ful. No, my money is on a student — a boy, I'm sorry to say — someone who is troubled at home or maybe the product of an un-pleasant divorce, a boy for whom the daily annoyance of school feels like the last straw.

I let Teddy go into the building first before I go in to track down Mr. Noah or Grace — whomever I find first — which turns out to be Grace. Same zip-up fleece; same beverage-equipped nylon knapsack; same plastic container being snapped shut with a loud and proud freshness-burp. She waves, friendly and conspiratorially, as I open the glass door to the office.

"Have you decided about the People Pup-pets?" she coos.

"We need to talk first."

"Of course," she whispers, pulling me off to the side of the office. "The tuition credit. Now, if you're able to take *two* People Puppets, we can give you more money. Close to a full month's worth, which would bring your account almost, but not quite — *but almost!* — current." She opens her knapsack, takes out a file folder, and quickly flips through the papers inside. "Nick and Phoebe, who lead the puppet company, are a couple," she says, rolling her eyes and shrugging, as if to say, *Young people! Who knows?!* Then she shows me printouts of each of them, like mug shots. "So they'd be a logical pair to take."

I ignore the pages she's holding up. "Tell me about the Secret Pooper."

"Excuse me?"

"The Secret Pooper. The Mysterious Defecator. The Crazy Shitter. Whatever you're calling the person who's gone to the bathroom on the floor of the middle school. *Twice.*"

She lets out a short panicked gasp. "Who told you about that?"

"My son, of course!" My voice is suddenly shrill but I don't care. "Why haven't you informed parents? Why haven't you told us? We have a right to know that our kids could be in danger." I want to poke her but I don't.

"I'm sorry, Judy, but I'm late for Spanish," she says, racing now around the big teachers' table, collecting her things — folders and books and a big ceramic mug of tea that produces so much steam I wonder if it's full of dry ice. Unlike last week, when she chased me down the hallway and wouldn't leave me alone, she barely looks at me now.

"I can't believe there's been no official word about this extremely disturbing situation. I mean, how many emails went out to parents last year about acceptable brands of organic non-GMO gluten-free pancake mix for the annual pancake breakfast?" When she doesn't answer, I do. "At least twenty."

"Accommodating dietary restrictions is something the administration and the school community take very seriously."

"More than informing parents and protecting children from a potential psychopath-situation?"

She stops and makes a frownie-face by pulling down on both sides of her mouth with her fingers. "Oh, Judy. I can't believe you're that kind of parent."

My mouth drops open. "What does *that* mean?"

"It means you're totally overreacting. It's not a 'situation.' It's a small problem that we're taking very seriously. We're trying to get to the bottom of it."

I make a frownie-face with my mouth, too. "Pardon the pun."

She doesn't laugh and neither do I. I get the distinct feeling that she's hiding something — at the very least she's minimizing the problem. Willful ignorance and denial seem to be their only strategy.

"Do you know who's doing it?"

"No. But we're looking at every single middle-schooler, since they're the ones with access to this building. Even the quiet kids." She doesn't blink. "*Especially* the quiet kids."

My stomach drops. I suddenly remember everything I told her that day after my presentation — how worried I was about how introverted Teddy had become. "What does that mean?" I'm so afraid she's referring to him that I'm tempted to apologize.

"It means, no one is above suspicion." Grace stops at the glass door before opening it. "Oh, and Judy?" she says, pointing to the sling. "Next time, leave the dog at home. Without an official therapy vest and the accompanying paperwork, pets are not allowed in the school."

"The dog's name is Charlotte."

"I don't care, Judy."

"Well you should."

"Well I don't."

"Well that says a lot about why this place is turning to shit. Literally."

"Don't let the door hit you on the way out."

I give her the finger, but only from inside the sling and only after she's turned around to leave her office.

THE ARRIVAL OF THE PEOPLE PUPPETS

The following week, two full-size People Puppets wearing costumes constructed from everyday recycled materials sit across from us in the living room — People Puppets on one couch, humans — and a dog — on the other. The scene is freakish enough, but I'm still unnerved by the creepy encounter with Grace — tempted even, out of an abundance of caution, to cancel the housing-in-exchange-for-tuition-credit deal we'd made. What would stop her from sending the People Puppets into our house with cameras or recording devices to get information on us? (*"Someone could be — and probably is! — spying on you right now — with their smartphone"*), I'd thought while I tried, and failed, to fall asleep. But I decided not to. Canceling seemed like an escalation, and while I didn't like her and didn't trust her, keeping our agreement in place seemed like a de-escalation. That, and the fact that we still needed that stupid tuition credit so that Teddy wouldn't have to leave school.

"So, I'm Judy, and this is Gary." I can feel myself break into a big nervous smile.

The puppet on the left answers first. "I'm Phoebra the Zebra. Well, Phoebe in real life. And this is Nick the Llama."

I repeat the words slowly, and so does Gary — *Phoebra. The. Zebra.* Then: *Nick. The. Llama.* — but nothing poetic happens. We exchange glances, afraid we're already doing it wrong.

"Don't worry," the Llama says. "It's not you. It doesn't rhyme. But for whatever reason, that's my name anyway." He leans in for Gary's hand, then stops short. "Oops. Let me take my 'hoof' off first." They shake, and then he puts the hoof back on.

Gary looks from one puppet to the other. He's so confused he doesn't even know how to form a question, but I know exactly what he's thinking: *let's leave.*

"I thought you were" — he searches for his words — "puppeteers. Like the Muppets."

"No. We're the actual puppets."

"We don't just hold the puppet," Phoebe clarifies. "We become the puppet."

I point to my sling. "Kind of like me and my dog!"

The first of many birds appears on my head.

"Exactly!" Nick says. "See, I'm the llama and the llama is me. But who am I and who is the llama? Where does one end and the other begin?"

There's a bird on Nick's head.

Gary nods. "Not to be an asshole, but I have no idea what that means."

"It's okay. Most people don't get it."

Gary leans forward. "But you work with children. Isn't it important that they get it?"

"Children *do* get it!" Nick says. "Because life is still full of mystery and magic for them!"

Gary snorts. I ignore him. "Teddy used to totally be into magic," I blurt. "Back before he became a joyless teenager. We still have his black satin cape in the basement."

Teddy turns sideways in the doorway, as if he's trying to slip in between the molding and the wall. "See?" I point, and everyone turns. "He's trying to make himself disappear right now!"

"Mom. *Stopppp.*"

Nick waves at Teddy. "Do you like puppets, dude?"

Teddy shrugs, smiles shyly. "They're okay I guess."

135

Nick turns to Gary. "Do you like puppets?"

Gary's mouth actually drops open. He shoots me another desperate look. I know exactly what he is thinking: *Seriously. We have to leave. But how can we leave early from our own house?* Since he's not answering Nick's question, I decide to talk for him, thinking, ironically, that in doing so he's like my puppet. "In theory, Gary likes puppets," I say. "But in reality, Gary is terrified of puppets. He's actually terrified of all costumed characters."

"Judy —" He tries to stop me, but it's too late — I'm already blurting the alleged origin story of his phobia: one of Gary's first jobs in college, at a Chuck E. Cheese-style restaurant, as one of three costumed mice playing on a tiny stage in front of families eating shitty pizza.

"He told me that he got almost all the way through his first shift, but suddenly the music stopped and he pulled off his giant mouse costume head and started screaming: 'I can't breathe! I can't breathe!' "

There's a bird on Gary's head. "The air-tube-mouthpiece-thingy inside the head part was *blocked.*"

"With anxiety," I whisper.

"I couldn't breathe, man!" Gary erupts,

before catching himself and looking around, embarrassed. "Sorry."

I adjust the dog on my lap and pretend everything is fine. "So, how did you get into puppetry, Phoebe?"

"My moms were founding members of this puppet theater at Bennington College," she explains. "They still perform — in fact, they just did a puppet adaptation of *The Vagina Monologues.* They wear these huge vagina costumes, made out of dark red velvet, and ohmygod it's totally embarrassing."

Nick turns to Gary, man-puppet to man. "Dude. You have no idea."

I can see Gary doing the math in his head — dog sling, vagina costume, same thing. "I think I do."

"Not that there's anything wrong with vaginas, Teddy," Nick explains, a sage in llama's clothing. "They're beautiful. I mean, I'm not sure how much you know about stuff like that." He turns to me and covers his mouth with his hoof. "Sorry."

"No problem," I lie, as if I'm totally fine discussing vaginas in my living room with Teddy blushing in the doorway. I quickly change the subject. "Were your parents into puppets, Nick?"

"My father was. He loves everything to do

with theater. Which is pretty much why my mother divorced him. Which was kind of a big deal. At the time."

"Well, that's something you two have in common!" I say, elbowing Gary. "Gary's parents got divorced and he still hasn't gotten over it!"

Nick points down at his costume shamefully. "Neither have I. Hence the career switch."

"You weren't always a puppet?" Gary asks.

"I went to law school because my mother wanted me to but I never practiced because I never took the bar. I hated it. It just wasn't me."

"It wasn't me, either," Gary says, softening. "I dropped out after my first year at Georgetown to play music."

"I didn't know you went to law school," Teddy says. I watch as something — surprise? confusion? disappointment? — crosses his face. "Jackson's dad is a lawyer." It's the first time I realize that Teddy is deep in the age of comparison — seeing himself and his family in relation to others, though what he thinks about those differences I have no idea, except that I'm sure I come up short compared to other moms who don't wear the family dog.

"I thought I'd told you," Gary says absently. He's a terrible liar. "Sometimes you just know that something isn't for you and law school wasn't for me. I couldn't take the pressure. I was practically hospitalized after the first year." He laughs to make it sound like a joke, even though it's fairly close to the truth. After dropping out, years before we met, he'd spent the summer living with his mother in his old bedroom in New Hampshire, the one with a twin bed and airplane wallpaper, and decided to go back to music, his true passion. If not for his anxiety, which got more and more debilitating, he would have had an amazing career, I'm sure of it.

"And a year after that he opened for Aerosmith!" I say super enthusiastically, citing his résumé highlights from memory, since aside from a few grainy old videos, pre-iPhone quality, I've never seen Gary perform live in a big venue. Except for small bars and coffeehouses, he'd stopped playing with his band before we met, and I've always wished I had known that version of him.

"Our band did," Gary corrects.

"Dude! Impressive!" Nick says.

"It was a long time ago," Gary says, changing the subject. Reminiscing always makes him uncomfortable — how does he explain to people what happened to his promising future, how does he square the present with the past, when he barely understands it himself? "I'm in snacks now. Ordering, stocking, and restocking beverages and crunchy, chewy, salty, and sweet nut and protein bars. It's a low-pressure job. Relatively. Unless you run out of Kind bars right before the four o'clock rush." He pauses, then lowers his voice to an intense whisper. "But I do miss playing sometimes. I went to hear a band last week and I was like, *man,* I want to do that again someday."

"Last week?" I'm confused. "Before or after couples therapy?"

There's an awkward silence.

"You guys go to couples therapy?" Teddy asks, inching into the living room.

Gary sighs. "Thanks, Judy."

I turn to Teddy. "We just go once in a while. For maintenance. Like going to the gym."

Teddy's eyes narrow. "You guys fight all the time, so I don't think it's working."

Everybody laughs, and Teddy's face relaxes, brightens. Even adolescents love the power of cracking people up.

"We do not!" Gary says.

"You're scaring the People Puppets, Teddy! Now they're not going to want to stay here!" I turn to Nick and Phoebe. "We absolutely do not fight all the time, I swear! Plus we have a great dog!"

"We love dogs!" Phoebe says.

"Not that any dog care will be required, since, as you can see, I've got that covered." I hug the dog through the cotton, then stick my hand inside the sling for a calming hit of fur. *Yum.*

"As you can see," Gary says, "Judy wears the dog."

Nick and Phoebe shrug inside their giant costumes. "That's cool. That's cool," Nick says. "Everyone has their thing."

"It's a long story," Gary explains, "which I'm sure Judy will eventually tell you — she tells everyone at some point."

"Because I've worked past my shame."

Gary nods. "Yes, she's worked past her shame."

"Shame was very big in my family."

"Shame is big in everyone's family, Judy."

I ignore Gary. "I used to be embarrassed about the sling but I'm not anymore. This may not be who I am forever but it's who I am right now." I have no idea what I'm talking about. (*"Professional social workers 'meet people where they are' and so should you: how self-acceptance is the secret sauce of self-help."*)

141

"We certainly hope it's not who you are forever!" Gary says, elbowing me lightly.

"But it's who I am right now," I repeat. (*"Looking for a life anthem? Edie Brickell FTW: 'What I am is what I am.'"*)

"Indeed it is."

The bird on my head has a bird on its head, which I take as my cue to stand up and head toward the kitchen. "How about a house tour?"

I won't lie: it feels strange to have giant costumed characters in our house, knowing they'll soon take over the snoring room, which will force Gary and me to share a bedroom again, albeit temporarily. The sound of their hoof-shoes on the wood floors, the way the fabric of their oversize clothes catches on doors and stair banisters, how they need to bow their papier-mâché heads under light fixtures and entry moldings: it's what I do all the time, too, I realize now. Maneuvering the sling in stairwells and around furniture, I'm always conscious of my width in tight spaces and squishing the sling when necessary — and this ability to navigate daily life encumbered by such a protrusion suddenly feels like an actual skill, one I could list on a résumé, which I should probably start sending out at some point to supplement the Well/er work. But for now I try to stop looking at them like they have birds on their heads, and try to remember instead why they're here and why we're doing this: for the money. And for Glenn. And to move past our still point.

We all head toward the kitchen, but before I can even finish showing Phoebe our "open pantry" (which is really just a closet that was missing a door when we bought the house and which we never bothered to fix and ended up filling with makeshift shelving) and brag about our love of organic grains and commitment to #MeatlessMondays (in truth, we had just one vegetarian Monday) to help save the planet — all lies — Teddy peels off to go back upstairs, and the men — Gary and Nick — slip down the other stairs to the basement, where they will undoubtedly be up to no good in no time.

I raise an eyebrow to Phoebe. "I guess Gary is going to show Nick his etchings."

Behind her I suddenly see the side of a giant box of Frosted Flakes, Gary and Teddy's favorite, sticking out from behind a small prop-box of the ancient grain farro, its florid electric-blue packaging screaming ignorance and a complete and willful disregard for health and nutrition, and making me wonder yet again what kind of parent I am. I want to reach behind her head and cover it with the nearby box of polenta and two cans of pinto beans, which are probably expired, but there isn't time, and if she caught me it would only make things worse. How would I possibly explain that I was pretending to swat at a nonexistent fly or clear away a nonexistent spiderweb because I was trying to hide some stupid highly processed food?

"Nick's not gay, if that's what you're thinking," she says, sweetly, without a trace of annoyance or rage, the two main emotion-molecules that make up most of everything I feel when I'm around people. "Not that there's anything wrong with that."

I wave my hand a few times too many, trying way too hard to backtrack. "Of course not!"

"Just because he's a People Puppet — someone who likes to walk around in a big costume — doesn't mean he's hiding under there. In fact, the costume allows him to be more himself."

I nod vigorously even though I'm not entirely sure what she's talking about and how that's possible — how wearing something that separates you from the world could possibly be considered anything other than insulation or protection or a way to hide — *I should know!* — and because I've just spied a package of Paul Newman sandwich cookies that I stupidly hid in an abundance of caution when I didn't even have to and that could have made us actually look good, since all proceeds from his products go to charity.

"Sometimes what starts out as protective gear turns out to set us free," Phoebe adds, looking down at my stomach area. I follow her gaze and absently realize, yet again, that I'm wearing the dog — which is almost always a complete shock, so much a part of me, like an extra limb, or a pregnancy belly, the dog has become.

"Therapy dogs are so cool."

I laugh out loud — the demented caw of the delusional, of the perpetually misunderstood — still reeling from Grace's awful parting words to me yesterday and the haunting threat of her possibly suspecting that Teddy could be the Secret Pooper. "She's not a therapy dog! She's just a dog! That I wear! Because she's really anxious! All the time!" I lean up against the canned goods section of our fraudulent health closet and something sharp sticks into my back, but I ignore it. The nerve of someone I'm trying to help with free housing — someone barely out of college in a zebra costume and papier-mâché hooves — accusing me of

145

having a therapy dog. It feels like an assault. I'm tempted to change my mind and clear the bad puppet-energy out of the house.

Then Glenn and her bald head appear like a flash, and I stare down at the sling, put my arms underneath it, and hug the dog toward me. I feel the urge to tell Phoebe everything — about the farce of my marriage, about having a teenager who doesn't seem to need or like me anymore, about having a friend who's dying, but all I say is: "Not that there's anything wrong with therapy dogs."

Phoebe searches my face, sees the tears forming, shakes her head. "I didn't mean to offend you. I don't even know you and I shouldn't have assumed anything about you."

I wipe my eyes and wave her away. "I assume things all the time, and even though I'm almost always wrong, it's my guilty pleasure. I can't help myself. Like, for instance, I assumed you didn't get my 'etchings' reference because you're so young."

"But I watch old movies. And one of my moms' favorite *New Yorker* cartoons is the one that says, 'You wait here and I'll bring the etchings down.' "

We both laugh until I get quiet. "You have

two moms," I say, more a statement than a question. "That's cool."

"You think?"

I shrug. "I don't have a mom anymore. Or a dad. And my best friend who kind of felt like a mom is sick now. Which is probably why I wear my dog." I stick both hands deep inside the sling, into all that warm fur, until the tears stop.

Phoebe's face falls, and she reaches to squeeze my arm. "I'm sorry."

"I shouldn't have said anything. I'm just a big old Debbie Downer sometimes."

"No you're not. Sometimes life is just really, really sad. Like, I have a friend who's dealing with a really heavy thing right now in his family. It's hard to imagine what's going to happen, but I guess he'll just get through it, right? I mean, that's all you can do. Do your best to survive the bad times."

There is something so comforting in her words that I'm thrown back to the days right before my father died when I knew the end was coming. I couldn't bear to go through the final decline — first slow, then swift and shocking — again, so soon after going through it with my mother, so for one week I just stopped visiting him in his assisted living apartment. It was the holidays, cold and dark and icy, with colored lights twinkling everywhere. I had barely seen Teddy, there had been a ton of snow, and Gary told me I needed a break before I burned myself out completely and that the private nurses we'd hired would take care of things for a few days. But I'll never forgive myself for shutting down when his illness suddenly escalated. When I saw him next, he could no longer stand without help, and he barely recognized me. After all I had done right, I couldn't get past what felt like selfishness for taking that short break, for not being present during that part of his descent. It nearly ruined me. A few months after he'd died, on a cold March morning when I was walking around the reservoir with Glenn and the dogs, I was still consumed with guilt.

"You did your best, though, right?" she asked. When I couldn't even nod, she asked me again. "Tell me. Did you do your best?"

I thought back to the suddenness of his diagnosis — the reason he had been mixing up day and night was because of a tumor that had sprung up seemingly overnight in his brain like a big spongy mushroom — and surgery; the rush to get him placed in a good rehab hospital and then into a good assisted living facility that would agree to take such a short-term resident — they'd said he had a year at most, but it was exactly half that. As the dogs played in the tall grass along the path — Charlotte was still on a leash then — I thought of all the paperwork, all the trips back and forth to visit him during the day and in the evenings, sometimes taking the dog with me, or Teddy; how Gary would sometimes meet us there and we would have dinner with my father in the resident dining room, pretending that we were like all the other families at the surrounding tables, enjoying time with a healthy senior who had merely downsized from a big house to independent communal living. I thought about all the trips with him downtown for chemo, all the MRIs and phone calls to doctors, and to the insurance company, running, always running, from home to Teddy's school, to my father, back to Teddy, then home again. Those days and months were a blur, as opaque as the white sky that March day at the reservoir. I couldn't see past it.

"Then I will answer for you," Glenn said. "You did your best." When I didn't respond, she dug her fingers into my arm. "Say it. It's important that you say it. Because it's true."

"I did my best." The words came out with my breath and hung in the air.

"And?"

"I did my best and I was a brave bear."

"A very brave bear."

Today, with Phoebe, I nod. "That's exactly right. All you can do is do your best."

"Well!" Phoebe says, half-laughing half-crying, wiping tears from her eyes. "Now I'm the Debbie Downer! Let's get back to Nick! What else did you assume?"

I shift my weight, move my back away from whatever was sticking into it. "That he's probably about as big of a pothead as Gary is."

"Gary's a pothead?"

"He's supposed to be quitting. Again. Really soon." In my dreams.

"Well, you're certainly right about that," Phoebe says.

"I am?" I feel like I should win a prize, but she just grins at me benignly. I guess this is what a normal conversation is like: one measured, appropriate sentence after another. "How long have you guys been together?"

"A year this past August."

"A year!" I want to tell her a year is nothing, that everyone's happy after the first year, that it's the years that come later that will crush you if you're not careful, but she's staring past my head suddenly, then poking excitedly at something on one of the shelves with her unwieldy hooves.

"Frosted Flakes!" she squeals, turning to look at me, and when she does I can picture her at five, or six, or seven, her face wide open and full of joy, the way Teddy's used to be at that age. "I love Frosted Flakes! My moms never let me have them."

I reach for the box and beckon her out of the fake pantry into the fading autumn light of the kitchen. "I'll let you have some."

What starts as one bowl of cereal for Phoebe turns into two (hers looked really good and I didn't want her to eat alone), and then four, after Nick and Gary come upstairs. We finish the first box, and then Gary comes back with a second one, secreted from a high cabinet over the stove that I can't reach and always forget is even there. God knows what else he hides up there.

"A spare," he says, ripping open the blue cardboard top instead of slipping his thumb under the tab the way the directions say. "You never know when the munchies will strike."

"Oh Gary," I say. "*Munchies* is such an eighties word."

"Well, I'm an eighties guy."

"Besides, we had an agreement." I point

at Gary from across the cereal box. "No. Smoking. When. Teddy's. Home."

"We didn't smoke!"

I stop, sniff, and realize he might be telling the truth.

"Edi-pulls," Nick whispers then, giggling, takes a tiny packet out of his pants pocket, under his billowing costume, and shows it to me. "Oedipal's Edibles."

I take that as my cue to start the conversation about logistics; the when and how of their stay — three weeks, starting Friday; going through the week or so after the end of Inhabitancy, which would put us into mid-November; how they'll stay in the snoring room in the basement and use the bathroom and shower on the second floor.

"You'll share Teddy's bathroom."

"I'm sure he'll love that," Nick says.

"It's good for him," Gary says. "He's an only child. He needs to learn to share."

After the cereal and after the tour, after we've forced Teddy to come out of his room to say "goodbye and see you soon" to the People Puppets, Gary and I walk Nick and Phoebe to their car, parked at the end of our driveway, right behind the Volvo — a People Puppet Theater minivan — the kind I'd refused to buy when Teddy was small —

with nylon animal hooves on the roof that inflate when the van is in motion. Nick presses his key, and when the side door slides open, he climbs in and stands, almost upright, in the middle of all the seats and cup holders and boxes of theater gear. Then he bends down and reaches into one of their costume cases — a big trunk with a fake padlock on it just for show.

"Now, here's something I think Gary would love," he says, pulling out a huge white sheet with a hooded beak attached. He gathers it up, hops down out of the minivan, and holds it up against himself, striking a pose. " 'Free Bird.' "

Gary stares at him. "No way."

"Way!"

Gary looks at me, then at Nick. "I love Lynyrd Skynyrd!" he laugh-cries. "How did you know?"

"I just had a feeling!"

"He's very intuitive," Phoebe says.

"Try it on!" Nick says, pushing the fabric on him.

"No. I couldn't."

"He really shouldn't," I add, remembering the massive Chuck E. Cheese panic attack.

"It's just fabric!" Phoebe says, reassuringly. "No one ever got hurt by a little fabric."

"You have no idea," I say under my breath, but she ignores me, moves over toward Nick, and helps him put the costume over Gary's head. What I assume is a panicked struggle to resist — arms jutting out, then up, hands pawing frantically at the claustrophobic hooded beak — to keep the costume off — turns out to be an excited effort to get the costume on. I know this is happening because Gary is high, but even so, I can't help but cheer him on. "Go, Gary, go!" I mutter under my breath so as not to put too much pressure on him to be successful. "You can do it!"

Draped in white, and looking remarkably like a giant bird, Gary is triumphant on the sidewalk, taking a few steps forward, then back; his wings flapping, billowing in the chilly late-afternoon wind. Dying for a glimpse of himself, he races over to the minivan windows and strikes a pose, then turns to us. Phoebe snaps a few photos with her phone, which she shows to Gary. He has a little trouble focusing his eyes under the big head, but once he does, he erupts.

"I love it!" he laugh-cries again, then hugs himself with his wings.

"It's yours, dude. Keep it."

Gary gasps. "I couldn't possibly." Then: "Really? Can I?"

"I made it myself and I want you to have it." Nick nods meaningfully, and the puppets get into the front seat of the van. The engine starts and the side door slides shut.

Gary looks down, smooths the folds of fabric with his hands, shakes his head. He's too profoundly moved to speak. There may or may not be tears in his eyes. And in mine, too: even though he's doing this with the help of cannabis, his exuberance melts me.

"We'll be in touch," I say, for both of us.

They back out slowly, then wave as they drive down the street, the nylon hooves catching air and dancing on the roof of the minivan.

Gary watches in awe, waving wistfully until they're completely out of sight.

"I love that guy," he says. "I could really learn from him."

"Learn what?"

He shakes his head. "I have no fucking idea." He pauses. "Maybe we can be friends with them."

Clearly the edibles are talking again. "But you don't want friends. And you hate people."

He stares at me, mouth open, disbelieving. "They're not people, Judy," he says, seriously, reverently, ridiculously. "They're *puppets.*"

Therapy Dog

If I'm honest, which for some reason I hate to be when it comes to the dog, I'll admit that Charlotte's true origins were indeed as a therapy animal — for Teddy. We got Charlotte when Teddy was eight, around the time his sadness about being an only child and losing both of his grandparents began, or, intensified.

That year, having just started Morningside Montessori, having lost the few friends he'd made in public school as well as the comfort of a place and routine he knew — even if that school didn't know what to do with him, and now, in its sudden absence, it was loved and missed beyond expectation — a sense of being alone in the world consumed him. He saw people only in terms of the shape and size of their families: specifically, whether or not they had siblings. Which most of them did. And he did not.

The few only-children we knew — born

to couples who had, like us, started late and had decided to stop at just one — were our salvation, until each went back on their assurances to us that they would not have another child and all the other only-children in Teddy's universe became older siblings. The semicomical betrayal we'd feel when, over dinner, the announcement would come — *Sorry! We're pregnant!* — and after the baby itself arrived, that betrayal would turn on the fulcrum of Teddy's heartbreak. Becoming a sibling was a magical occurrence bestowed on other people but not on him, a fact that deepened the divide between him and the rest of the world, proving time and again to him that happiness was for other people, not for him. It was then that he started looking at the world with a sad hunger, a longing, a deep wish to be connected, to join, to be accepted into the arms of a big noisy happy family. Which we're not. Because we're just three. And three never felt like enough. It didn't when I was growing up. And it doesn't now.

Everyone else is lucky, he'd say. *They have siblings.*

I know, I'd say.

I really want one.

I know, I'd say again. Because I did know. I knew the longing, the solitude, the unbearable quiet of living in a house with no other children. And I also knew that I was too old to have another baby, because I was already almost too old when I'd had Teddy.

Sometimes we'd be driving when he'd talk about wanting a sibling — he'd be in the backseat because he was too young still to sit up front — on the way back from a playdate toward home, and a thick foggy sadness would creep into the car from the inside out. Sometimes we'd be in his room at night, me sitting on the edge of his bed and rubbing his back and talking to him about his day — a routine that is still in place, even now, despite all my complaining about the distance between us during the day, in public.

Sometimes it would be right after he'd come in for the night after playing all day with the kids on the street. He'd walk inside alone at dusk, and I'd catch him taking one last look over his shoulder to see everyone else paired, two by two, going home together for baths and dinner.

Sometimes, like when we'd leave from a visit with Gary's mother and sisters in New Hampshire — cousins and dogs spilling out into the backyard, all the kids in shorts swatting at mosquitoes, their bug spray and sunscreen long since worn off — there wouldn't be words at all. I'd see his face, full of joy at being part of a whole — at having a place in a big family — that feeling of fullness that comes from being in the midst of all that energy and activity, of all that life — right before it would fall, cheeks and eyes and mouth changing shape, dissolving, caving into itself like a dying flower.

It was always a cruel tearing away; his weeping would last almost an hour into the drive, when the crying would finally stop and the struggle between what he wanted and what he couldn't have, would never have, turned to silent resignation and to two unassailable beliefs:

Things will never change. I will always be alone.

Or, maybe those were my beliefs, projected onto him. If I'm being honest. I hated leaving, too — returning to our quiet world of three always felt like a punishment for something I'd been accused of long ago and didn't even do.

That's when Glenn suggested we get a dog. Why we ever thought a dog — just a dog — one simple animal — could fill that black hole, that dark space, for Teddy, I have no idea, but many people besides Glenn, including a psychiatrist we'd consulted about his learning issues, and Gary himself, who'd grown up with dogs, all thought that was the answer to our problem. I didn't grow up with animals, but Gary and Glenn swore it would help. Sure, we'd end up walking the dog and feeding the dog and training the dog and playing with the dog — no matter how much we'd try to teach Teddy the responsibility of pet care, Gary had warned — but it would be a long-term companion, a provider of love and affection, a protector against loneliness and sadness and grief.

I look down at the dog in the sling right now: *Check. Check. Check.* The dog is all of those things. For me. The law of unintended consequences.

And so it was after he started his new school, when he was the most bereft about being an only child, alone in the house with no one his age to talk to or play with or eat with; no one to eat cereal with in the morning and dinner with in front of the television as a treat on a Saturday night, or throw a ball with, or ride a bike with; no one to fight with and compete with and to feel less than or better than; no one to whisper good night to in the dark after rehashing the minutiae of his day — how he did at basketball, or video games, or skateboarding, or if he should even bother putting a crazy-expensive Star Wars LEGO set on his Christmas list or not because maybe there wasn't really a Santa — that we ended up getting a dog. Charlotte. I knew nothing about getting a dog, less about what I would do with it if we found one, but a few friends I'd made online were serious dog lovers who told me to start with rescue shelters. Every day after school, I'd pick Teddy up and every day we'd visit a shelter — in towns beyond his school, north and south; east and west — we'd park and get out of the car and he'd take my hand and I'd see his eyes close in silent prayer that we would find the perfect dog.

How will we know which dog is for us? he would ask. And I'd repeat what my dog-lover friends had told me: *we'll know.*

And so in and out of the shelters we'd go — leaving after a quick survey of the cages lining the walls — mostly pit bulls and rott-weilers and scrawny mutts and mixed breeds with missing eyes and paws and patches of fur. Hiding under his long hair and baseball cap, Teddy would look and shrug, which was his way of not saying that none of the dogs was our dog.

And none of them were. Until a cold January day — Martin Luther King Jr. Day — when he was home from school, and Gary was home from work — and when the house vibrated with so much tension between us that I took Teddy to the Harvard Museum of Natural History to look at the giant bugs and the glass flowers. Afterward, as I drove more slowly than usual in an effort to postpone the inevitable — I didn't want to go home and deal with Gary's jumpiness and anxiety, always worse in the winter when the weather was bad and we were all trapped in the house together — Teddy tapped me on the shoulder from the backseat: *Can we go to the pet store?*

The pet store was the same one that I had gone to when I was young — it's where my parents got me my first (and last) goldfish and the pair of gerbils that gnawed and burrowed in a glass aquarium until they killed each other and their litter in a crazy act of murder-suicide. For serious dog people, pet stores were evil sellers of dogs from puppy mills, but we were desperate: we'd been looking in shelters for over a month and hadn't found a single dog that called to us. Until that freezing cold afternoon when I opened the door to Debbie's Petland and saw, instantly, in the cages along the right wall of the shop, a perfect fluffy fur-ball — a tiny Lassie — and announced to Teddy and anyone else in the store who may have had designs on her: *that's my dog.*

I still remember Teddy on the floor of the pet shop playing with her, then just three months old, that cold gray afternoon — how he said he wanted to name her Charlotte because they'd just finished reading *Charlotte's Web* at school — a smile under all his long hair and looking happier than he had since preschool. So I bought the puppy, and the crate, and the food and the bowls and the leash and collar and the chew toys, over a thousand dollars' worth of pet and gear, loading everything — except the dog itself, who sat on Teddy's lap in the backseat — into the trunk. Which was a small price to pay for what would become my full-time companion; my life vest; my vine; my dog-baby.

Having the always-costumed People Puppets in our house feels strange and quickly creates a cloud of *should*s in my head: we should entertain them, we should treat them as special guests; we should put out snacks, make dinner with all their favorite foods, fix all the broken and leaky things (*"The top 10 'should's and why you should [see what we did there?] ignore them"*). But for the first few days of their stay, I'm off the hook: after they load in their giant duffle bags, stomping their hoof-boots on the front hall mat before scuffing the walls with their massive plastic storage containers on their way to the basement, we barely see them. They leave early in the morning and come home late, after dark, already working long hours at the school, building sets and sewing costumes. Morningside Montessori Autumn Inhabitancy is in full swing, apparently, but the only thing Teddy has told us is that the themes for the big finale "Spotlight" performance in a few weeks have been decided on: a combination of "Resistance" and "Together We Rise" — an echo of the country's pushback against the political turmoil in our country.

"Great," I say in the car on the way home from school, barely remembering what it was like to wake up without that sick the-world-as-we-knew-it-is-ending feeling in my stomach because every day it's clear from the news that the world as we know it is ending. "I especially love the positive message in 'Together We Rise' — how depending on others for support helps us survive difficult times." I practically tear up, thinking about how I shouldn't have to defend my sling ever again. Shouldn't everyone be wearing a dog for improved mental health?

"That's not exactly how Mr. Noah described it," Teddy says with a dubious head-tilt. "You're making it sound like a self-help book. He made it sound political. Like civil rights and stuff."

"The personal *is* political," I shoot back, as smug as a college freshman who did some but not all of the assigned reading. "Tell them to remember their history. It's Feminism 101." Fuck Mr. Noah and Ms. Grace, I think, moving beyond defending my dog

166

to more pressing matters. Together we will rise and resist our awful new government and the Secret Pooper, whether they help us or not. No wonder Teddy barely tells me anything.

But the strangest thing about the People Puppets' stay by far is how it has forced Gary and me back into the same room and the same bed, Gary's clothes and toiletries brought up from the basement and piled in a corner of the room and in a heap on top of my dresser without any thought to acquiring permanent drawer or shelf space.

I text Glenn.

We're like best friends sharing a motel-double on a longer-than-expected road trip. Side by side, absolutely no touching. Like we did that time we got snowed in in Rochester, after that huge "Bird" book signing.

Don't tell me you're making him sleep head-to-toe.

Good idea! Even safer!

Oh Judy . . .

Even Teddy is confused by the temporary

arrangement. On the first night of the Puppets' stay, he stops into our room with a made-up question about what time we're leaving for school in the morning — we always leave at the exact same time every morning — *late* — and then stares at us suspiciously, as if the minute he turns his back to go to his room we'll break character and dive into sleeping bags on the floor. The idea, frankly, is tempting, since I feel claustrophobic with Gary in the room and in the bed: he is so big and unwieldy, and noisy, with his anxiety-related constant throat-clearing — a sound that causes me such annoyance that I self-diagnosed myself with a mild case of misophonia (*"Is marital misophonia an actual thing?" "Can marriage cause misophonia?"*). I've grown so used to having the room all to myself that it's become a "safe space," a respite from the daily annoyances of normal marriage. Any infringement on it, however temporary, seems almost too much to bear. In the dark, very much on my side of the bed, I am already counting the days until the Puppets are gone.

On the second night, Teddy comes in to pet the dog, passed out on my feet, and then lingers, staring at us — Gary reading and me scrolling through the news feed on my phone. He is at a particular phase of his age where he won't voluntarily or spontaneously speak without being prodded to.

"Yes, Teddy?" I say, over the glow of my screen. I have a vague idea of what he's thinking before he says it.

"I thought you guys couldn't sleep in the same room because of the snoring."

Gary puts down his book and I put down my phone. "That's true," he says. "But there are extenuating circumstances. We have *guests.*"

"Yes. We have *guests,*" I repeat. A mantra, a magic word. Gary and I nod and smile cordially at each other, and then at Teddy — we're playing the parts of two good-natured adults in a romantic comedy, suffering in the short term — *housing People Puppets in our snoring room, which was really our separation room!* — to keep our son in private school and to spare him the true meaning of our arrangement. I feel my fake smile start to fade. Even Sandra Bullock couldn't pull this off.

"Okay, but what about the snoring?"

"It's not so bad," I say.

Gary snorts. I turn and elbow him hard enough for his book to slip out of his hands.

"How would you even know? You're the one sleeping through it."

"Um, Judy?" He elbows back. I've gotten

169

so carried away with my lie all these years that even I forget that I'm the snorer, not him.

"But if it's not so bad," Teddy presses, "then why can't you sleep in the same room when we *don't* have guests?"

There it is. The big question. If he were seven, or eight, or nine, that would be the end of it — I'd just say *because* and follow him down to his room, read him a book, or distract him with talk of a new longboard or whether his next guitar should be a Gibson SG like Pete Townshend, or a Rickenbacker like Paul McCartney, or a Fender Stratocaster like Jimi Hendrix. But I can't remember the last time he longboarded with friends or played music, or the last time we sat on his bed like that with the little train night-light on, the future paved with birthday and Christmas gifts and lit by the warm glow of a tiny bulb. But it's different now. I look at Gary for an answer, and when he doesn't have one either, I just shrug and say: "Maybe we'll try."

"Really?" Teddy says, almost breathless with hope. For a second he's a child again, unselfconscious and unafraid to express himself, to be vulnerable, to reveal what he wants.

Gary sits forward. "Does it bother you

that we don't sleep in the same room, buddy?" It's the first time we've asked him that question, and the first time in a long time that Gary has softened a question with *buddy.*

"Kind of." He shrugs. "Not really." He pets the dog. "It's just that everyone else's parents sleep in the same room."

"Well then, like Mom said, maybe we'll try."

"Were you serious about trying?" Gary says once Teddy is out of earshot.

"I don't know. Maybe." I shrug. "Were you?"

"I don't know. Maybe." He sits up against the headboard, looks around at the old photos on the walls and on my bureau. "It's weird to be back in this room."

"Maybe at some point, after the Puppets leave, we should switch back and forth with the basement. To make it more fair."

"I don't mind it down there, actually. It's peaceful." He shifts onto his side, then clears his throat. "There's something I need to tell you."

No good news has ever come from that sentence. For a few seconds, I don't even breathe. Even though this is what I want — for both of us to lead separate lives, even if we can't technically afford to live separately yet — I'm stunned, instantly paralyzed, a lizard on a rock.

"Better you should know than not know. And better you should hear it from me than from someone else. Even though we don't really know anyone anymore who could possibly tell you." He stops, restarts. "Isn't the conventional wisdom that a separated couple should be honest with each other about what they're doing outside their separation?"

"You're doing something?"

" 'Doing' is a bit of an overstatement. But I guess you could say I 'did' something." He sighs; I hold my breath again. The truth is coming. "I met someone. At work."

No good news has ever come from that sentence either, a trench digger, one of life's many dividers between then and now, before and after. Proximity, which once drove us apart, is about to bring us closer together. Not in the form of tentative kisses, or the accidental brushing of skin, or the sudden spooning in the dark in the middle of the night. We are not coming back together like damaged nerves regenerating after an accident or a fall; our marriage is transforming itself in an unexpected way: through kindness and radical honesty, which is what drives deep platonic friendships, and it seems, those who are consciously uncoupling.

"The snackology team catered a meeting," he explains, "and I use the word *cater* with extreme relativity here — one of the startups did a presentation. And, well, let's just say there was a lot of excitement about a new energy bar we debuted at the first break: dark chocolate maple bacon coconut almond quinoa Paleo Dream."

A month ago he didn't even know what quinoa was, or how to pronounce it.

"I know you're thinking that a month ago I didn't even know what quinoa was or how to pronounce it, and so how deeply ironic it is now that I'm trafficking in the stuff. But. Anyway. A fellow snackologist and I snuck off to the little stockroom and decided to put out the new bars." He sits up straight now. "We usually debut new snacks on Mondays, which had been the plan with this one, but the meeting was so dull and had run so long that we decided to ignore tradition and take a risk."

I thought he was the only snackologist, but no, he explains, there's a few of them, a small team — *team* being the new term for *department*. There is a lot of explaining going on. Including how crazy everyone went for the new flavor of the snack bar, which was apparently a big deal: having such a positive reaction to a new snack, right out of the gate like that, increases the visibility and the buying power of the person who ordered it because the risk of making a mistake is so high. Lots of explaining and lots of words. We still haven't gotten to the main story.

"You have to understand: *I* was the one who purchased this item, *I* was on the hook for that decision — I took a real flier — these people are serious about their nut bars, and if they don't like what we order, the snack just sits there and doesn't go away, while all the other snacks disappear quickly, requiring near-constant replenishment. There's nowhere to hide when you make a purchasing error like that — they're an everyday reminder of your failure to correctly assess the collective tastes of the companies we work for — and it gets factored into your job performance rating: lesser snackologists have been fired or replaced for misjudgments like that. So there was a lot on the line for me. It was impulsive, putting it out there like that, without any planning. Prematurely. But I have to say, it turned out great."

I watch a smile spread across his face at

the memory, and I start to realize that this is the part of the story that stops being about energy bars. "You slept with someone," I say. A statement, not a question.

"I kissed someone. Yes."

I feel the room — the bookshelves, the walls, the dog — recede. Even though we've talked openly about this possibility for a while now, it feels incredibly strange and unpleasant to actually be here now. Gary, who has always seemed like a completely open book, now has a secret life. He tells me that he didn't plan to do it, that it just happened, that he's sure he'll never see her again. That he's just some older dude who put out a great snack on an otherwise excruciatingly boring day.

"But of course you'll see her again," I say. "She's on your team."

"She isn't a fellow snackologist. She's the CEO of the startup."

"The CEO?"

"I know, right?" He shrugs, then laughs. "How crazy is that? She's thirty — *may*be — and she probably mistook me for some dude from MIT. Little does she know who I really am."

"And who are you really?"

A long slow breath comes from deep inside his chest, like he's blowing out a candle in slow motion. "A guy who loves his wife and his son but sleeps in the basement because he's too anxious and underemployed to find a place of his own."

ESCAPE

There's no easy way out — I can't make Gary sleep in the snoring room now, because the People Puppets are there — and as much as I want to, pulling my bedding into the living room and sleeping there — with strangers in the house — doesn't seem like a good idea, either. If Teddy were three or four I could bunk in with him, but now I'm trapped sharing a bed with someone I'm separated from who has just told me he's met — and kissed — someone else — something I thought I'd wanted; something I thought would free me. And maybe it eventually will. But right now, while his sudden confession has exhausted him — he's already asleep on the other side of the bed — I'm wide awake and rigid on my side, struggling with the sadness at the failure of our union and the strange guilt of relief: that he has moved a step away from me; that he will eventually end up with someone new who is far better suited for him than I have become; that one day we will both be happy again in our own way, together or apart.

So when I check my email on my phone in the dark and see that Sari Epstein has invited me for a special meditation-weekend — okay, when I receive her mass email advertising "only a few spots left" in her retreat, The Noble Journey: Creativity Unbound! at her Vermont farm this coming weekend — designed to "unlock your blocked artistic impulses and guide you toward free expression" — I decide to sign up. I know it's last minute and impulsive and financially irresponsible, but I also know that solving our problems, marital and otherwise, starts with me finding my way back to the person I was when I created *Bird:* if Gary and I are ever going to be able to split up it will be because I've finally been able to make some real money again, or at least get back on track for doing what I was meant to do. Doing "just enough" at Well/er will never be enough to save us. But Sari Epstein might.

It takes just seconds between telling myself I can't afford the seminar to justifying and rationalizing the expenditure beyond all measure — the $895 fee for the retreat itself (room and board for two nights at a plush nearby inn sold separately, and there is a link to a list of friendlier-priced Airbnbs and local hotels, too) isn't exorbitant, *it's actually a bargain.* What price could you possibly put on reconnecting with your creativity? I fill out the online registration form on my phone, find the one Visa card that hasn't expired yet and that I've been saving for an emergency like this. Well, not quite like this — more like a dental emergency or, god forbid, a medical emergency — most likely some kind of mental health emergency outside the bounds of normal coverage — but why not a creative emergency? I pull the card out from the back of my nightstand drawer, where I keep it hidden, and fill in the payment information. Then, in the "additional information box," I identify myself with my published-author credentials so that Sari Epstein will treat me with published-author respect when I get there. When I hit "send," I think: *Yes, this is why we're broke, but what the fuck.*

With the online purchase completed, I take a screenshot of the receipt and text it to Glenn:

Come with me on my Noble Journey. I'll drive.

The idea of it as a spontaneous and fun girls' weekend appears in my head like a fizzy bubble — but the fantasy of it pops and disappears when she declines with a single word:

Can't.

I know she doesn't have the energy to stay in a room and sleep while I'm out trying to cure my writer's block. Part of me wants to stop right there — if Glenn's too sick to go, then I don't want to go, either — but I know that's not an option. I have to start preparing myself for what's coming, even though I also know that's impossible. You can't ever prepare yourself for that.

In the morning, after drop-off, I tell Gary about the workshop — and how the timing of it actually provides the perfect opportunity for us to take a short break from each other. "Given last night's awkward revelation," I spell out, "it'll be good for both of us to have some time to think."

"To think about what?"

"About what we're doing."

"And what are we doing?"

"Well." I snort. "You're having an affair." I realize I don't entirely believe his story about it being just a kiss. What sexually deprived husband who's officially separated and has permission from his wife to have sex with other women would stop at just a kiss?

He snorts back. "I'm not having an affair! It was just a kiss, I swear!" He sits down at the table. "Look, nothing's changed. We're still separated. And we can't actually separate. Except for that one thing, our situation is pretty much the same as it was before. Let's not get crazy."

But something has changed. He's made a break for it. He's done us each a favor by taking that first step. Is it possible that I feel relieved?

"It'll be a quick road trip for Teddy and me, something we haven't done in years," I say, explaining that since Sari Epstein's farm is only two hours from Boston and a few towns over from Gary's mother's house, which is right near Dartmouth College and on the Vermont/New Hampshire line, I'll figure out an Airbnb or a cheap last-minute hotel, then drop Teddy there for two nights while I'm busy writing and drawing and coloring and meditating. "It'll give us a chance to have time together in the car and go to all his favorite diners on the way there and back."

It'll also give me a chance to be without

181

the dog for a weekend — now that the People Puppets can act as part-time dog-sitters, I can practice being slingless for when Lucy comes to live with us. I'll tell Teddy after dinner. I know he'll be as excited as I am.

"No, Mom."
　"What do you mean 'no'?"
　"I'm not going."
　"But you love our road trips!"
　"I used to, but I don't anymore."
　"Why not?"
　"Because I'm different now. I just want some time alone!"
　"But you're always alone!"
　"I'm not! I'm always in school! And when I'm not in school, I've got homework! I haven't even started the outline of my yearlong Immersion Project, and the last thing I want is to be trapped in a car for a million hours."
　"Three hours. At the most."
　"No!"
　"I'm tired of 'no'!" I'm starting to understand how frustrating it must be for Gary to deal with me.
　"And then there's everything else."
　"Like what?"
　"Like the Secret Pooper."

"Has he pooped again?" I ask, then wonder about my use of the male pronoun — my assumption that the Pooper is a he.

"No, but everyone's waiting for it. Every time you leave the classroom you have to sign out, and then they watch you walk down the hallway to see where you're going. If you say you have to go to the bathroom, they check the bathroom after you come back. I feel like they're always watching me. Like they think I'm guilty. Like they think I'm the Pooper. But I'm not!"

"Of course you're not! But this is all the more reason why you should come with me. Get away! Take a break from everything! You'll get to miss a whole day of school!"

Teddy shakes his head vehemently. "No, Mom! I don't want to be stuck at Grandma's for a whole entire weekend! She never has any food and she's always trying to get me to hike and I hate hiking! Remember that time she lost me?"

Which time? When she walked so far ahead of him on a birding trail because she was in hot pursuit of a stupid blue heron that it took him fifteen minutes to catch up to her and he almost didn't because he was six? Or the time she came to Boston to visit and lost him near the swan boats in the Public Garden because someone asked for directions to Beacon Hill and she decided just to walk them there, without saying more to him than "Wait here — I'll be right back"? (Which he didn't, because she wasn't. And because he was eight.) "Please. Don't remind me."

So maybe he's safer if he doesn't come. But hearing his refusal, seeing his face contort in misery at the thought of spending an extended amount of time with me — *"a whole entire weekend?!"* — is too much for me. Remembering the road trips we'd taken over the years — to the tip of Cape Cod, throughout New England, down to New York — and how many hours we used to spend together so peacefully and without conflict in hotel rooms and diners, over pancakes and chicken fingers, makes my throat seize and the tears start. When Teddy goes upstairs I duck into the bathroom, forgetting to turn on the overhead fan before the trumpet of nose-blowing starts.

Not that it matters: the People Puppets aren't stupid. They're witnessing their first family fight, and there's nowhere for any of us to hide. Whose idea was it to have complete strangers in the house?

Back in the living room, with the dog in the sling in my lap and a fistful of Kleenex, I pretend to be hard at work on a new

Well/er piece (*"Is communal living good for the soul?" "Why long-term houseguests can be good for your marriage [no really!]"*), when I'm actually checking Sari Epstein's feed. Sari in child's pose. Sari painting with watercolors. Sari deep in an evening gratitude meditation by candlelight. Sari drinking tea and journaling before bed. Sari with her palms together, head bowed, telling everyone to sign up for the Noble Journey creativity workshop this weekend because space is limited. I creep on all the photos, watch the short videos, spy the expensive couches, rugs, the diffuse light from the vast high ceilings in her home yoga and art studio, the foot-high bed with super-fluffy down duvet and far too many throw pillows. Except for the ridiculous throw pillows and the stupid journaling, she is perfect. I would trade my life for hers in a second.

I'm still sniffling when Nick sits down on the couch across from me. For once he's not in full costume, but he's still wearing his hoof-shoes and hoof-hands, which he taps, like a drummer, on his legs. I think of Sari Epstein in her perfect yoga pants in her perfect house with her perfect steady-creativity-seminar-income lifestyle, which does not require her to house hoof-wearing People Puppets to pay the bills, and I want to die all over again. I can tell that he means well, that he wants to try to make me feel better — to tell me about how, when he was Teddy's age, he didn't want to spend time with his parents, either — how it's normal to separate and differentiate.

But I don't want to hear any of that. My son doesn't want to go away with me. My husband has a girlfriend. My best friend is dying. I'll never be Sari Epstein. Haven't I suffered enough for one day?

"So," Nick says with a percussive tap of his hooves. "What's with the dog?"

I stare at him, then down into the sling. "What do you mean?"

More tapping. "I'm just curious about it. It's pretty unusual. I mean, I don't think I've ever seen anyone *wear a dog.*"

"No one's ever accused me of being un-original!"

"Exactly! I'm just really curious about how it started and why you do it. And like, if it bothers Gary. Does it bother Gary?" He's sitting on the edge of the sofa, as if it's children's story time at the public library. Isn't that why he has taken his hoof-hands off and has a sketchbook out and is starting to draw me with a big soft pencil, making smudges to the lead with his thumb?

"So many questions!" I lob back, but I'd

186

be lying if I said I'm not just a little bit flattered to be asked. Not to mention giddy at the opportunity to talk about it. No one ever wants to talk about it. No one ever wants to talk about anything to do with me, I've found, now that I'm fifty and invisible. The fact that Nick does makes me almost teary with gratitude — especially after I misjudged his curiosity for nosiness. I start at the beginning: the day I found the sling, the red cabbage and the bath towel and the cans of tomatoes, and the sudden epiphany about wanting to carry something around because I missed carrying around a baby and because it somehow made me feel better after so much loss and sadness.

Nick nods. "Wow. I had no idea."

"Yeah, well, watching both your parents get sick and die within two years of each other really kind of takes it out of you." I clear my throat. "Sorry. I didn't mean to get so grim."

By the time Phoebe sidles into the room and onto the couch, tilting her head and sizing me up, as if she's trying to figure out how much I weigh and what shape my body actually is under my sweater and T-shirt and sling — I'm telling them about Grace barring me from bringing the dog into the school.

187

"Unless I register the dog as an official support animal and show her the paper-work."

Nick shakes his head. "What. A. Bitch."

"Seriously," Phoebe adds.

"I know, right?" I'm so grateful for their support that I find myself holding my pose of outrage — mouth open, hands in the air — while Nick flips to a fresh page in his sketchbook.

"I've never liked her," he says, still sketch-ing.

"You know her?"

He looks up. "She's my dad's girlfriend."

"Noah is Nick's dad," Phoebe explains. "And Noah and Grace are a couple."

I feel like my head is going to explode. "Wait, *what*?"

Nick puts his sketchbook down and puts his hoof-hands back on. "That's why we got the job. My dad put a good word in for us and the teachers all voted us in. I like to think we would have had a chance without the nepotism, but I'm not stupid. People Puppets are a hard sell without someone on the inside."

I'm still trying to absorb all the connec-tions I hadn't known about when I take that as an opening to keep the conversation go-ing. "So, speaking of 'hard sell,' what's with

188

the costumes?"

Nick seems confused by the question.

"You asked me why I wear my dog. So now I'm asking you: Why do you wear . . . *that*?" I'm not sure what animal he's dressed as, or is *becoming through dress*, but it's a symptom of something larger. "Clearly there's a story behind the need to cover oneself up and the desire to become something else."

"Sure there is," he says, matter-of-factly. "My dad. It's all his fault."

I nod slowly. "Oh, okay." I hadn't expected an actual answer.

"No seriously. He's ruined everything for me."

I look at Phoebe. She makes a sad face, then rolls her eyes. *"Everything."*

"Everything I've done — dropping out of law school, starting this puppet company — has all been because of him. It's all his fault."

I feel like the ground underneath me has shifted the way it does when total validation appears for long-held seemingly insane opinions. Like thinking the soft and fuzzy man-bunned teacher was a phony. I feel like calling Teddy back downstairs to prove that I'm not actually crazy: Mr. Noah is not who he pretends to be.

"I'm sorry to hear you have such a troubled relationship," I say, my voice dripping with empathy. "That can't have been easy for you."

Suddenly, they both fold over with laughter. "My dad?" Nick says. "I'm kidding! He's the best guy ever. *Ob*viously!"

Phoebe nods her confirmation, then taps her heart with her paws. "A total sweetheart."

I'm so confused. I pull away from both of them, leaning as far back on the couch as I can, hugging the dog in front of me like a protective shield. Who *are* these awful people? How could I have been so stupid to invite them into my home?

"I love my dad," Nick says. Suddenly there are tears in his eyes. His voice cracks. "He's basically my best friend. He ruined everything for me because he made me think the world would be as accepting and loving as he is, and it's not. It's been a long, slow, rude awakening." Phoebe puts her hoof-paw over his until he clears his throat and regains his composure. "So to answer your question," he says with his hooves in the air as a signal that everything's fine, "I pursued this art form because I was looking for a way to hide for a while. I was miserable after my parents' divorce. I never felt like I fit in with other kids because no one else had a dad who was such a free spirit. And, I may have gone through a slight chubby phase."

Phoebe's sad face returns, as do the paws to her heart. "He was so cute. But so chubby." Then she laughs, blushing. "But not anymore."

"Nope. Underneath the costume I'm rock-solid."

They fold over laughing again.

Oh. "Guys," I say. "Let's have this conversation another time. Like when you're both not so high."

Upstairs, I slip into bed, making sure to carefully stay on my side. In the dark, once my eyes adjust, our two separate figures under the blankets, peaks and valleys, look like one of those special sectioned plates where all the food is separated so that it can't touch.

"Teddy won't go with me on the trip."

Gary turns toward me, leans up on an elbow.

"I thought it would be fun," I say. "The old Teddy would have jumped at the chance to have an adventure and miss a day of school, to eat out at diners along the way, but he refused. I'm kind of devastated."

"I'm sorry. That sucks."

"I miss the old Teddy."

"So do I." In the dark I know we're both thinking about how perfect he was then — the skinny skater jeans he used to wear, the long hair that always covered one eye and almost reached his shoulders; the willingness to do anything to make us laugh, including running around with his pants off.

I sigh. I'm so lonely I think I might die. I could reach out to Gary, but the divide between the past and the present feels too far, too deep, too wide. It is too late for us. It's been too late for a long time. And besides, the dog is there, sprawled between us. I pull the blanket to slide her closer to me, then put my arm around her, tucking my hand under her paws and chin and bringing my knees up around her until we're spooning. I instantly feel better. Which isn't surprising, given what I've learned since starting to wear the sling. (*"Newsflash: new study shows that women who interact with their dog for twenty-five minutes have a 58 percent increase in oxytocin, also known as the 'hug hormone.'"* " '*An Examination of Adult Women's Sleep Quality and Sleep Routines in Relation to Pet Ownership and Bedsharing' is the study we've been waiting for, proving that women have higher-quality sleep when they share their bed with at least one dog."*) But I don't really need scientific studies to tell me what is already so obvious and intuitive, like the fact that women who sleep with their dogs may actually be disturbed as often by the dog as they are by the human they sleep with, but they self-report being less bothered or less aware of the dog-disturbances than the human disturbances. Though sometimes I do wonder what all this forced human affection feels like to the dog. If Charlotte were interviewed and could talk, what would she self-report about sleeping or slinging with me? Does she also get a boost of oxytocin and higher-quality sleep or does the dog-human closeness make her feel more claustrophobic than comforted?

"I'll go with you," Gary says.

I look at him over Charlotte's ears. "To the workshop?"

"I'll drive with you. You can drop me at my mother's — I'll get points for visiting her and raking some leaves — and then you can pick me up when you're done with the seminar. The Puppets can watch the dog and Teddy."

"Maybe I'll stay at your mother's the first night to save money, then find a cheap hotel for the second night."

"Good. It'll give us time to talk."

"Time to talk about what?"

He flops onto the pillows, then rolls over and away, back to his side of the bed. "Oh Judy. I give up."

OFF TO SEE THE FOREHEAD

Two days later, on a chilly, bright blue morning, we're packed and ready for the weekend — we've done a huge food shop for us and a smaller one for Glenn, including making sure she has all her meds and that friends are coming to check on her while we're away; left Gary's mother a voice-mail about our last-minute visit; let the school know that the People Puppets would be driving Teddy to and from school today; taped a list of our cell phone numbers and emergency contact numbers — pediatrician, veterinarian, and take-out vegetarian — to the refrigerator. Gary takes our bags out to the car while I throw a notebook and a bunch of Sharpies into my bag just in case inspiration strikes early and I start writing or drawing before the workshop. Then I wave at Phoebe, who's lurking just outside the kitchen, to come in. I have things — important things — to show and

195

tell her before we go.

"We got you a whole bunch of new food," I say, opening the refrigerator door. "Healthy food! Vegan food! Puppets-from-Vermont food!" I don't register Phoebe's frozen and fading smile. "Kale-this and quinoa-that."

Phoebe blinks, looks miserable. "Great."

I touch her lightly on the arm. "Don't worry. We'll only be gone two days."

She looks at me like I have a bird on my head.

I open the freezer and the cabinets above it. "Teddy eats regular food. Frozen pizza. Chicken fingers. Cereal. You know, teenage-boy stuff." I roll my eyes like I can't believe he's related to me, even though just saying all those words makes me suddenly want to eat all his food. "With kids you just have to pick your battles sometimes."

She seems oddly interested in what's in the freezer and the cabinets now, trying to peer around me and my hair, but I assume it's because she's horrified by my parenting and is making mental notes to regale her puppet friends later. "Here are all the emergency numbers," I drone on. "Our cell phones, and the vet's number, though I'm sure the dog will be fine.

"Speaking of the dog." I lift the sling off

and put it over Phoebe's neck. She tries to extract her ponytail out from under the back of it but the sling is too heavy and she gives up. I feel weightless and empty and anxious suddenly without the extra twenty pounds of living breathing pet on me. The dog doesn't look much better: inches away from me, hanging from around Phoebe's neck, she looks terrified. Or maybe she's completely relieved. Like every Yelp review I've ever read (*"It's the best restaurant!" "It's the worst restaurant!"*), there's simply no way to tell — it could be either extreme.

"So I really have to wear this?" Phoebe asks, trying again to free her ponytail and finally succeeding.

"You don't have to, but you might want to throw it on once or twice a day. For, like, a few minutes, or an hour, or two, or three. I find it actually helps me feel centered. I just wouldn't want the dog to feel totally abandoned and have to go completely cold turkey by not being worn at all. That would be weird. For her. Don't you think?" I rub my stomach, since I can suddenly. I could swear Phoebe rolls her eyes but again I'm not entirely sure. When there's nothing in the house left to show her, and nothing left to say, I leave her alone in the kitchen. Free of the dog, I run quickly, moving easily down the basement stairs to check on things before we leave. I haven't been down there since they moved in.

There are no boxers or bras hanging from the lampshades; no bongs, still warm and fragrant, in plain sight. Just duffle bags spilling with socks and sweaters and sweatpants, and a soft pile of sheets and a comforter on the floor instead of on the bed. I step over and around things as I peek at the room, and then, as an afterthought, I pick up the Emily Dickinson book, which is still on the coffee table. I flick the rubber band guiltily: it's been years since I read poetry, let alone this poetry, but the notion of transformation during this road trip seems to be sticking. I put the book in my bag, along with the other props of my nascent artistic life, and head back up the stairs.

After we say our goodbyes to Teddy — I manage to plant a kiss on his cheek and extract a half hug out of him before Gary forces a bear hug — we get into the car. Gary backs out of the driveway slowly, while they — Nick and Phoebe and Teddy and the dog — our doppelgänger family — wave from the doorway. We wave back. I can't help but think, sadly, that this is the first time we have ever left for a road trip without having Teddy with us, either strapped into his car seat or belted into a booster seat behind us. The vision of him on the front steps — lanky, awkward, turning back toward the house before we're even gone — makes me sad, and Gary, too, though he won't admit it. It's why, halfway down the street, neither of us has said a word. Suddenly, The Forehead's retreat doesn't seem like such a great idea. What was I thinking, leaving Teddy — and the dog! — alone with virtual strangers who will probably ignore our pet and starve our child. What is wrong with me?

"Well this is fun!" Gary says as he pulls onto the highway with a lilt in his voice. The false cheer means he's lying. "And if it's not fun, we can always leave early!"

"We can't leave early. Not for what I paid for the workshop and spent on vegan food for the Puppets at Whole Foods."

Gary looks at me. "They're not vegan."

"Of course they are. They're puppets!"

"They're not. In fact, Nick asked me where they could get ribs."

I fling myself back against the headrest. "This is why we're broke."

"You should have told me you were doing a shop!"

"You should have told me you had the food-preferences talk!"

I recline the seat and try to close my eyes, knowing I should check my hotel app for last-minute lodging for the following night, but it isn't long before I feel the car slow to a crawl. Sitting up, I see the traffic stalled, snaking along the posted signs for scheduled construction. Gary grabs his phone and opens his favorite GPS app — Waze — which is the opposite of my favorite GPS app — Google Maps. In minutes, he's being bossed around to get off the Mass. Pike and rerouted onto secondary roads.

"Why bother?" I say. "It's always wrong."

"It's not always wrong."

"Why do you always defend her?"

"Because she's always right."

But within minutes, just as I'd predicted, we're lost, miles past the last strip malls and gas stations and fast-food outposts. I turn my app on instead, which leads us back onto the same highway his app had instructed us to leave. Gary turns to me, expecting a snarky remark, but I say nothing, and we drive in silence: him looking at the road, me looking out the window at the blur of colorful foliage whipping past us. When Gary's phone buzzes with a text notification, I'm tempted to grab it and see if it's from the CEO, but he grabs it first, turning it off before either of us can see it.

"So let's talk," I say.

"Later."

"Suddenly you're the reluctant one."

"I'm not reluctant. I just don't see what the rush is. We've been in the car for five minutes. Neither of us is going anywhere."

I pretend to be annoyed but secretly I'm grateful for the reprieve. Anything to delay the inevitable parsing of our marriage. I hand him a piece of the nut bar I've just torn open from our snack bag — dark chocolate maple bacon coconut almond quinoa Paleo Dream. "It's really good," I whisper, though it tastes like wood dust and broken dreams and death.

In an hour we've crossed the state line from Massachusetts into New Hampshire, and an hour after that we're in front of Gary's mother's once-grand Colonial, peeling white with green shutters, circular gravel driveway, dormers and gables and mullioned windows and old rugs in tatters that always fascinated me, someone who was exposed to the color-coordinated wall-to-wall carpeting and drapery and scalloped window shades of the Early American Jew decor of the late seventies. Despite the vestiges of the glorious fall now fading — pumpkins shrinking on the steps to the house; the last of the unraked leaves, red and orange and dry and noisy, blowing against the side of the house and into the scrubby bare bushes — there are no signs of life: no lights on inside; no car in the driveway. When Gary calls her from his cell phone, we both hear the house phone ringing and ringing inside the house.

"You're sure you told her we were coming today?" Gary says.

"Of course I'm sure. I said Friday the twenty-sixth."

He rolls his eyes. "Today's the nineteenth, Judy. The twenty-sixth is next week."

"Oh shit."

"And now I really have to pee." He starts looking around at trees and bushes, but I shake my finger at him.

"No way. Remember what happened last time?" Who knew that public urination in the woods off a dog park trail was considered indecent exposure in New Hampshire and carried with it the fine of $1,000. (We didn't.) "Can't you wait?"

"Do I look like I can wait?" He is hopping now, his voice an octave higher.

"Do you have a key?"

"No, but sometimes she leaves the back door open. Maybe she just went to the supermarket."

We walk around to the side of the house, and while Gary makes another call I try the mudroom door, but it's locked. Gary's hopping gets even more frantic and I tell him to just go in the bushes already.

"No! I'm not taking any chances this time."

I drop my bag on the ground and eye the mudroom window, then struggle to push the storm window up, then the window itself. Just as I get them both open and wave at Gary in triumph, I hear the distant sound of a police siren and Gary shouting at his mother.

"You're staying *where*? I can't hear you! For how long?" He covers the phone and turns to me. "Her house is being sprayed tomorrow for *termites*!" The sirens are getting louder. But as I get closer to Gary I can hear his mother telling him she can't talk now — the alarm company just called to tell her that somebody is trying to break into her house and the police are on their way.

"It won't be much longer," the officer says from the front seat, eyeing us in the backseat, in the rearview mirror instead of turning around. He has the heavy-voweled accent of a native New Englander, but he doesn't drop his *r*s with the savage disregard of a Bostonian. Unfortunately. "As soon as we reach the alarm company, you'll be on your way."

"Great." Gary rolls his eyes just at me.

"Sorry," I whisper out of the side of my mouth, then shrug, as if it's not really my fault that I messed up the date of our visit. Before Gary can complain about my shitty nonapology-apology, another officer approaches the car, holding my shoulder bag — the one I'd dropped outside the mudroom window.

"This must be yours," he says, opening the bag and peering inside before he hands it over to me through the open backseat window. I open it up and Gary sees what's inside.

Gary's eyes widen. He's panicked. "You brought the book?" he whispers.

The cop points at the bag, then at me. "Just make sure everything's in there."

I reach into the bag, take each thing out to confirm its existence: "Wallet, keys, phone charger, Emily Dickinson."

Gary grabs the book out of my hands, holds it against his chest inside his jacket.

"I think the officer has been through enough already with our false alarm! Let's not assault him with *poetry*!"

I look at him like he's insane until sounds of static and then an "all clear" come from the police officer's radio. They tell us we're all set and to have a good trip.

"But no more breaking and entering, Thelma and Louise!"

Out of their car and on our way to our own, we smile warmly at the officers, then quickly drop the act. Gary continues to hug the book until we're back in our own front seat.

I swat at him. "What's wrong with you?"

"Why'd you bring that book?"

"For old times' sake!"

Gary tries to shove the book under the front seat, but I wrestle it from him and hug it to my chest with both arms like a flotation device.

"Why were you trying to hide this?"

"Because it's got *my shit* in it!" he whisper-hisses.

"But it's medical marijuana! It's legal!"

"Not this shit — it's Nick's! A special road-trip blend!"

I glare at him. "Really, Gary? Really? The first book you ever gave me and you put *weed* in it?" I remove the elastic band, open the cover of the book slowly, and see a deep square cut into all the pages. A miniature Altoids tin sits like an embedded jewel in the middle. I shake my head, hand him back the empty book and elastic band, then look out the window.

"God. How old are you?"

"I'm sorry."

"Just drive."

"Where?"

"You figure it out."

At first I assume we're going to simply turn around — our usual trick of leaving early before even arriving somewhere we never really wanted to go to in the first place would never be so perfectly timed — but we head toward the highway. I'm not sure if Gary has a destination in mind — a plan B for the free lodging at his mother's — or if he's just continuing to move forward because forward is somehow easier than backward this one time.

As we slowly approach the highway, my hotel app is showing either zero local vacancies or super-high rates for a few available rooms — clearly there's a Dartmouth home game that I failed to take into account — so now we're really in a bind.

I text Glenn the current marital calculus: the emotional and logistical coordinates and debts owed — I owe Gary for giving his mother the wrong date: he owes me for cutting the guts out of the most sentimental object of our relationship: I owe him for insisting the People Puppets stay with us: he owes me for embracing them more than I'd planned and for bringing his weed with us on the road and almost getting us arrested: I owe him for turning our marriage into a platonic relationship and for the fact that we're on a trip we can't afford. Plus minus plus minus plus minus. I spare her the news about the CEO; why should she have to see Gary in an unflattering light right now? Though she was divorced once and widowed once and considers herself a failure at marriage, she is the most decisive person I know. Her response is quick and definitive:

Stay over at The Forehead's.

But we haven't been invited. And I have a plus-one: Gary.

Tell her the inn lost your reservation and everything else is booked because her incredibly popular retreat has taken up all the available rooms.

Flattery, as we both learned at Black Bear Press, always works.

But it's less about the awkwardness of asking to stay with Sari Epstein and more about the prospect of socializing with her and her husband that is my concern right now. Since our "separation," Gary and I have stopped going to other people's houses, and we don't invite other people to our house for dinner, either. This voluntary curtailment of our social life just happened to dovetail with the fact that we've run low on friends anyway: the older Teddy got, and the further away from the preschool and elementary school years we've moved, the fewer obligatory back-to-school nights we have to go to and the fewer Saturday or Sunday afternoon paintball or indoor-rock-climbing or bowling parties Teddy is invited to. In fact, he hasn't been invited to any this year, and maybe not last year, either.

Gary is thrilled to be relieved of having to behave well and maintain the ridiculous pretense of being interested in other families with whom he's always felt that he has absolutely nothing in common except a child the same age at the same school or one who has a shared extracurricular activity. But it's different for me. I face the empty calendar every month with sadness — wondering why, when other families routinely have to turn down invitations because of being double or even triple booked, not a single one of us seems to have a social life.

It was always torture for Gary to listen to another dad describe, in mind-numbing detail, an ongoing do-it-yourself project — a bathroom redo or the installation of new kitchen cabinets, or a drain-snaking method found on YouTube to circumvent the plumber. Gary would stare at me over bowls of hummus or plates of bruschetta, making *Let's leave early* eyes as he was led out into the backyard like a hostage to see a recently installed firepit or a raised gardening bed using recycled wood, or to hear about some magnificent adventures in organic composting. He didn't want to see anyone's reorganized toolshed or a family's dirt bikes suspended from a garage ceiling; he had absolutely no interest in bending down to inspect a fully insulated cat door lined in felt weather-stripping or hear about how a snowblower could be retrofitted to run on canola oil instead of gasoline. Being forced to interact with people he didn't necessarily like or care about made him feel trapped and anxious, then angry.

I struggled less with these interactions myself: during Teddy's elementary school years I was always in demand as a friend — obviously! — my résumé practically guaranteed that I would be the first picked for coffee dates or yoga class invitations — I'd written a children's book, after all, that had been turned into a PBS animated series! All the women I met had children who read children's books and watched children's television. I loved inspecting the reorganized kitchen cabinet project, the newly alphabetized disappearing rolling spice rack, the gleamingly clean refrigerator vegetable bins, the perfect basement home office or home gym — I loved escaping into the fantasy of how such a well-ordered world must correlate precisely to a well-lived and happy life — how women who had been smart enough to pick solid-earners for husbands were now reaping the many benefits of such sage decisions — even though I knew better about all of it. But I couldn't enjoy any of it, knowing that Gary couldn't bear it, that as soon as the quinoa was cleared and the gluten-free cupcakes were devoured and the fair-trade decaf was served, he would make it clear it was time to go.

I'm never doing that again, he'd say in the car, vibrating and agitated. *I'm never going to another dinner like that again. I can't take it.*

I would close my eyes, and sigh, and look out the window. Did other couples suffer this much? Did all husbands unravel after only an hour or two of harmlessly annoying parents? I'd stare out into the darkness, trying to focus on houses and trees and storefronts and street signs, but I could never see past those questions.

Sometimes I wished I'd married someone who loved to entertain, who filled the house with people every weekend, dimming lights and pouring drinks and explaining where the cheese was from and how we'd first discovered the wine we were serving. But every part of that fantasy was ridiculous: when we'd met, Gary was already sober, and people had annoyed him even then. And maybe it was for the best, since once my career started to wane, I found it easier not to have to explain why yet another book I'd written hadn't been reviewed or wasn't being stocked in giant stacks at Costco, or why another television possibility wasn't going to happen. So when we stopped having anywhere to go, and anyone to go with, I couldn't help but think that, like everything else I had somewhat willingly given up, it was almost better that way. Leaving the social scene early had made things easier for both of us.

It was Gary's idea to stop socializing as a couple — for the simple reason that we weren't a couple anymore — wasn't that what separation was all about? — so the idea of having to socialize with Sari and her husband is making me nervous. Not only are we out of practice, but it's also entirely possible that given Gary's recent truth-bomb of telling me about his fling with the young CEO and the stress of the trip, we could make a scene. It's entirely possible that the center will not hold.

"Tell me again how you know Sari?" Gary asks. We're at a Dunkin' Donuts, drinking coffee, eating Munchkins, taking a break to strategize and recalculate.

"Sari Epstein," I correct.

"That's what I said."

"No, you just said 'Sari.' But you have to say her first and last name. *Sari Epstein.*"

"Why?"

"Because she's one of those people where you have to say both names."

He rolls his eyes — *okay. Anyway* — then repeats his question.

"She's a really successful creativity expert."

"Define 'successful' and 'expert,' " he says while I glare at him. "Does she have a TV show?"

"No."

"Has she won awards?"

"Not exactly."

"Bestsellers?"

I shrug. "She's never written a book. Unless you count coloring books."

Gary stares at me. "Then how is she so successful?"

"She has a podcast."

He snorts. "Everyone has a podcast."

"And she's on social media. She has really big Twitter and Instagram followings that focus on authenticity and courage and how to unlock the creative spirit."

Gary's eyes glaze over. "Sounds like bullshit to me."

"It's not. She's really pretty and really smart and totally committed to what she does. I could learn a lot from her."

He looks at me with mild disgust and a tinge of intrigue. "Maybe you guys should get a room."

"Maybe we will."

"Maybe I'll join you."

"Maybe you won't be invited."

We each have another Munchkin.

"So what kind of a name is 'Sorry'?"

"It's 'Sari.' *S-A-R-I.* Like the traditional Indian dress."

"Well, it sounds like 'sorry.' The traditional English apology word." He laughs at his own dad-joke, which, I try, but fail, not to laugh at, too. "Is she from India?"

I stare at him like he has a bird on his head. "She's from Long Island. And, like I said, she's really really pretty. Except for the forehead thing."

"What forehead thing?"

"Glenn is obsessed with the fact that she has a giant forehead."

"She knows Sorry, too?"

I explain that she doesn't know Sari Epstein in real life either — that she's just seen pictures of her on social media. "And it's not *just* that she has a giant forehead: it's that she has a giant forehead and wears her hair parted in the middle, making her giant forehead even bigger."

"As opposed to?"

"Wearing her hair parted on the side, or with bangs, either of which would minimize the giant forehead instead of strangely emphasizing it."

"I bet that's the real reason you're going. Because she's obsessed with someone's giant forehead."

"Pretty much."

"Anything for Glenn." We both laugh, then, thinking the same thing, stop abruptly. "God, what are we going to do without her?"

214

Our smiles fade and we both sigh heavily, then look away, drinking our coffee, poking at the box of picked-over doughnut holes, inexplicably stale so early in the day. He gathers our trash, then nudges my foot under the table.

"So what's the plan?"

I check my phone and see that Sari Epstein has responded to my text, which I share with Gary:

We can put you up here in our incredible guest quarters. And we promise not to look at you like you have a bird on your head!

I've never heard anyone brag about their own guest quarters — or even call their guest room *guest quarters* — and it's unclear if they're going to put us up for free or charge us for our stay, but I'm so flattered that she references my book — that she knows who I am — that I Google "expensive florists near me" as we head toward Woodstock. It's clear we're going to need to show up with a very special hostess gift.

An hour later I'm leaving a place called Mattahorn, where I easily drop $150 in under ten minutes, despite Gary's pleas to get something small. But since I don't want to appear cheap, especially in light of these allegedly incredible guest quarters, I opt for a giant orchid, the biggest one they have, which is now even bigger wrapped for transport and gift-giving in a cellophane-pod tied at the top with green grosgrain ribbon (the salesgirl, in fact, had to jump up onto the shop's sleek cement counters, ducking her head under the halogen lamps and plant misters, to staple the wrapping shut and tie the bow).

It's also almost impossible to carry, now that the wind has picked up and Gary is circling for a parking space. Waiting for him on the sidewalk, I feel like I'm windsurfing and that with one more strong gust I could end up airborne. When Gary comes around the corner and spots me, he pulls up and I open the trunk, but we quickly realize that the orchid won't fit upright in the trunk (too tall) or lie flat in the back (too delicate). The only way to get it to Sari Epstein's is to open the sunroof and drive with the plant sticking way out of the top of the car, like a scene out of a Dr. Seuss movie.

"Seriously?" Gary says, staring at the giant orchid. He's surprised but not surprised.

"That's all they had," I lie.

Gary looks at me, shakes his head. "See, this is why we're broke."

"No, we're broke because I'm taking a

weekend writing seminar with a creativity specialist to help me get unblocked so I can get my career back so we won't be broke anymore."

"Is that what Glenn says?"

"That's what I say."

"I'd rather know what she says."

I hand him my phone. "Then ask her yourself."

He snaps a picture of the plant sticking out of the sunroof and texts it to her with the caption Hostess gift.

Seconds later, Glenn replies with a string of emojis — hands clapping, hearts beating, champagne glasses, dogs, unicorns, balloons — and then another text arrives with just one emoji.

I show it to Gary before he pulls out into traffic. "It's for you."

THE SLEEPOVER

Sari Epstein's house — a low-slung expansive midcentury ranch — sprawls atop a gently rolling hill, all white and glass and steel under a cloudy, gunmetal autumn sky — but the long driveway is blocked by huge shrubs, each wrapped in burlap and trussed like rib roasts. Confused, Gary slows, then parks on the side of the road. We get out of the car and stretch, then he gets our bags out while I crawl into the backseat to carefully extricate the orchid.

It's a hike up the long driveway to the front door, and we don't suffer it in silence — there's eye-rolling and sighing and even a grunt or two as I struggle with the plant swaying in my arms. We would have never lasted a week at Plimoth Plantation or on the American Frontier, I think, as I shift the weight of the plant from one hip to the other. Gary looks at me and shakes his head. "If it's not the dog, it's a giant orchid." He's right. What is it with me and giant barriers to the world?

When we finally reach the door, we freeze. This has happened before to us — whenever we arrive somewhere, usually for dinner years ago, there would always be the tempting moment to forgo the knock; to back away silently from the door, to return to the car — the desire to leave before arriving has always been strong. Back when we were still in love it was because we preferred our own company to that of others; now it's that being with others makes us feel worse than being alone.

My finger hovers over the doorbell. For the first time since I hatched this plan and we started executing it I'm realizing the full scope of the stupidity of what we're doing.

"Whose idea was this again?" I say, with a lame little laugh. I should apologize now to get it out of the way, but I just can't. Not yet. "What if we hate them?"

"What do you mean, 'what if'? Of course we'll hate them."

I try to shake off the dread. "It's only two nights, right?"

"Unless we leave early."

We both try to laugh but can't.

"What's his name again?" Gary asks.

"I forget."

"Hers is *Sari. Sari, Sari, Sari.*" He practices as his finger slowly heads for the doorbell and presses it.

"At least this absurdity will be an icebreaker," I say, trying to get my face around the cellophane on the plant.

I close my eyes and try to breathe deeply. When the door finally opens all four of us freeze. I'm trying to get past my shock and awe at actually seeing Sari Epstein in person after only seeing her on my phone screen all this time — and trying to gauge, for Glenn, whether or not her forehead really is as prominent as it seems (it is), until finally we all awkwardly wave and start talking and shaking hands. Sari and her husband are probably trying to figure out how they got roped into housing us the night before a retreat.

"Gary," Gary says.

"Gregory."

"My wife, Judy," Gary says, turning to me, and then to Sari. "And you must be Sorry."

" 'Sari,' " Gregory corrects.

Gary stiffens. "Isn't that what I said?"

"No. You said 'Sorry.' "

"Sorry!" he says, without a trace of sincerity, until my elbow hits his rib and he tries again. "That must happen all the time. The Sari-Sorry thing."

Gregory sniffs humorlessly. "Actually, it doesn't."

I wait for Sari to give Gregory a similar elbow to the ribs — we're wives, after all, trying to make our dudes behave in an uncomfortable social situation — but she barely seems to register the tension. You'd think she'd pretend then. Doesn't she want me to like her?

Gary and I look at each other, then at the birds on both our heads. I push the orchid plant on Sari, harder than I intend to. Then, too loudly, I blurt: "Thanks so much for inviting us even though you didn't actually invite us since we invited ourselves! Sorry about that!"

Sari Epstein's face finally registers an expression. I think she's overwhelmed, but it might just be Botox. Whatever the cause of her placid expression, she seems to be struggling under the weight of the plant, which is understandable: it's almost twice as big as she is. As am I. How can she be so small? Are her bones actually smaller than mine or do they just seem that way? Does she buy her clothes at Gap Kids or Janie and Jack?

Finally, she speaks with the breathless, practiced gratitude of the professional guru. "Thank you," she says, adding the flourish

221

of a bowed head. "Orchids are my favorite."

An opening. I lunge for it as if my life depends on it. Which it does. "We wanted to make up for the fact that we forced ourselves on you. Especially on the night before the start of the retreat when you probably have a million things to do."

"A million things," Gregory says.

I ignore him. "The woman wrapping it actually had to jump up on the counter with a staple gun because it was so big!" I mime the scene, pretending my arms over my head are the two big flaps of cellophane, and my hands opening and closing quickly are the staple gun.

No one's laughing. Gary and I exchange looks. We want to die. "Then we drove with it sticking out of the sunroof!" Gary adds, joining the ill-fated pantomime, his entire torso becoming the plant swaying in the wind.

Still nothing. My fake smile fades to panic, as does Gary's — *we are so fucked* — but Sari Epstein barely seems to notice. Is she dead? Does she have a pulse? She turns around and pads down the slate floor toward a huge open kitchen. "Gregory will show your husband to the guest suite," she says, having so clearly already forgotten Gary's name. "It's over the car-barn."

222

■ ■ ■

A few minutes later, Sari hand-hugs a mug of tea while looking out the window over the sink. Vast fields roll as far as the eye can see. I think of our own tiny yard at home, with the previous owner's compost heap we never got rid of and the lawn we never graded and seeded and cover instead every year with cheap dark mulch. I force myself to compliment her, when really I'm wondering how they can afford such a spread.

"So this is all yours!" I say, my voice lilting a little at the end, but you can't disguise jealousy. My tone is brittle and forced, and I'm pissed that I feel less than her in the midst of her affluence.

"My coloring books and workshops and private coaching do really well, so Gregory and I — he's a sculptor — get to do what we want to creatively. Everything changes when art becomes about money."

"Everything!" I'm trapped in a nightmare of my own making.

"It must be the same for you, right? Your *Bird* book was a bestseller and the animated series didn't hurt."

"It certainly did not hurt!"

"See? I know who you are." It's like she's

reading my mind already, and I can't help but be slightly awed and flattered again. "Just because you disappeared creatively doesn't mean your fans did. There are lots of us waiting for your next *oeuvre.*"

I cringe. She just misused *oeuvre.* How is that possible? Is Gary right about this whole thing being total bullshit? I nod and try to follow her continued gaze out the window.

"And yet, for all my success," she says with ethereal self-absorption, "it's still a struggle. I think writing is the hardest job in the world."

"Posting, you mean." Confused, I blink. I'm thinking about the tiny Instagram paragraphs she writes under her daily meditation and yoga selfies and how not hard they are. But maybe I'm wrong. Maybe they're even harder to compose than actual writing.

"Posting is writing."

"On a small scale."

"Whatever the scale, skill is still required. And effort. And it's the hardest thing I do."

My $895 is already gone, so I decide to stop fighting. "The hardest." I relent. I'm all in.

"Harder than working in a mine."

"*So* much harder."

"Or digging ditches."

I shrug. "They're just big holes!"

The back door opens and a woman in chef whites enters the kitchen. "Andy will get dinner ready while we go into town, Judy," Sari says, putting her cup down on the counter. "I'll show you around and we'll pick up some wine and cheese."

Andy has chin-length violet-silver hair, a pierced lip, and a full sleeve of tattoos on both bare arms. She looks at Sari and then at me with sadness, then pity. It takes me a few seconds to realize that we are too ridiculous to even bother hating. I blink in horror. I have crossed a line I never even knew existed. I want desperately to disappear.

"Thank you, Andy!" I say, gushing. Then, as if that's not weird enough, I wave and walk toward her with my hand extended. "Hi! I'm Judy!"

Andy looks at my hand like it has a bird on its head. "Judy. Chill," she says calmly, before heading toward the refrigerator.

Sari and I get into a huge SUV — the kind you have to actually step up and hoist yourself into — so that we can go into town to buy wine and cheese. She backs out and drives all the way down the lawn to the road, passing our car.

225

"Sorry you had to park so far from the house. We had a muddy thaw." She shrugs with faux frustration. "Country living."

"It was good exercise."

"That's why it'll be great to start yoga this weekend. It changed my life. I've cut my Xanax in half."

"I know," I say. "You posted a lot about that last year."

She ignores me. "So I never did ask you what you're working on now."

I shrug. "Work."

Sari looks confused.

"I have a day job," I explain. "I write for a health and wellness site." I tell her a little bit about Well/er — the founding brodudes, how young everyone is, how I get my inspiration for "researched" pieces from my everyday life. "Maybe I'll write about this trip!" (*"Is country living actually like chicken soup for the soul?" "The science behind how a daily walk in nature can boost the quality and quantity of your creative output."*)

"Creating isn't work for me." Sari sniffs. "Creating *is* my life's work. There's a difference."

Sari pulls the SUV into a gravel lot in front of a slate sign hanging from a lamppost: VERMONT COUNTRY PROVISIONS. We jump down out of the car and pad across the gravel, her clogs digging in with each step. Inside the dimly lit shop with sawdust on the wide-plank floors, multiple blackboards show cheese and wine specials written out in colored chalk, while wealthy weekenders fondle delicately wrapped hunks of triple-crème from local dairies and artisanal crackers. If Gary were here he'd tell me it smells like feet. Though we have been apart for less than an hour, I miss him desperately.

Sari puts a few things in her hand basket — two bottles of light pink wine; a tiny log of herbed goat cheese; and a small container of olives — and just as we turn toward the front of the store to pay, I see Gary and Gregory coming in. I now know the true meaning of the gratitude Sari is always tweeting about.

Gary and I make *Save me!* eyes at each other, while Gregory and Sari air-kiss and whisper into each other's hair, like they're at a cocktail party. Which they kind of are: within seconds they see more-important friends and drift away from us. Gary and I move toward each other like magnets.

"I hate them," he whisper-blurts.

"Me, too!"

"He asked me if I wanted to drive his BMW. Which is sad, since it's a 3 Series. I mean, it's a nice car, but nurses lease 3 Series! What's the big deal?"

"Did you drive it?"

He shakes his head, lowers his voice. "We got high before we left the house and I didn't want to be responsible, so he took their Prius."

"So the trip hasn't been a total loss for you."

"Some free shitty pot notwithstanding, Judy, it has been a total loss. No visit with my mother, which always yields some highly entertaining gossip about my sisters. No opportunity to meet chicks." We both laugh. "Seriously. What are we doing here?"

"I have no idea. It's all my fault."

"Yes! It is!" He stops, in delayed shock. "That was so truthful! You're never that truthful! What happened?"

"I don't know! It's just — I shouldn't have spent all that money on this stupid weekend." I don't want to admit that I think he was right. That this whole thing feels phony. That Sari Epstein's creativity retreat is just a slick way for her to make money off vulnerable people who think they need her help. Which I do, but still.

He looks around the store and signals to me: they're heading back our way, slowly threading a careful route through farm tables laden with foods marked as WEEK-END PROVISIONS. "At least my exposure to them will end tomorrow."

I ask him what he'll be doing while I'm busy.

"Taking a tour of the glassblowing mill and visiting the local lutherie — the guitar-building school," he says. "My own personal creativity retreat."

Back at Sari's house, we wait in the living room for dinner, looking at their books, mostly of the health and wellness variety, and at their photos — some little, some big, some hanging on the walls and some lining bookshelves and in silver frames adorning side tables. We see Sari and Gregory through the years: her hair morphing from long to short to long again; Gregory from bearded, to clean-shaven, and back to bearded; together and apart; with students and without. We walk around the room as if we're in a gallery that's showing art we're not sure we like — we look, move along, look again. We see their marriage, vacations, work, evolve, in pictures; and yet who knows what happened in between the seconds caught on film. How it all wove together to make the whole of who they are. I think of our house, how we have only a few family pictures on the walls downstairs or on the bookshelves. Most are upstairs in my bedroom, photos of Teddy when he was two, and three, and five; asleep in his bed in plaid pajamas; pushing a toy plastic shopping cart in Gary's mother's yard; sitting on Gary's lap on a bench by the Charles River with his hand inside a bag of Goldfish. If strangers came in one day and tried to figure us out from the photos on the walls, what would they learn? Would they be able to see the holes in our cloth? Would they be able to tell that we're not at all who we seem to be?

Sari and Gregory go out to the barn. We watch them through the big windows, setting up the chairs and creativity stations — drawing pads, writing pads, little metal buckets full of crayons and markers and colored pencils. It looks like the setup for a big birthday party or an after-school daycare center — but instead of readying the room for hyper six-year-olds, they're prepping for expressive adults in desperate need of artistic guidance. While I watch them drag cushions and mats and heavy woven blankets out of storage closets, then arrange them masterfully in a pile that looks inviting but not messy, I'm uncomfortably conflicted: drawn to the possibility of being helped; embarrassed by the props and tools to be used in that effort. Instead of naps and sippy cups, it will be guided meditations and Noble Journey–branded reusable water bottles.

Eventually we'll sit down in the dining room, where Andy will lay out dinner — a big green salad, a platter of grilled fish, a bowl of ancient grains, along with the weekend provisions we'd gathered. In spite of ourselves, Gary and I will get through the meal without incident. At one point I think it's even possible that we're almost enjoying ourselves. As we help clear the dishes, Sari will get a text on her phone — a cancellation for a spot in the weekend workshop — and she'll turn to Gary and invite him to take it, for free, a gift from them to us to celebrate our new friendship.

"Sometimes things happen to make the impossible suddenly possible," she'll say, with a heavy sigh of mysticism. "Clearly it's a sign that Gary is meant to be here tomorrow, too." And that is how Gary and I will end up attending the seminar together.

Before we can think of a way to say no, she and Gregory will turn to each other and kiss on it. As we watch their lips touch, Gary and I will smile awkwardly, then look away. We never like being reminded that other

couples still feel and do what we don't
anymore.

NOBLE JOURNEY

Before we sit down at the tables Sari and Gregory arranged last night, we — the attendees — approach a low teak credenza in the barn, in search of our place cards. They are arranged on wooden slabs, like cutting boards, formally but casually, as if we're about to be seated for a wedding reception or luncheon. Each of the off-white cards has a raw edge and is written in Sari's perfect script, which I recognize from her calligraphy posts on her Instagram feed. They are like little tiny individual works of art, and I wonder how long it took her to make them.

"Nice font," I say under my breath, to Gary, who I realize too late is not the one behind me.

"It's called Noble Journey," Gregory says. "Sari designed it herself. She takes great care with every aspect of the workshop. Nothing is an accident."

"Wow," I say, my voice full of wonder.

"People want a completely curated experience when they come here." He drones on like a press release. "That's what they pay for and that's what they get. It's her brand."

"That's why Judy's here!" Gary says, rescuing me finally. "She loves curated experiences." We look for our cards, and when we find them, we realize that we've been separated, seated at opposite tables.

"You're at table two and I'm at table one," I say.

"It's probably a mistake," Gary says. "I'm just the last-minute add-on."

Gregory, who has remained within earshot of us to my great annoyance, shakes his head. "No mistake. We always separate couples. They need to learn how to disconnect from each other and form bonds with other people. To achieve their own noble journey. It's all part of the creative process," he says, drawing out the *allll*. "Learning to trust others and to trust ourselves instead of always leaning on our spouses."

We both laugh.

"What's so funny about self-differentiation?"

Gary fills a heavy earthen mug with coffee from a thermal pitcher and grabs a sticky bun from a platter that no one else has touched. There are small bowls of brown sugar and honey and what I think is agave, and I pray that he doesn't accessorize his bun with condiments clearly meant for the beverages, something he often does either accidentally or on purpose because he loves sugar so much.

"It's just a private joke, my dude," Gary says humorlessly, his voice edgy, then reaches to grab a napkin. "Judy and I aren't like other couples. We're actually quite disconnected from each other already." It sounds like a joke, and Gregory's face softens just enough to assure me that we're not going to be asked to leave. "In fact," Gary continues, his tone slightly warmer, "we're experts in 'self-differentiation.' We're officially separated but we can't afford to live separately, so we just live in opposites parts of the house so that we can continue to co-parent our son as if nothing's wrong. So if you guys get tired later we could probably run things for a while."

I'm grateful when Gary finally bites into his sticky bun and stops talking. And then I do what I always do when things get awkward with people we barely know: I thank Gary for his honesty.

"We're supposed to be honest here, aren't we though?" he says, suddenly loud enough for everyone at the place-card coffee table to hear. Clearly he's been triggered and we're not done yet. "Why shouldn't Gregory know the truth? I'm not ashamed of us, Judy. Are you?"

"This guy!" I roll my eyes and laugh, then motion for him to wipe the crumbs and stray pecan from his chin. Of course I'm ashamed!

People are staring now. They always stare. Today it may be because Gary is the only male seminar attendee, or because he is the only one eating the proffered carbs. But usually it's his energy and the differential in our demeanors. He vibrates with the hyper-vigilance of the superanxious — his eyes are always scanning a room, assessing his fight-or-flight options, while I'm completely contained, almost reptilian in my stillness. Which is my own version of hypervigilance: I'm always waiting for Gary to panic, to make a scene, so I try to take up less space and air than he does. It's like I've been holding my breath since we met, unable to fully inhale or exhale; as if there isn't enough room in the world for both of us.

Two small wiry women with short gray hair wearing big sweaters over black leggings and clogs with wool socks stop to pick up their cards and heavy mugs of tea. I feel an instant wave of something — sadness — jealousy — anger. They look like Glenn before she got really sick; what she would still look like now if she weren't sick. Four more younger women, all blondes, wearing thick knitted ponchos and shawls and pom-pom hats like some kind of private tribe, pick up their cards and beverages. Another group of women, weekend warriors in fleece and boiled wool slippers here to tap into their potential, find and hand each other their place cards, then pass around the basket of protein bars. Each group is separate but together, looking after each other, getting ready for the day ahead, like they're at base camp, preparing to summit.

Sari finally appears, in leggings and a white cashmere poncho-cape. She smiles wanly as she moves through the room, catching up on what she's missed. Gregory fills her in like a senior aide to a politician whose been working the room in her absence; she nods as he whispers in her ear, then cues up her response: first going over the basic logistics of the morning session, the "creativity warm-up," and then addressing the elephant in the room.

"We have one couple here today, Judy and Gary, but I know that many of you, if not most of you, are married or have been married at one time, so it's worth talking about the role that relationships play in the creative process," Sari whisper-lectures. "The culture wants us coupled, and yet coupling can often keep us from our true noble journey — our creative process. Our spouses mean well, but in the daily dance of marital obligation we can get locked into unproductive cycles." She clasps her hands together. "Unproductive cycles that we need to break out of." She pulls her hands apart. "Which is why you're here. And why I'm here. And why Gregory is here." Here she cracks a wry half-smile. "He knows firsthand how hard it is to be married to a creative person."

Gary shoots me a look, and we lock eyes. If he could, he would move a finger toward his mouth. If we'd been allowed to bring our phones into the seminar, he would be texting me our favorite emoji 😵 or our second-favorite 🐵. He's dying to leave early and so am I, but there is no way out. Yet. But despite his misery, I suspect there's a part of him that's into this, that deep down he wants to form bonds and connect with people other than me. He's already going back for a second sticky bun and making conversation with one of the tribes of women.

Sari touches my arm with a mixture of

kindness and sympathy. I assume it's because my husband is embarrassing me — she must know the feeling, given her own husband's omnipresence, even if they do present as a team. "How are you holding up?"

"I'm great!" I chirp. "But I hope Gary will be okay."

We both watch as a group of women surrounds him, then quickly absorbs him as one of their own. Someone hands him a big mug of tea and he takes a tiny tasting sip, then shakes his head in disbelief. "Who needs sugar when there is ah-gav-AY!" he exclaims.

"A-*GAH-vay*!" they correct, before all dissolving into laughter.

Sari tilts her head. "Gary seems to be doing just fine." An understatement. "I don't think you need to worry about him."

I'm not worried about him. I'm worried about me. I wasn't planning on him tagging along. I wanted to focus on myself, not spend my day worrying about him fitting in and finding common ground with a bunch of weekend artists he's never met.

"This is an opportunity to disconnect from your daily life and reconnect to your inner life so that you can eventually push past your creative block."

I nod. I'm trying to disconnect, but I can see him and hear him. I feel like we're home except we're here, wasting time and money. Now, on top of being blocked, I'm worried that I'll have gotten us further into debt for nothing.

"Just let go, Judy. Let it all go." She takes a cleansing breath, touches my arm again, then lifts her hands out from under her poncho-cape to capture the scene with her phone. I know that shortly she'll post pictures and videos in all of her social media feeds, braying about another group of brave souls embarking on their noble journey, and that within minutes hundreds of people will respond with thousands of emojis. Only this time, instead of being at home lurking and feeling envious, I'm actually here, about to experience the magic firsthand. So why do I still feel separate?

Turning now toward the attendees, her sinewy arms once again appear out from under white cashmere when she raises them to motion us into the room with the crayon tables. "Let's get started."

"Starting" starts with sitting on the floor, on meditation cushions, in a silent group "breathe" — a way for us all to get centered "together and apart" to start our "sacred work." Sari and Gregory take their places on pillows with us. I can't quite keep my eyes closed during the five-minute meditation, and neither, it seems, can Gary — we catch each other peeking several times a few minutes in, and then point at each other, silently, through clenched teeth, to stop fucking around. But then, something happens: Gary succumbs to the meditation. I peek a few more times to see that his face has softened, giving way to the appearance of complete relaxation. Gone is the furrowed brow, the darting eyes, his tense shallow breathing. Practically snoring, he has surrendered to the first steps of the noble journey. He is letting go. He is all in. I have never been more tense in my life.

Once the meditation is complete, we take our assigned seats at the round tables. There is the noisy removal of clogs and slippers and moccasins, the guzzling of water bottles, the loud sipping of tea, the rewrapping of woolen wraps as Sari stands before us, about to guide us through our first creativity exercise. People hold crayons and markers above their sketch pads. Through several heads of hair I see Gary, fully engaged with the women on either side of him. They are helping him choose a crayon because he can't decide on his own. "The colors are all so beautiful I can't pick just one!" he says, his voice a sudden joyous soprano, and the table erupts in laughter. He is like an ebullient child they are all looking after. I roll my eyes to the woman next to me.

"Sorry!" I say.

"For what?"

I shrug, then point. "My husband. He wasn't supposed to be here but we had kind of a travel emergency." Then I whisper, by way of explanation: "He's not even really a struggling blocked artist."

She tilts her face at me, bird-on-the-head style. "But he told us on the way in that he's a musician who doesn't play anymore," she says gently. "Being here could be a really transformative thing for him."

A complete stranger — part of the group of women who taught him how to correctly pronounce a natural sweetener this morning — sees him for who he is: the creative person he once was but stopped being. But making such an obvious connection hadn't occurred to me. I stare down at my empty pad, blinding in its whiteness from the tiny halogen spotlights high up along the exposed ceiling beams. I pull out a red crayon. *What. Is. Wrong. With. Me?* Though I hadn't planned on it, this creativity retreat has suddenly turned into a private hellish marriage workshop, one I'm not quite ready to sur-render to. I rip out the page from the sketchbook and fold it up. Then I sit on it.

The first hour is spent doing various ten-minute exercises — using writing and draw-ing prompts that Sari delivers ("Draw your earliest memory." "Write ten five-word plot-lines for the directions your life has taken." "What color is your mood right now?"). Then we return to the floor for a longer guided meditation on creativity, and a thirty-minute mini yoga class. While Sari leads us through each activity, Gregory prepares the necessary props and tools: set-ting out and putting away pillows and mats; replenishing art materials; refilling water bottles and tea mugs with cold and hot water. While I'm coloring or writing, and later when we break for lunch — helping ourselves to plates of vegetarian salads and stews — I can't help but watch how the two move around the room, silently doing what needs to be done with barely any words. Their communication seems effortless, nonverbal, entirely spiritual. I am both full of disdain for and deeply jealous of their apparent connection. The only person who would understand my feelings is Gary. I long to catch his eye, but he is fully absorbed by the latest activity: creating something —

a drawing, a poem, a story, anything — to express one of our biggest frustrations.

I'm still struggling with what I'm working on — a combo-prose-poem-cartoon of me struggling, and failing, to write — what else? — when Sari reappears, calling us all together on the pillows on the floor.

"It's time to share."

At first there is nothing but silence. Then shy giggling. Then Gary's hand shoots up. "I'll go first."

"That's superbrave of you, Gary," Sari says. "What will you be sharing with us?"

"I wrote a song. Well, part of a song."

Sari nods, impressed, then puts her hands together under her chin, bows her head slightly, and whispers, *"Namaste."* I roll my eyes at Gary —What does *namaste* have to do with creating and sharing something? (I would later learn, and write about for Well/ er, that *"ICYMI: namaste directly translates to 'The divine in me bows to the divine in you.'"*) But he is struggling to stand up in the tight space on the floor without losing his balance. The women from his table who are still sitting around him give him a little boosting push on his arm and back, then laugh — but not unkindly. "Go, Gary!" one says, and the others repeat, "Go, Gary!"

Gary — taller than almost everyone anyway — now towers over the room because he's the only one standing. Looking beyond Sari, he points to a ukulele on a shelf. "May I borrow that?"

"Of course," Sari says. "Anything for art!"

We all watch as he steps around pillows and people to reach it and tune it before sitting back down to play. But after strumming a few goofy chords, he stops.

"I think I'm feeling kind of shy," he whispers, tucking a strand of hair behind his ear. "It's been a really long time since I wrote or performed anything. Years, actually. My anxiety has robbed me of what I love for a very long time."

"Sharing one's art is a courageous act. We are all here to support you, fellow brave-warrior-soul." She bows her head again. "We are so grateful to receive the gift of your sharing."

Every time Sari says something ridiculous, which is essentially every time she opens her mouth, I want to catch Gary's eye — want him to validate the extremely high bullshit quotient going on here, the way we normally do at home. This is not who we are. We are not joiners. We are not suckers for this kind of emotional group-think manipulation. We don't belong here. But something is happening. Gary is absorbing

245

whatever it is that the group is offering him — beyond just the "empathic solidarity of the artist's spirit," as described on Sari's website. They are supporting him, shoring him up, seeing him for who he is. He closes his eyes, then picks up the ukulele again.

I'm sad with you.
You're sad with me.
You're distant, and quiet, until you see the
    dog.
Suddenly you coo, you kiss, you've found
    your bliss.
The way you are with her is how you
    used to be with us.
Why do you love the dog more than me?
I'll be frank: I'll tell you why I pout and
    what this is all about:
I feel left out.
How sad it is to have to admit
That I'm deeply jealous of our pet!

Again, I'm blindsided. It never occurred to me that Gary would be jealous of the dog, though it's completely understandable, since I show the dog way more love and affection than I show him. I'm also mortified, but at least I left the dog at home so no one knows about the sling. I barely breathe as I glance around the room — the women

246

convulsing in laughter, delighted by his song. Several of them nod, recognizing themselves in his lyrics.

"I spoon with our dog every night and my husband gets *so* pissed!" one of the women says, before falling over facedown into a pillow, her poncho spread out all around her. Another covers her mouth guiltily: "My husband calls our dog 'the boyfriend.' "

Gary rests the ukulele in his lap. He seems relieved by the positive reception to his song, but I can tell that he's also surprised and confused by the lightheartedness of their reaction: here he was, baring his soul about the deep pain he feels because of the loneliness of our relationship — how he's competing with, and losing to, a dog, which his wife now wears. But the pathos of what he wanted to communicate got lost in translation, stripped away in favor of the adorableness of his performance and the fact that so many women can relate to the topic of preferring dogs to husbands. He wanted that pain to be acknowledged, seen, felt. Instead, it's being eclipsed by relatable marriage-humor.

Gary stares at me as the compliments flow around him. I know he wants more than anything for me to acknowledge what he just put into words — everyone else may have missed the point, but he knows I didn't. He waits for me to throw him some kind of bone — a word of understanding, a promise of improvement, a sign of love. Immobilized by the public awkwardness of the situation, and truly impressed by his impromptu performance, I give him two thumbs-up and a big smile. "Great job!"

It's not enough. My response is yet another disappointment. He turns away from me and, instead, turns back to his group. I get a funny feeling that we have crossed a line — as if something has shifted and he knows, finally, that who I once was is gone for good, that I'm never coming back.

After lunch, when we return to the afternoon session, I can only come up with a half-finished paragraph and a stick-figure sketch about the torture of writer's block. When it's my turn to share, I clear my throat, but nothing comes out.

"I can't," I say.

"Yes you can," Sari says. "Just relax."

I glance over at Gary for some encouragement, but he looks away, refusing to meet my eye. He's done. I'm on my own. I stare at my pad again, but still nothing. "No. I really can't."

"Okay, Judy." Sari turns to the woman

next to me. "Go ahead, Ann, brave-warrior-soul."

And just like that, I'm off the hook.

We're back in our room, getting ready to go to the big group dinner to celebrate the completion of the first day of our Noble Journey. Gary's pawing through his small overnight bag, trying to decide which sweater to change into, when I tell him that I think Sari's methods are a crock. "When I said I couldn't read my thing, she should have pushed me. Instead, she took the easy way out and just went on to the next person."

He stares at me. "You're kidding, right?"

"Actually, I'm not."

"It's not Sari's job to push you, Judy. It's your job to push yourself."

"No, actually, I'm here because I paid her to push me. If I could push myself to write I'd have stayed home!" He shakes his head, which only makes me dig in more. "Look, just because you were the star of the day with your song doesn't mean that her approach works across the board. Not everyone can just perform on cue."

"Judy. I haven't 'performed on cue' for almost ten years. You know what a big deal that was for me. You know how I battle in

249

my head to get through every single day."

"I do know," I say quietly. "And I admire you for it."

"I don't want your admiration. I want something else."

I sit down on the bed. I don't know what that means and I'm really not ready to find out. The idea of leaving the room is suddenly more than I can handle and I tell Gary that I'm going to skip the dinner. "Just tell Sari that I don't feel well. Which is actually the truth."

"Good. I'll go alone. Which will make me feel less alone than if you were there but not really there with me."

It's quiet after Gary leaves. Too quiet. I look around the room and realize Sari was right — it's a beautiful space: high ceilings, big windows with the same kitchen view of rolling fields; linen couches and overstuffed armchairs and walls of bookshelves. For the first time since we got here, I touch things — big glass paperweights, the topstitching on throw pillows, the frames of happy-couple family photographs — and I'm sad suddenly, missing Teddy, and the dog, and Glenn. I'm just about to open a desk drawer out of habit — I've always been a compulsive snoop, curious to know the mundane things about people — what they eat, what they read, how they arrange their clothes and their closets, the kind of toothpaste and floss they use — my fingers are looped around a heavy brass drawer-pull when Andy appears in the doorway with a dinner tray.

"Looking for something?" she says eyeing me, before explaining the soup. "Sari said your husband said you didn't feel well."

I know that if her hands were free she would have pumped air quotes around that entire sentence. I drop my hand from the drawer-pull. "Just chocolate!" I lie.

"You won't find any in this house. Skin and Bones wouldn't eat chocolate unless her pills were covered in it."

We have a nickname. I can't wait to tell Gary. When we start speaking to each other again.

Andy puts the tray on the desk, then bends down and slowly slides the bottom left-hand drawer open. She reaches in, behind what looks like a stack of envelopes, and pulls out a fat white joint. "Is this what you were looking for?" I don't answer, so she sniffs the rolled joint, lights it, takes a long slow drag, then hands it to me. After all the times I've said no to Gary, I take it from her without hesitation. Why not? It's

251

been a shitty day. I take a second drag when that's offered, too, but refuse a third.

"So tell me about these people, Andy. Sari and Gregory." I lean back against the desk, and close my eyes. Something is definitely happening to my brain already.

"You don't need me to tell you what your eyes can plainly see."

I inhale, then nod. "They seem like such phonies. Such narcissists. Peddling confidence and snake oil and big dreams to the disenfranchised and downtrodden."

Andy raises an eyebrow. "Don't get crazy."

"Sorry. I mean, the creatively disenfranchised and downtrodden."

She stares at me and shrugs. "All I know is that they're in the business of telling people what they want to hear and these people are hungry for it. They eat it up."

"I hate myself for being here."

"Then why did you come?"

I tell her that I came because I'm desperate, that I'm stuck, that I have writer's block. I tell her that I know it sounds like a First World Problem except that it's how I used to earn a living, for my family. I try to guess Andy's age — she's probably twenty-five, or twenty-eight, definitely under thirty. She probably has no idea what I'm talking about. I wouldn't have at that age. "This was a last-ditch effort to restart my career, but I barely wrote anything today, despite a million different prompts that seemed to work for everyone else. Including my husband, who was the star of the day. And he wasn't even supposed to be here!"

Andy says that I sound pissed. And I guess I am. I'd wanted some time to myself, to clear my head. But there we were, attached at the hip, as always. It's such a shitty, ungenerous thought to have so I tell myself it's the pot talking.

"Some couples like that togetherness-thing," she says. "You must like it, on some level, if you ended up here together." I shrug, and then she shrugs, and then she says she's not interested in any of that straight-cis-married-shit. "I'm single. By choice."

"You're smart."

"I know."

"You have no idea."

"I do."

"You should stay that way."

"I will."

In minutes, after she leaves, I feel awful for being so unkind about Gary's breakthrough, especially since I only want him to do well, to thrive, to conquer his anxiety. I just wish that we both had it easier. I often wonder, as I do right now, if I'd known how much Gary and his anxiety might eclipse me — that being in his orbit might pull me away from my work, my thoughts, my own private world, the dissociated place in my head I'd always gone to that made it possible for me to think and work — whether I still would have married him. I think back often to the beginning, to when Gary and I first met, as if there is an answer I will find there. If I'd known how hard things would be now, would I have made the same choice? Would he? Doesn't every married person ask themselves this question?

Sometimes, when I'm with Glenn, waiting for a doctor to see her or for a drip to start, and I tell her the latest with Gary — a new anxiety trigger or symptom, the possibility of an untried therapy, even more pot — she shakes her head.

"I told you," she says. "But you didn't listen. And now you're stuck."

She means "stuck" in the best possible way, though. She means: *stuck together, like birds of a feather.* She means: "You're not just married. You're family now. Because that's what happens."

That is what's happened. It's why we stay. I look away from whatever nurse or needle is closing in on her, out a window if there is one, at the patterns on floor and ceiling tiles, and think back to the early days, when I first met Gary. He's temping in the publicity and marketing departments of Black Bear Books, coming and going for weeks at a time, during our busy periods — opening boxes, packing up Jiffy bags, collating binders for sales meetings, organizing shipments for trade shows. I notice him — who didn't? — because he's tall and funny and straight — a unicorn in New York publishing.

"I love the guy, but no," Glenn says when I ask about him.

"I don't care that he's still a temp at his age."

"I don't care either. I meant that he's too complicated."

"Everyone still single is 'too complicated.' That's why we're still single." I roll my eyes for good measure, but in truth I'm concerned. Glenn's warning reminds me of the time a friend wanted to fix me up with someone she'd met at a wedding. "You should meet him," she said, "but he has glasses." I stared at her. "How big are the glasses?" The friend had cleared her throat. "Very, very big." Which they were, when I finally met him because I didn't believe her. I'm not sure I believe Glenn now, either, even though I know I probably should. "*How* complicated?"

"He's divorced. Brief marriage, right after college, no kids, but still. Who needs that? Better to start fresh with a first-timer. Someone with no history of failure."

I shrug. It doesn't feel like a deal breaker to me. In fact, the idea that he was married once means he might marry again. That he can commit. So this is actually good news. "What else."

"He used to drink. And there may have even been a few visits to rehab in between temp-stints here. But to be fair, it's because of his anxiety and the musician lifestyle: you stress about money, whether you're any good, whether anyone's going to show up to hear you play, what the reviews will say. And you drink. Self-medication as opposed to simple degenerate behavior. There's a difference, of course." She is only half-kidding.

Addiction doesn't run in my family and I have never dated an alcoholic. But I've seen some on TV and in the movies who have successfully quit, like Paul Newman in *The Verdict,* and I believe strongly in the power of change. I'm undaunted. "And?"

"*And,* he's Catholic. And you need a Jew. I've met your parents. You're their only child; their parents were survivors. You have one job in life and that is to marry within the tribe and perpetuate your people."

That may have been true at one time, but it isn't true anymore. All they want now is for me to bring home someone decent and kind, someone good-looking, and someone taller than me because they're of that generation that does not go for a nontraditional differential in height. Gary would fit that bill on all counts.

"Look," Glenn says. "I love Gary — you will not find a kinder more hilarious guy on the planet. But, he struggles. Which means you'll struggle. I just want you to have an easier time than I did."

She has been married twice — the first time to an alcoholic she'd met in graduate school who died a drinker long after their divorce — he simply could not stop drinking — and the second time to an editor who died young of Parkinson's ten years into their marriage. By the time I meet her she is single and living alone, like me. "Both times I thought I could handle it, and both times I underestimated what I was taking on. I'm not saying I regret either husband, but they each took a lot out of me. Sometimes I wonder what my life would have been like if I had chosen differently."

I get it but I don't get it. I'm still young

enough to believe that we don't choose who to love — love chooses us. I'm drawn to Gary's troubled past, attracted to it even. I want to save him. I'm a giant cliché, but I don't care. I'm also reading the tea leaves of his past and future differently: that as someone who's struggled, he's resilient, a fighter, a survivor. Couldn't that be the story that will eventually unfold?

And so against Glenn's advice, when I run into Gary a year or two after his last temping stint, I say yes when he asks me to go bowling. We meet on a snowy night after Thanksgiving when almost no one is back in the city after the holiday. He teaches me how to bowl with the big balls and big pins, even though he grew up in New England, like me, candlepin bowling, with small balls and tall narrow pins. He stands behind me, almost a whole foot taller, shows me how to put my three fingers into the three holes and swing my arm back and then forward and up. He models it for me, vamping up and down the lane like a pro bowler on TV. He looks ridiculous, but he hits strike after strike, while I throw mostly gutter balls. In between strings we talk about people we used to know at work and we die laughing. We close the place down. With our coats on, heading down the stairs to the street, I congratulate him on his victory.

"We're tied. Because you won, too."

"What did I win?"

We are out on the street now, on University Place, and it is cold and dark and quiet. For a few seconds, the only footprints on the sidewalk are ours. He looks up at the sky, takes my hand, and kisses it. "This."

Within a month we will practically be living together at my place, a block away from the bowling alley. I will have no regrets. He'll be nothing but loving, and kind, and honest — dependable and present in ways no previous boyfriend has been before.

When I call to tell Glenn the news, she laughs through the phone. "I am so happy to be wrong!"

But she is not wrong. He has his first panic attack on what seems like a perfect Sunday afternoon. We've seen *Harold and Maude* at the Cinema Village on Twelfth Street and afterward walk a few blocks down to a diner for an early dinner. It is late December. Dusk had fallen while were inside the theater and Christmas tree lights twinkle in almost every window. I slip my arm inside Gary's and lean into him. Despite the gloaming, the movie has left me in an unfamiliar state of being: squishy and warm;

full of love and hope; open to possibility. If Maude, a Holocaust survivor, can embrace life, then I can embrace it, too.

My life is already improving. Though Glenn doesn't live in New York anymore, we still talk and email daily. I'm finishing a first draft of *Bird* and hoping to show it to her soon. And after years of living alone in between failed relationships, enviously staring at couples walking around the Village on the weekends, I am finally one of them. I gaze up at Gary in his dark blue peacoat with his big shoulders and his giant green eyes and am just about to tell him how happy I am, how great this is — how being with him on the street in my neighborhood after a movie feels like a tiny miracle — when he suddenly stops moving.

"I can't go in there."

I think he's kidding. We're standing right in front of the door of the restaurant — people are rushing around us to get inside where the windows are steamed with heat. But when he steps away from the door, disengages from my arm, and looks up and down the street, his eyes are wild. He is terrified. I feel like I'm with a stranger.

"If you make me go in there, I'll die."

"I'm not going to make you do anything." The street telescopes, goes quiet. He looks like a cornered animal. I stand perfectly still, trying not to make any sudden moves.

He tells me he's serious. He's not kidding. That he can't take it anymore.

I have no idea what he's talking about, what's happening, what the "it" is. I wonder for a split second if I should call someone, someone who deals with this kind of thing, but I don't know who deals with this kind of thing because I don't know what this thing is.

He takes a few deep breaths, then shakes his head. "I'm sorry. I hate Sundays." He is pacing now, back and forth, then in circles around me.

I blink, trying to piece things together. I know about his father's drinking, the volatility of his home life during and after his parents' divorce, the hypervigilance and anxiety that came from that kind of uncertain and traumatic childhood — and I'm convinced that our relationship will be enough to save him. That together we'll get past his childhood, that with someone to take care of him and look out for him, he will survive and thrive. I'm sure of it. My naïveté is staggering in retrospect, but at the time, I believe my plan will work.

Back then it is easy to comfort him, to distract him from himself, to make things better. When he is calm I take his arm again and lead him away from the restaurant and back up University Place toward my building — into the lobby, past the doorman, and up in the small creaky elevator, into my apartment. After an hour in bed, he is better. Back to normal. He gets up and gets dressed, opens the refrigerator, then closes it. "Where should we go? I'm starving!" he says. Like nothing happened.

But something did happen. Because now I'm the one who can't move. I'd felt so good after the movie, but taking care of Gary took everything out of me. It's like we've traded places. Glenn was right when she said that he's too complicated — maybe I am making a mistake, maybe saving him means risking getting pulled under myself. But it already feels like it's too late. I already feel like I'm in too deep. He already needs me. How can I leave?

Helping the drowning is noble work, the most noble journey, but it can cost you almost everything. I think of Teddy, our one true joy. How can I say I would have chosen differently when Gary has given me this beautiful boy, this good life? How can I be anything other than blocked when I feel so conflicted and confused?

LEAVING EARLY

It's only nine o'clock, but it feels like a million hours go by as I wait for Gary to come back up from dinner. I haven't been high since college, and while I didn't like the feeling then, I realize I actually hate it now. Whatever was in that joint is nothing like the harmless low-tech pot we used to smoke. I'm wired and exhausted, anxious and paralyzed, almost like I'm tripping. I have no idea when Andy left the room and what we talked about before she did. I'm trying to get my hands to work on my phone — trying to text the People Puppets to make sure everything is okay back home — that Teddy has left his room at least once and that Phoebe has worn the dog for at least an hour — but while I'm fumbling I can't shake the feeling that I've lost track of time. All I sense is that at some point this evening I had a desperate urge to draw.

The next thing I know, Gary is back. He's

standing over me, asking me if I'm okay.

"Maybe it's all the crayons and markers we used today, but I've been dying to get creative." I'm talking either superfast or superslow. Am I actually talking or are the words just in my head?

Gary stares at me, then sniffs. "It smells like pot and Sharpies in here," I think he says. He looks down and then so do I: there's my open tote bag on the floor, most of its contents spilled out onto the rug. Fragments of memory are coming back to me: I remember digging around in that bag for the handful of pens I'd grabbed before leaving the house yesterday morning. I smirk at the possibility that I had a delayed reaction: after producing nothing in the seminar all day, I may have had a burst of creativity tonight.

I'm groggy now, and headachy, but vaguely aware that something isn't right. Gary is moving in slow motion around the room, his mouth open in horror. He's pointing at the photos on the walls, and at some of the framed pictures on the bookshelves. His lips are moving and words are probably coming out but I don't hear anything until finally he grabs me by the shoulders and yells:

"Jesus, Judy. *What did you do?*"

What did I do? Apparently, in his absence, and under the influence of whatever kind of cannabis was in Gregory's desk drawer, I took my supply of Sharpie pens and marked up Sari Epstein's happy-couple photos: big Dalí-mustaches on the glass over some of the faces; devil horns on others. And then there's the reprint of the *New York Times* Style section piece on Creativity Gurus where I drew arrows pointing to Sari's head and then wrote, in big block letters, THE FOREHEAD. Next to that are several caption bubbles filled with I HAVE A "CREATIVE" IDEA: GET SOME BANGS! and OR: HOW ABOUT A SIDE-PART?

More of my memory is coming back to me: I now remember making those mustache flourishes and writing those caption bubbles; the glee that my old book signing and illustrating pens were no longer going to waste and were finally being repurposed — punishing someone *who isn't even a writer* because she had a framed print of a famous Norman Mailer quotation on her bookshelf: WRITER'S BLOCK IS ONLY A FAILURE OF THE EGO.

A failure of the ego. Her ego is so ridiculously huge that it's eclipsed the fact that her only true creative talent is marketing creativity retreats. Which didn't even work for me.

The more I blink awake, the more the rage comes back to me. Gary is pointing at a big poster-size blowup of the two of them, Sari and Gregory, from the back, running down a beach holding hands. I've scrawled THIS IS SO UNFAIR on the glass at the top of the photo, with a flurry of at least ten angry arrows pointing at them. He sighs, rolls his eyes. "Jesus, Judy. Please don't tell me you're jealous of them."

"I am, but it's not what you think." I'm jealous of their ease. I'm jealous of his mental health, of her physical health. "Why do you have to struggle every single day and he doesn't? Why does Sari get to live when Glenn's going to die?" It's the first time I've said this out loud, and it only makes me feel worse, not better. "Why do some people get to be healthy and others don't? It's not fair." The words come out of me in a low growl, and then in the deep howl of a wounded animal. "It's not fair."

Gary exhales and his shoulders slump. The day has gutted him, too, but somehow he is still standing. I cry until I can't anymore.

"I want to go home," I whisper, wiping my nose. But I know that's not possible.

There's still another day of the seminar, and the minute Sari sees what I've done, she'll post about it on social media. I'm paralyzed with shame and fear.

Gary looks down at all our stuff, then at the clock on the desk — it's almost 10:00 P.M. — and then out the window. It's pitch-black out, and he can just make out the car under a big white rising moon. He picks up all of our bags at once and, with his free hand, lifts me by the elbow. It seems we're leaving early.

We tiptoe down the stairs and edge around the kitchen door. Andy is clearing the table and Gregory and Sari are drinking wine and talking in hushed tones — their practice of "checking in" with each other after students have left for the night, both of them glowing from the activity of creativity, from the apparent joy they take in the community of artists and writers they've built; in the people who come and go from their house struggling to express themselves. All I feel is loneliness — every cell in my body and brain is empty and devoid of what's supposed to connect me to the rest of the world — and to Gary — and I am full of a strange new grief, that of a nonjoiner who suddenly sees what they've been missing out on all these years: community, connection, the quiet comfort of others.

But there is no time. With the stealth movements of a scene from a *Bourne* movie, Gary signals for me to follow him down a few more stairs, into the "car-barn," otherwise known as a garage. There are the three cars — the SUV that Sari drove to the cheese store, the BMW Gary refused to drive, and the white Prius Gregory drove earlier. He takes a set of keys off a nail on the wall and pops open the Prius's trunk, then loads our bags in. He motions for me to get into the car, and then he does, and, with a press of the "start" button, the dashboard lights up. Gary turns off the interior lights and the headlights and backs out of the garage without a sound. In our perfect battery-operated getaway vehicle we float silently down the lawn all the way to the Volvo.

With everything transferred into our car, and the keys left in the ignition of the Prius, Gary leans in through the driver's door and puts the Volvo into neutral, runs to the back of the wagon and pushes it down the road past Sari's house. Once we're in the clear, Gary gets behind the wheel and shifts the car into drive. At the end of Sari's road, he guns it toward the highway. I enter our destination — Home — into his phone, then put it on the holder on the dashboard. In seconds it lights up with our mapped route. We'll get back just after midnight.

In the dark silence between us I remember another similarly dramatic night-escape — years ago, before Teddy was born, when we visited a college friend of mine in Maine. Clara had invited me countless times to see the beach house that had been in her family for generations, and one summer weekend a year after I'd met Gary, I finally agree. I print out her directions and pack up the car. I promise him that it will be fun.

Gary only reluctantly agrees to go — he prefers the impersonal feel of hotels to the awkward closeness of staying with friends — travel in general and being in situations he can't control, like being someone's houseguest, makes him extremely anxious — but as we get off the highway north of Portland and follow the coastal roads into town and toward a huge shingled house on a craggy hill, he suddenly perks up.

"See?" I say. "And you didn't want to go."

But then we pull into the driveway and arrive at the back of the house, which is a dump. Gary parks on a burned mound of dry grass next to two dead station wagons and several feral cats. The cats glare at us, and then Gary glares at me. "We're not staying. You know I can't handle this kind of thing. The unknown, the unclean, the unsafe."

Clara, plain and preppy in flat sandals and a faded Lilly Pulitzer–style skort, comes running out to greet us before we can plot the details of an escape. She takes us through the back of the house — from the kitchen that hasn't been touched since the avocado-green-and-brown-appliance-seventies, to a grand foyer where flies enter in through a sagging screen door, to an upstairs guest room. Inside the bedroom with sea foam–green walls, Gary's eyes fixate on the bed itself: a mattress on the floor, a short stack of stained pancake-thin pillows waiting for pillowcases; the buzzing of bees and more flies outside in the dead summer heat.

Clara adjusts the window fan leaning up against a broken screen like a scrappy nurse improving the angle of a bed or a splinted limb. "If you just angle it like this," she says, almost pushing it out the window, "you can get a nice cross breeze. And it keeps the mosquitoes from coming in. Who needs air-conditioning?"

"Not me!" Gary says theatrically, hitting

his head on the swaying chain hanging from a bare lightbulb on the ceiling. He grits his teeth then digs his nails deep into the soft flesh of my palm. "We're leaving," he mouths.

"I know," I mouth back.

It only gets worse when Clara leaves us alone. "Oh look, Judy!" Gary shrieks. "A litter box! In our bedroom!" He covers his eyes with both hands. "We're not staying. I can't sleep here. I won't sleep here. It's hot. There are mosquitoes. And —"

"I get it, Gary. Don't panic. I'll think of something."

We hug, then laugh hysterically into each other's necks, trying to snuff out Gary's rising anxiety, which lasts until after dinner, when we go back to our room and pretend to go to sleep for the night. Instead, in the moonlight, with the bleating of crickets in the background, Gary and I, much like we did tonight, tai chi our way out of the guest room, down the stairs, and out the kitchen door to the car. If Gary hadn't knocked over a trash can while I left a note on the kitchen table, thanking Clara for her hospitality and apologizing for our hasty departure, we would have made a clean getaway. Instead, we peel out of the driveway while all the lights in the house go on. Seconds later, driving on a road that traces the ocean like a finger, we stop at the first beach parking lot we pass.

"What did you say in the note?" Gary asks, breathless, tearing at my clothes.

"That you forgot your little Claus von Bülow bag of insulin," I say, tearing at his.

"Diabetes! *Brilliant!*"

Tonight, in the dark of this autumn evening, we drive under another giant moon, but we will not pull off the road after this escape the way we did then; we will not tear each other's clothes off. I watch Gary drive, study his face lit by the yellowy lights of the dashboard and briefly by the occasional oncoming car for clues for what to say.

"What's wrong with us?" I whisper. I'm not sure if Gary doesn't answer because he hasn't heard me or because he doesn't know how to answer. "We're not like other people. We're always escaping. We're always fleeing in the middle of the night."

"No we're not like other people. And maybe you'd be better off if you finally accepted that."

"Maybe I don't want to. Maybe I don't want to be different."

"But you *are* different, Judy. You have a different kind of marriage than most people have. And so do I. Maybe we both wish we didn't — maybe we both wish we had a 'normal' marriage, whatever that is — but we don't, and that's how it is. That's our reality. The longer you fight it, the worse it will be. For you. For me. And for Teddy." He shakes his head. "I get it. I get that Sorry and her stupid husband have it easier than we do, or seem to anyway. I get that it sucks about Glenn — there is no justice when it comes to who lives and who dies — but you still could have used this weekend to jump-start your work. But maybe me being there ruined it for you, so you just shut down and didn't even try."

"You didn't ruin it for me."

"Sometimes I wish I'd married someone else, too. And the weird thing is, I'm not even that unhappy, Judy. Even though we don't fuck anymore, and even though we sleep in separate rooms and have this weird arrangement that's kind of a fake marriage and kind of a very real marriage, I still love you. And I probably always will, no matter how things eventually end up."

I turn my head and rest my forehead on the cold glass of my window.

"You've got Teddy, and the dog, and me. You may wish you had more than that, but that's not bad."

I don't want more than that. I've never wanted more than that. I've just wanted things to be easier. Is that so wrong?

"No one cares how weird your life is, Judy. Or all the ways you think it's failed you," Gary says. "Your mother's gone. No one sees the bird on your head except you."

■ ■ ■ ■

PART THREE:
BRACING FOR
CHANGE

■ ■ ■ ■

MICHAEL WASSERMAN

Trying to distract myself from the emotional hangover of our disastrous trip to Vermont, I'm at Costco a few days later, fondling a twenty-count bag of small avocados, while Teddy is off in the video game aisle. I'm hoping to find even one avocado that is soft enough to eat tonight, or tomorrow night, or maybe this month, which I know probably isn't going to happen, since finding an avocado that's ripe when you want to eat it is nearly impossible. Everything in life is about timing, about patience, about having faith in the future, but I've never believed in any of that. All the cigarettes I smoked before meeting Gary because I was convinced I'd never meet anyone and thus would never have anything to live for; all the times I've tried to get back to my work — the writing and the drawing — and failed. Maybe I wasn't ready. Maybe I'm still not ready. Maybe instead of blaming myself for what happened at Sari Epstein's I should accept the fact that I'm pushing myself to do something I don't actually want to do anymore. Maybe I should just move on.

Moving on (*"Is 'moving on' like 'giving up' but with a better publicist?"* *"When accepting failure is a Good Thing"*) is what I'm thinking about when I think I see Michael Wasserman from Hebrew school looking at a jumbo pack of tomatoes. Michael Wasserman, who I'd had a secret crush on all those years ago because of his slim chinos and thick brown hair and perfect teeth and always-white Jack Purcell sneakers, but who had never liked me back. At least I didn't think he did. Was it possible he'd liked me, too? Probably not, especially since he'd started dating Janie Levy, who also had perfect teeth, during our bar/bat mitzvah year, and to my knowledge, they had never broken up. But now that I'm technically separated, I force myself to question all my default negative thoughts — especially that he could never have liked me because of what I did to him all those years ago by accident.

Almost forty years ago I caused Michael Wasserman's Passover-themed shoe box diorama depicting Moses receiving the Ten

Commandments to fall off the teacher's desk when I stupidly reached for another piece of matzo that I wasn't even hungry for. Wasn't it just yesterday that everyone turned and stared at me without helping to pick it up and put it back together? That he saw the shoe box on the floor; all his hard work, all his careful gluing, his tiny precision handiwork — ruined? We were eleven or twelve then, the age when boys still show their feelings, the age that Teddy used to be when his face would soften and fall with every passing sadness. That day, in the few seconds it took Michael Wasserman to register the accidental demolition of his construction-in-miniature, his eyes had welled with tears like something actually hurt. He looked crushed. I'm certain I'd gasped and covered my mouth with my hands in shame. Was there anything worse than destroying someone's art project?

But before I could apologize, he'd bent down in his chinos, carefully picked up the shoe box, put it on top of the pile of books and notebooks he was carrying, and left the classroom for the carpool line. All without saying a word. I didn't move. My face was red-hot, my stomach churned with embarrassment and self-loathing and recriminations I was convinced would last forever:

Why hadn't I just sat down in my stupid chair with the little side-desk attached? Weren't my braces already filled with enough chewed-up matzo? If only I hadn't reached for that second piece, none of this would have happened. I was wearing my favorite powder-blue ski jacket, which meant that it was sometime between March and April, during New England's tease of changing seasons that never fails to trick and disappoint — there must still have been a chill of winter in the air, despite some light in the sky. The principal, Mr. Wrath — which was really his name and really how he spelled it — poked his head into the classroom and told me that my mother was in the carpool line, waiting. It was six o'clock, time to go home. He didn't seem to notice the debris on the floor, the accident that had just happened, how time had suddenly and completely stopped.

Instantly I'd had a flash of my mother's blue Buick Skylark idling in the chilly dusk while the other mothers — it was all mothers back then, no "helpful" dads — pulled around her and gave her dirty looks — a scene I knew I'd hear about on the ride home, and during dinner, and for years to come: how it was hard enough for her to teach inner-city seventh-graders all day, go

280

food shopping after work, bring the groceries home and put everything into the refrigerator and freezer, and then make it to the temple in time for the mad crush of children desperately pushing through the doors toward freedom, only to have me be late and put her in the incredibly uncomfortable position *of holding up the line.*

It never occurred to me, as I got into the front seat and drove off with Mandy Adelson and Rhonda Schlossberg in the back-seat, to explain to my mother why I was late that day — just as it had never occurred to my mother to ask me why I was late. We didn't do that in our family — relate to each other in the moment, with curiosity or empathy. We didn't interact in an interactive way. My grandparents had all survived the Holocaust and there had always been a very high bar set for true suffering. We never shared even the most basic facts of our days: *"I just ruined Michael Wasserman's diorama and now I want to die." "One of my students called me fat when I was passing back their spelling tests."* We never would have said those things. We didn't know how to commiserate or comfort each other. We were three circles, occasionally just barely overlapping, a Venn diagram of connected separateness. Which had always seemed to me to be the loneliest feeling of all: having people around you who you could see but couldn't ever reach.

Even if my mother had asked me, I probably would not have had the language to explain the sadness I felt when I looked at what remained on the floor after Michael left the classroom — the little bits of uncooked elbow macaroni and broken Necco wafers and the focal point of the diorama — the Ten Commandments itself — that the janitor would sweep away. To confess how inanimate objects could sometimes make me feel incredibly sad, those two Bit-O-Honeys stuck together to look like Moses' tablets from God that had landed under the chair. That right before running out of the classroom I'd picked them up and slipped them into the pocket of my ski jacket, the one I'd never actually skied in because the Jews in our world didn't actually ski, and noticed that the number "10" had been etched into each beige sticky candy rectangle, maybe with a paper clip or a pocketknife or the tip of a dead ballpoint pen to make the indentations. Michael Wasserman, whose mother had died the previous autumn of breast cancer, right before the High Holidays, had taken the time to etch numbers into his pretend Ten Commandments and I had ruined it. How could I ever have explained the sadness of that?

Even if I could have, I wouldn't have: telling only made things worse. Reassurance, the erasure of worry, the absorption of anxiety — for the most understandable and saddest reasons, those were not part of my parents' skill sets. They were barely part of mine, though I'm working on them. I will always be the survivor of survivors, of catastrophizers; always the one to say the darkest, bleakest thing at a moment when a shred of levity could save the day. Just ask Gary.

"Oh, Judy Hope Vogel, the irony of your middle name," he always says, when my negativity bleeds unexpectedly into a conversation or an exchange, a permanent marker through paper. But for me it's never been irony. It's always been the weight of that middle name, the burden of being the one to carry a positive life force for the three of us. Which is why my *Bird on Your Head* success had been so sweet, and why my now-descending star is that much harder to bear. I'm letting my whole family down, not just myself.

Today, I inch away from the rock-hard avocados toward the organic pitted fruit, already out of season and just out of reach, and the berries, to try to get a better look at Michael, to confirm that it's actually him. It is. I'd know his teeth anywhere. I watch him while he looks intently at his phone — maybe at a text, maybe at a shopping list — maybe at an email from his wife — until his shopping cart finally starts to move.

"Excuse me," he says, staring at me like I have a bird on my head. It takes me a few seconds to realize that my cart is blocking his way past me.

"I'm so sorry!" I smile expectantly but don't move. I'm waiting for him to recognize me, to say something awkward and adorable and perfect, something we will brag about in the retelling of this moment at the small but intimate rehearsal dinner before our small but intimate wedding exactly a year or two from now. But when my fantasy scenario doesn't materialize, I realize suddenly what I must look like to him: just another middle-aged female warehouse shopper, oblivious to everyone around her because she feels like she's invisible anyway. I clear my throat, then force myself to break through the scrim of intense discomfort. "I'm sure you don't remember me" — I clear my throat again — "but are you Michael Wasserman? From Temple Shalom Hebrew School?" And then, before he can answer that no, he doesn't remember me, I preempt the possibility of disappointment by blurting: "I'm Judy Vogel. I broke your Ten Commandments diorama. By accident."

He smiles slowly, cautiously. It's all coming back to him now, I'm sure of it, and we will each live better, less burdened lives once this painful memory is cleared up and we each get the closure we so deserve. Such is the magic of living where you grew up, I think: the opportunities for soul-cleansing do-overs are endless. "I *am* Michael Wasserman," he says, "but I have no memory of a Passover diorama."

"Oh wow. Okay. Great. What a relief!" I lie. I feel oddly disappointed. How is it possible for that incident to have meant more to me as the destroyer than it had to him as the destroyed? That's not how it's supposed to work, is it? "I can't tell you how many times I've thought of that day and felt terrible about it. I had this whole awful scenario in my head about how a neighbor had helped you with the project because your mother had just died and your father was too busy being in mourning."

When my mouth finally stops moving I reach down into the sling for self-comfort. But I remember that, for once, I've left the

dog at home. Which must be why I'm saying things I shouldn't be saying. And why
I've insisted on reintroducing myself to
someone I used to know, even though
Gary's been advising me against that kind
of thing for years: *They're strangers,* he'd
say after each humiliating episode in a
restaurant, a mall, or a movie theater, when
someone either didn't recognize me, didn't
remember me after I'd explained our connection, or didn't care.

Michael Wasserman, a virtual stranger, is
still staring at me, but he hasn't walked
away yet. I take this as a good sign, or at
least as a sign that all is not lost. Yet. He
nods his head slowly. "Mrs. Shapiro." He
edges our carts out of the line of rabid shop-
pers desperately foraging for dinner at the
nearby whole-roasted-chicken counter, then
speaks slowly, a memory gelling with each
word he adds: "She lived next door, with
two girls, so her house was full of arts and
crafts stuff. We sat at her dining room table
the night before the diorama was due and
she helped me do the whole thing." He
pauses, then smiles, all teeth. "Actually, she
did the whole thing while I just watched."

I'm as sad now for him as I was years
earlier. "I didn't mean to bring up a painful
memory."

"I'd completely forgotten about the diorama until now. Clearly I'd blocked it."

As a crowd at a frozen pizza sample counter continues to gather, we move our carts out of the way again.

"So what did you do after I destroyed your diorama?"

"I became an orthodontist."

"No way."

"I know. So boring."

"Are you kidding? When you're a writer there's nothing boring about a normal career with a steady income." I haven't self-identified as a writer in ages and I have no idea why I did just now.

"That's right," he says, smiling again. "Congratulations on all your success!"

I wave him away. "That was such a long time ago."

"Was it really?"

"It feels like it. It feels like a million years ago!"

"Well, my kids loved the book. And the show. I used to tell them that I knew the girl who created them, that I sat next to her in Hebrew school."

I roll my eyes. "The girl with the bird on her head."

"That's not how I remember it. I remember you being the supercool girl that I was

287

too scared to talk to."

"Shut. Up."

"Remember what you used to say to the principal when he told you to smile? You'd say, 'It's *my* face.' " He laughs. "It's *my* face. That was really something."

"Smiling was not part of my skill set back then."

"Well, you're smiling now."

I blush, then look in his cart: cereal, organic macaroni and cheese, peanut butter. "Tell me about your kids."

He taps his phone and then shows me — three adorable dark-haired children in various stages of toothlessness, against a backdrop of epic foliage. "This was a few years ago. They don't like to be photographed now. They're in their tweens now."

"They look just like her," I say, with a wry smile, remembering Janie Levy. She was the prettiest girl at the temple, and she and her twin brother, David, were the bat mitzvah circuit heartthrobs. I remember Michael and Janie dating around the time of all those awful parties, her perfect hair and his perfect teeth, neither of them needing braces, and how awkward and unsightly the rest of us seemed by comparison. "I can't believe people actually marry their Hebrew school sweethearts and live happily ever after."

He looks at me like I have a bird on my head. "I didn't marry Janie."

"Then who did you marry?"

But before he can answer, Teddy materializes as if out of thin air from the video game aisle. I reach for his arm. "Teddy, this is Michael, an old friend of mine from when I was your age." I prod him to shake hands, then whisper into his ear: "Now smile. With teeth."

He pulls away. "Why?"

"Because Michael is an orthodontist. And I think you need braces."

Michael smiles and manages to get a glimpse of Teddy's mouth, and then mine. He hands me his card. "He does. And so do you."

ADULT BRACES

"Your bite is off," Michael says, a week later in his office, his gloved fingers in my mouth, my chair tilted all the way back and the bright examination light blinding me. His mini metal dental pick taps lightly on my offending lower teeth, then hovers above my lower lip. He offers me a little hand mirror so I can participate in the conversation about the possibility of a second round of orthodontia, instead of being a passive victim like I was the first time. "You see that?"

Actually, I don't. I'm too busy admiring my hair, which I blow-dried for once, and the perfectly thin and straight coat of eyeliner that I somehow managed to apply with a steady hand despite wearing the dog — all in preparation for my date with my orthodontist.

"I'm kidding. He's not officially my orthodontist," I tell Glenn when I call her from the parking lot with Teddy trailing far behind me. "I'm just going to ask him before Teddy's appointment what he meant by his remark that I need braces, too." As usual, I'm all over the place.

"I thought you said he was married."

"I did, but now, in retrospect, I think I also got a divorced vibe."

"Based on what?" Glenn always wants me to provide specifics, to show my work. In the manuscripts of the books of mine she edited, that need for substantiation appeared in the form of notes in the margin — queries on Post-it notes — *Why would she say this?* Or, *How does she know this is what her mother is thinking?* Or, *Do we know if the bird on her head has thoughts and, if so, what they are?* If I couldn't answer to her satisfaction, she would make suggestions on how I could rework something to make it deeper, richer, or clearer. I can tell she doesn't quite trust my divorced-vibes — if this were a story I'd written, her marginalia would include, *Was he wearing a ring? If he told you he hadn't married Janie, why didn't he tell you who he did marry? Even though he didn't tell you who he did marry who wasn't Janie, why wouldn't that give you married-someone-else-instead vibes?* At the very least, she didn't understand what I was basing my cues on. And indeed I couldn't articulate them — now or then, when Teddy and I were driving home from Costco and I'd replayed our encounter in my head. It had been years — decades even — since I'd done that level of conversational parsing and analysis, holding every word up to the light and shaking it to see if it had meant something more than what it seemed: a chance encounter with a childhood acquaintance who I used to have a giant crush on. At the time, it hadn't, but in the days since, my mind, so desperate to avoid reality, swelled with possibility. The possibility that maybe Michael, not the dog, is my true vine.

The light poking and tapping of the tiny dental tool bring me back to the present.

"Your teeth are starting to crowd. Which means you need braces."

"But I already had braces. Isn't once enough?" I look in the mirror again, this time biting and rebiting, baring my teeth like an angry baboon, trying to grasp the fact that there's a seismic shift — *mesial drift* — going on inside my mouth, especially in my lower teeth.

"The older you get, the more your teeth move to the front of your mouth," he explains. "It's called 'relapse,' and if you don't stop it, it just gets worse."

"Maybe they don't want to be alone. Like that final scene in *The Mary Tyler Moore Show,* remember?" I describe how, after their final broadcast, everyone in the newsroom comes together in a group hug, and then stays in that formation as they scuttle across the floor to answer a ringing telephone. He laughs, and when he does I look at his teeth. "How come yours aren't relapsing? How come your teeth still look perfect? We're the same age. I don't understand why I need braces right now and you don't. It's not fair."

"It's just luck." He pokes my lip with the metal pick and I open, and close, one last time.

Passing quickly through anger and denial, I now enter the bargaining phase. "If I decide to do this, can I get the invisible kind of braces, like Tom Cruise?"

He scoots a few inches away on his seat with wheels, snaps off his gloves, and tells me that invisible braces aren't as good, which means you end up wearing them for twice as long as the regular kind. And, they're more expensive. "Nothing beats good old-fashioned metal hardware."

"How long would I have to wear them?"

He tells me that we could probably correct what's wrong in eighteen months, then scoots back. "It's not so bad."

"Easy for you to say. As I recall, you never even had braces once. Unlike the rest of us, you were born with perfect teeth."

"I could have used some minor correction, probably just a few bands on the front tops and bottoms, but there was a lot going on at home at the time. As you know."

I watch him move around the office putting tools away for later cleaning, his back to me. I want to ask him about that time, what it was like, those dark teenage years, but I can tell he'd rather not talk about it, so I don't. "How much would it cost?"

"Why don't you set up an actual consultation on your way out today so we can have more time to go over your options and I can answer all your questions."

"I know. I ask a lot of questions."

"You should."

My eyes dart toward the waiting room, where Teddy stares into space at a muted cartoon on a wall-mounted flat-screen television. His teeth are the priority here, not mine.

"Actually, I think I'll pass." I sigh, restraining myself from explaining that money is tight and that this is the first time in five years that someone hasn't been diagnosed with something awful or dying in hospice. *Look at me, keeping my mouth, with its relapsed bite and its crowded lowers, shut.*

He shrugs, then takes the crinkly paper bib off my chest, flips the light away from my head and angles my chair back up. "Okay, but don't blame me in a few years when your teeth start falling out."

I sit in on Teddy's consultation, then sign the proposed but nonbinding treatment and payment plan for his braces — a minimum of two years with the probability of an extra year, depending on the growth of his chin and subsequent exacerbation of his pronounced under-bite. We schedule his appointment — the big day — for the second Wednesday in November, after Inhabitancy ends — and then, since the idea of my teeth falling out is still haunting me, we schedule an official consultation: there has been a cancellation for tomorrow, the receptionist tells me. Do I want it? I reluctantly accept. Why not have all the information before probably saying no?

Back in the car Teddy is quiet. I can't tell if he's glad to be getting braces like everyone else did two years ago, or if he's horrified to be joining the adolescent masses so late. I know I could ask him — *shouldn't I just ask him?* — but sometimes I think it's easier for both of us if I just leave him alone with his feelings, instead of making him share them with me. Because maybe he doesn't want to share them with me: maybe he'd rather process things himself, silently, without parental intrusion, the way I did.

On the way to school I don't bother telling Teddy that my appointment with Michael was not to continue our trip down memory lane, but to talk about the possibility of braces for me. Why does he need to know, ten minutes before school, that the same mother who wears the family dog for comfort and mental stability might soon have a mouth full of embarrassing metal bands? Hasn't he suffered enough? Instead, when we pull up in the blue zone, I hand him a note to give to Grace excusing his late arrival that I've scribbled on a piece of paper I rip from a notebook in my bag:

> Please excuse Teddy. He had an orthodontist appointment even though he doesn't have braces yet.

The next morning, though I don't want to leave the dog, I decide to try going it alone again. It will be good to hear my options before committing either way without the

296

distraction of the dog — and I'd be lying if I said I wasn't just a little embarrassed to face Michael again wearing my neurosis in my sling. While the subject of his marriage, or divorce, didn't come up in the few quick minutes I spent hyperreclined in his examination chair, I'm still somehow convinced that running into Michael and his encouraging me to come back to his office — for the second time — might be fate's hand. Maybe there will be a way out for me. Maybe Michael Wasserman and I are meant to be.

I ask Gary to take Charlotte to the reservoir for a walk today before work.

Unencumbered, Teddy and I make the drive to school with considerably less tension. He seems more relaxed, now that it's just us two in the car and I don't have to drive with my seat pushed back as far as it will go in order to give the dog room between me and the steering wheel. When we pass the house getting the big stupid addition, I slow down the way I always do, only this time, Teddy looks, too.

"Isn't that house big enough already?" he says.

"Seriously." I breathe deeply, full of wonder. My work here is done.

After dropping Teddy, I get to my 9:00 A.M. appointment with Michael exactly on time, though it requires speed-walking from the parking lot to the waiting room. When I catch the young receptionist staring, I realize I must be beet red, or sweating, or both.

I fill out paperwork — financial and insurance information — then get shown to a chair in a different examination room — this time, one with more advanced equipment in it. When Michael arrives, he and his assistant take X-rays, then do a series of close-up digital pictures of my potential new virtual "smile." They hand me an iPad so I can watch a time-lapse version of my teeth in motion: what they'll look like and how they'll get there.

I nod, marveling at the technology that can animate the seamless transition from my now-teeth to my future-teeth. Even after the iPad is taken away, the loop continues playing in my head. My teeth in motion, going to a better place. Maybe they'll take me with them.

But the big decision still looms: full metal braces and brackets — the old-fashioned kind — or translucent ceramic brackets — both of which get cemented to the front of the teeth with wires threaded through them that get replaced every few weeks when the tension gets worn out. I ask Michael to explain it more — how it all works — how teeth actually get coaxed into moving — so he sits down next to me with a plaster model of a braces-filled mouth in his hands.

"The power is in the wire," he says, pointing. "That's where the movement comes. The brackets sit low on the teeth, but instead of tightening the wire like we used to, we switch out the wire at every visit so that each new tight one pulls the teeth to where they need to go. Not too fast, not too slow."

I look behind his elbow to the framed photos of his three children on the wall beyond the swing-arm light, two boys and a girl in the mountains, at the beach, on bikes. I wonder why Janie isn't in any of the pictures and notice suddenly that there's no wedding ring under the purple latex glove. Why wouldn't he have just said that he was divorced?

I try to focus on the photos Michael is showing me of my orthodontic options — always so many choices, too many choices in life — but after I see the translucent brackets, I make up my mind.

"The invisible ones. *Ob*viously," I say.

"Just so you know, they're a lot more expensive than traditional stainless brackets."

I sigh, then agree to the more fiscally responsible choice. It doesn't really matter. I'm not a teenager. No one's looking at me anyway.

The final step is taking impressions of my teeth, top and bottom. Michael leaves to see another patient while his assistant looks for the right size metal arch trays for my mouth and prepares the gloppy mixture that goes in them. I settle in, play with my bib, and think of Charlotte.

"I left my dog at home," I chatter nervously to her as she spreads the amalgam into the two trays. "She's kind of a therapy dog but not really. She's an unofficial therapy dog. She doesn't wear a stupid vest and I don't walk her — I wear her, in a sling."

The assistant looks at me. There's a giant bird on my head. I'm just another weird person her mother's age babbling about something totally gross and embarrassing, but I'm too distracted by sling-withdrawal — *I should have brought the dog. Why didn't I bring the dog? Isn't this exactly the sort of stressful event when I should have the dog with me?* — to really care. We're both clearly relieved when Michael finally returns.

"So," he says, rolling toward me on his wheely-stool, clasping his gloved hands together. "Have you decided? Are you going to stop the entropy and control the chaos of tooth regression?" I don't know if he's trying to sound like a dental brochure on purpose or not, but it's time to commit to a yes or no.

I think of Glenn's body, her chaos, cells dividing everywhere. Suddenly my physiologic mesial drift and malocclusion don't seem so bad. In fact, I'm lucky to have my chaos, the relapse of shifting teeth, so minor and harmless by comparison. I reach for Michael's arm. I tell him I'll do it, but only if he can squeeze me in now. "Before I change my mind."

I wait, reclined, with all the comforts of modern dentistry — fancy headphones blasting Enya into my ears, which I'm too lazy to change and too embarrassed to admit, even to myself, that I actually like — the little remote that controls the wall-mounted flat-screen television where any number of movies are available for distraction — it's all too complicated, just like the one at home that I always have to beg Teddy to show me how to use.

But who needs a flat-screen when the flashbacks are coming, fast and furious, inside my head: I'm eleven, twelve, thirteen;

the metal brackets are fitted around each tooth, not just affixed to the front of the teeth the way they are today: the tiny dental pliers thread the wires from tooth to tooth, on uppers and lowers, the gums bleeding. All while my mother sits in the waiting room, distracted behind a copy of *Better Homes and Gardens,* in which she's folded down pages of rooms with wallpaper she liked and recipes for easy weeknight chicken, even though she will always leave the magazine behind the minute I come out and even though she never cooked from recipes anyway.

After the impressions are taken and the cementing phase has started, I'm given a few plastic masks full of nitrous oxide to stop my squirming and complaining, and my constant apologizing about the squirming and complaining. And at some point after that, I start asking Michael questions.

"Bang and Olufsen," I slur, pulling the headphones off my ears and trying to look at them as they flop against my neck. "Are they from Sweden?"

"Denmark," he says through his blue paper mask.

I don't buy it. "I think they're from Häagen-Dazs."

Another question: "How old are your kids?"

"Eleven, nine, and seven."

My eyes fill with tears. "I remember eleven, nine, and seven," I whisper. "Teddy still liked me then."

Then the real question: "So why did you get divorced?"

Michael's brow tenses over his mask. "What makes you think I'm divorced?"

"It's obvious," I slur, trying to point with my floppy hands, at the walls and at him. "There's no Janie in the photos, and you don't wear a ring."

"You're a real Columbo."

I nod, then point to my brain, smugly. "I'm a writer. It's my job to notice this stuff." I let a few moments pass, then I ask again. "Seriously."

"Seriously what?"

"Seriously why did you and Janie get divorced?"

"Oh Judy," he says, smiling, with the tiny pliers still in my mouth. "Wasn't it enough that you wrecked my Passover diorama?"

I laugh, and close my eyes. I'm floating in the chair, my head a swirl of cotton candy. "Then let me ask you this," I say, forcing my eyes open again. "How did you both know you were making the right decision?

When did you go from thinking *maybe* splitting up was the right thing to do, to *knowing* it was? My husband and I are separated but we still live together, and there's a weird kind of shame about not being brave enough to leave."

"Judy."

"Yes, Michael."

"I didn't marry Janie. I married her brother. And we're still together. Very happily so."

I drive home with my mouth closed over teeth already hurting from being pushed and pulled, reluctant participants in the drama and chaos that I'm trying to control. I'm deep in the black hole of shame for how badly I misread the situation with Michael, thinking he might be my vine, my way forward, the perfect ending to my sad story. Isn't this what would happen in the movie version of a person who moves back to their hometown? Wouldn't this have been the perfect plot point?

I suddenly wish I'd kept some of my mother's OxyContin to dull the tooth pain and erase the humiliation and disappointment of the death of a tiny fantasy. Just a few pills, or a handful of pills; maybe just one container from the drugstore, that giant-size refill she was getting at the end, which wasn't enough and required the addition of a fentanyl patch. How easy it would have been to slip a few pills into my pockets at the end, in hospice, when they sat unused in the overnight bag my father and I had brought for her, because there was no time to wait for pills to work when liquid morphine under the tongue was so much faster and didn't require swallowing. For five days we moved that bag, full of other things we didn't use — Enya CDs, slippers, hand cream, a bathrobe — from chair to closet to chair again — packed because I'd glanced at a few end-of-life websites and taken the advice of the home hospice nurse to bring nightclothes and soft sweatpants and socks; family photos to put around her temporary room; things to remind her of home, of her happy life, to make the phase of active dying — her transition — her passing — easier. To make it easier for her to let go.

But she didn't want to let go. She didn't want to leave early. Not even a little bit early.

Unlike me, my mother was always the last one to leave: birthday parties, dinner parties, get-togethers of any kind. She always stayed to the very end of everything, as if to get every drop of whatever experience she'd signed on for. Growing up, while waiting to go home, I'd always find my mother in somebody's kitchen with a dish towel in her hands, helping to clean up, laughing and talking and smiling, flushed with energy and life, so unlike the way she was in our kitchen, in our house. Sometimes I'd watch her from a doorway, from another room, from where she couldn't see me — *Who was this delightful social fun person?* — wishing that version of her could come home with us and be my mother. But somewhere on the ride home, on the highway or on the quiet side streets that led past all the Victorian houses that surrounded our modest street of tidy Colonials, the air would seep out of the balloon. The world, our world, deflated back to its normal size. Back in our own driveway, in our own house, we were once again ourselves: quiet, disconnected, passing each other like strangers in the kitchen or on the stairs on the way to bed. Did we ever say good night to each other when I was growing up? We must have. We should have. Isn't that what families do?

There at hospice, in a big room with a view of a Japanese cherry tree in full bloom and a giant bird feeder hanging from its branches — though she was drugged and

306

her mind and body were already shutting down, slowly at first, and then all at once — her eyes were still wide open, taking everything in. Until she was gone, she was somewhere she didn't want to leave, not until the last possible second.

In bed now with the dog in the sling, my tongue running over the sharp brackets glued to the front of all my teeth, I think about everyone who has left early: my parents and, soon, Glenn. Not to mention Teddy, who will go off to college in a few years, and Charlotte, who will, like all pets, eventually expire. I think about disconnection, and how I've been trying to find ways to keep Teddy and me from growing further and further apart. It hasn't occurred to me until now that going through the same experience of getting braces right along with him could help him, or me; that our circles could overlap instead of floating next to each other; that we could suffer together instead of alone.

Maybe we can stave off drift and relapse. I fall asleep thinking about Teddy and me in big white sheets, dressed as giant People Puppet teeth, connected at our waists by chain-link belts, our braces, keeping us together forever.

Walking the Reservoir

I get out of the car and walk toward Wheeler's Field off-leash dog park, where I always take Charlotte first before we do a long loop around the reservoir. The usual suspects are all here — Lady, Atticus, Poppins, Ogi, Bazel, Shelby, Cooper — dachshunds and Bernese mountain dogs and border collies and mutts and shepherds, all running and jumping and chasing balls under a perfect blue autumn sky while their owners, in layers of crewnecks and fleece vests and quilted jackets, stand along the sidelines, making awkward small talk. As always when I approach the group, I feel both ignored and deeply scrutinized. It reminds me of the awful playground years, when Teddy had to be dragged kicking and screaming whenever it was time to leave the slide or the sandbox and all the parents rolled their eyes in judgment.

It's a bracingly cold fall morning. I watch

the dogs play, and Charlotte, poking her head out of the sling, watches, too. This moment is always a nice transition before I take her out of the sling and let her join the fun for a while, before we go off on the walk. It's an especially welcome moment of peace today after so much stress: the disastrous trip to Vermont; adjusting to my braces and being in the black hole of shame for what I said to Michael Wasserman; Gary and I not talking further about the kiss since he first confessed to it in our bedroom. Not to mention: Glenn's steady decline. Despite it all, I force myself to follow the advice I've prescribed in twenty or fifty or a hundred of my Well/er pieces: gratitude. *I'm grateful to be outside on such a glorious New England fall day; I'm grateful to have my dog with me; I'm grateful to have a supportive husband, even if that husband isn't technically my husband anymore, and even if that husband is in-like with another woman.*

But today, before I can take the dog out of the sling, a troll of a woman — big-haired and wild-eyed, with giant hiking boots made for mountains, not urban trails — makes a beeline for me. I ignore her, trying to blend into the sea of puffy coats, but her eyes are on me and on the sling. She weaves through the crowd until she is right on me. She taps me on the shoulder.

"Is that a baby sling?"

"Excuse me?" I try to keep my teeth covered when I talk so that she won't make fun of my braces.

"Is that a baby sling? You're carrying a dog in there, not a baby."

"It's none of your business what I'm carrying in there."

"Is the dog injured?"

"No, the dog isn't injured."

"Then why are you carrying it?"

"Because it's my dog. And I can carry her if I want to."

She nods, all-knowing, seething. "I've seen you here before, carrying your dog around like a baby. It's not good for the dog."

"How do you know?" I want to hit her.

"Because I know."

"Are you the animal police?"

"I'm a concerned citizen."

Another woman joins the conversation. "She's right. You should let the dog out."

"Who are you?"

"I'm her friend." She points at the troll. "And I agree with her: let the dog be free."

"She is free."

"No, she's not. She's trapped."

"She's about to go for a walk, so you can just relax."

"When? When is she going for a walk?" A third person has now appeared.

"When she's ready."

"She's ready now."

"How do you know? Are you a dog psychic?"

"All I know is that I'm not comfortable with what I'm seeing. I'm not comfortable with you confining a dog against its will."

"Neither am I." A fourth person has appeared.

"And neither are we." Two more, a couple of some kind, have joined the conversation.

I feel like I'm in a creepy online chat room that has suddenly come to life. "What are you, dog lawyers?"

"If you're not doing anything wrong, why are you so defensive?"

"Oh for fuck's sake," I say, but the minute I utter the f-word, even more of a crowd gathers.

"Now, wait a minute," a dude wearing spandex bicycle shorts says to me. "That was uncalled for."

"Who the fuck are you? The fuck police?" I do a big theatrical shrug and look around for support. No one is with me. Instead of deterring me, it only emboldens me. "I'll tell you what's uncalled for," I say, pointing at his encased thighs. "That outfit."

"That's it. Let's call animal control."
Everyone in the mob takes out their phones
and starts swiping and tapping.

"Animal control?" I snap. "Are you fucking kidding me?"

"No, we're not kidding you. Let's get
Ranger Molly down here and we'll see if
this is even legal."

"If *what's* legal?" I bray.

"Wearing a dog."

While we all wait for Ranger Molly I pace,
trying to calm myself. I stare off into the
trees and at the water, which today is gray
instead of bright blue the way it sometimes
is. It's then that I think I see Gary coming
off the trail. I'm squinting, trying to see if
maybe it's not him — *It's Wednesday morning. Isn't he supposed to be at work?* But the
closer he gets the clearer it's him.

Only he's not alone. He's walking with
someone. A woman. Tall, no makeup, black
turtleneck under a zip-up fleece, jeans.

He's laughing now, and talking using his
hands, animated. He's telling her a funny
story — maybe about how I wrote all over
Sari's photographs and our escape from
Vermont — which I still feel bad about and
expect any day some kind of public shaming about in Sari Epstein's social media

feeds. Or maybe not, since actually that's not a funny story. That's a sad story. One that proves the true grimness of being stuck in a marriage you wish you could leave, is what he would be telling her if he were telling her that story.

No, they're having far too much fun for him to be telling her about me. He must be telling her something else because she's laughing so hard she stops midtrail and throws her head back, then holds her arm out, as if to say, *No. Stop. It's too much. I can't take any more of this brilliant hilarity.* I almost start to laugh, too, as if we're all friends and I am in on the joke, too, but I don't want to witness something upsetting that I won't be able to un-see: like if he kisses her, or gathers her up in his arms, or takes her hand as they walk farther along the path.

I know I should stop watching them and that I should instead turn back to the mob of accusers pawing at their phones, texting and calling and waiting for Ranger Molly to show up and cite me for *unlawful confined restraint of an animal,* or so I overheard one of them say. I know I should protect myself from seeing something that could change everything. Would I survive secretly, but accidentally, watching Gary on a great date?

Whether from the dog-mob or from spying on Gary, or both, my hands are shaking from the adrenaline and my legs are weak. Couldn't I have just one normal uneventful day when I'm not being accused of something like torturing my dog, or my son's not being suspected of pooping in public, or I'm not acting like a complete and utter lunatic in someone else's home after one or two hits off a joint? After everything that's happened, is my only reward really getting a full set of unsightly adult braces and having to watch my husband fall in love with someone else in real time?

I stare at Gary and his girlfriend like they're Martians, their body language so alien to that of ours at home. They're holding hands now, and Gary kisses her on the head. If I weren't about to be arrested for animal cruelty, I would probably run away into the woods and vomit. But instead, I force myself to watch them, to see the result of my ambivalence and disinterest. *Isn't this what you wanted? Your husband has found a woman who likes him and wants to date him. Isn't that what you wanted for both of you — freedom? Shouldn't you let him go and be happy? Shouldn't you stop your "confinement and restraint" of not just the dog, but of him, too?*

I finally force myself to look away. I realize, when I hug Charlotte before taking her out of the sling and putting her leash on, that I'm crying. My eyes blur with tears as I turn back toward the water, but when I do I still manage to see, in the other direction of the trail, the strange figures of a couple, shrouded in oversize puffy parkas and hats and scarves. I wipe my eyes and blink, trying to get a clearer view: if I were the paranoid type, which of course I am, I would say the couple looks like Nick and Phoebe — something about their theatrical movements as they flee from my line of vision, ducking behind trees and now running toward the parking lot. If it is them, aren't they supposed to be at school — rehearsing for the evening Spotlight, which is less than a week away? What are the chances that they'd be here, at the same time as me, and at the same time as Gary and his new girlfriend — all while I'm about to be arrested for some arcane animal cruelty infraction — unless they'd followed me here? But why would they do that?

Before I can even concoct an answer to such a bizarre and unlikely question — I'm probably just seeing things — Ranger Molly arrives. She's wearing her usual forest-green pantsuit uniform with an army-green windbreaker, carrying a clipboard. A heavy black radio hangs from her belt. As she gets a quick briefing from the outraged mob, I stare at my phone and pretend not to notice while Charlotte strains on the leash. She wants to leave. A wave of sorrow for the weird un-pet-like life I've forced upon her overwhelms me. She should be running and playing with other dogs, not awaiting possible punishment for my sins. But no good dog goes unpunished; she did nothing to deserve any of this and yet she is stuck paying the price for all of it.

They're pointing at me now, while I stand there, the empty sling hanging from the front of my body like a big empty bra. "The dog is on a leash now but before she wasn't — she was confined to that instrument of torture." I can hear someone say these words, carried on a breeze that blows through Charlotte's fur and makes her, for once, look like a wild animal. As she should.

Ranger Molly takes notes, nods, then walks toward me. Her big boots crunch the gravel on the path.

"So much for cool heads prevailing," she says with a thick Boston accent and a half-smile that makes the wrinkled skin on her cheek look like a skate wing. "These people over here are claiming that you're abusing your dog."

I shake my head. "Oh. My. God."

"I know, I know. Everyone's an animal cruelty activist, but I'm the one paid by the city to make sure no one's actually harming their pet. Now, because I didn't see anything — right now what I see is a dog on a leash, with an up-to-date city permit on her collar — I'm going to let you go."

"Thank you."

"But because they're a mob of entitled crazy-people, I'm going to pretend to write you a citation." She winks at me, then flips to a clean piece of paper on her clipboard and takes a pen out from behind her ear. "So I'm going to write it like this — *All work and no play make Jack a dull boy* — *The Shining,* that's my favorite movie — and then I'm going to do a big John Hancock at the bottom." She winks again. "And now I'm going to make a big deal of handing it to you like this and you're going to look at it and nod like I'm explaining it to you."

After we each play our part in an exaggerated pantomime of justice being meted out, I fold the "citation" up and put it in my pocket and tug on Charlotte's leash to head back to the car. With their activism a success and nothing left to see, the mob backs away and returns to the mundane daily business of dog park small talk.

I shake Ranger Molly's hand through the window of her van. "Well, thanks for saving me."

"If I were you, I'd take a break from this place for a while," she says, backing out, the tires of her van crunching the gravel as she turns the wheels.

I wave, then get the dog back into the car. *Don't worry. I won't be back.*

CONTAINED

Getting braces only compounds the collective misery at home after the Vermont trip. Gary and I are barely speaking despite still sharing a bed, and Teddy seems touchier than ever: simple questions about homework elicit near-tearful grunts, then high-pitched pleas for privacy, then dramatic exits. I keep my mouth shut, literally, and keep to myself and the dog, working extra hard on Well/er, feeling the added financial pressure that our orthodontia is bringing — especially now that my fantasy of starting, let alone selling, a new project doesn't feel like it will ever happen. I had my chance. I could have buckled down over the weekend with Sari Epstein's coloring books and gotten to the buried core of my dormant creativity, but I let myself get derailed. Instead, I churn out five to six Well/er pieces a day now, which seems to be the perfect pace to keep me from thinking too much about anything:

money, Gary's new girlfriend, our increasingly miserable teenager, my terrible behavior that still hasn't been called out in any of Sari's social media feeds.

Midweek I'm supposed to bring Teddy in to see Michael — for dental impressions and more insurance paperwork so that the appointment on the day he actually gets his braces will be shorter — but when I pick him up at school on the day of the visit, he pleads with me to cancel.

"I can't today."

I tell him that yes he can. That two shorter appointments are better than one very long one. "Trust me."

"I can't! I'm too stressed-out!" He starts to breathe heavily and shake his hands out, working himself into a panic. When he stops, his brows furrow and he turns to me. "Do you think I'm becoming like Dad?"

It's the first time I realize that Teddy sees Gary's anxiety and worries about it, wonders if it is somehow catching, or communicable by proximity or observation. Which means we'll need to talk about it, just not right now. I reach around for his seat belt to buckle him in. "No, dude. You're not becoming like Dad. Being a teenager is just the worst. But braces really aren't that bad!" I lie, flashing him my mouthful of ugly hardware.

"No, Mom, you don't understand."

"How can you say that? I'm an adult with braces! How could I possibly feel your pain more?"

"You're not being watched constantly every day at school. You're not being made to feel like you're a criminal."

Criminal? "What are you talking about?"

"They think I'm the Secret Pooper."

"Wait. *What?* Who?"

"Ms. Grace. She watches me all the time and says if there's anything I want to tell her, I should. She says that being truthful is the only way to truly come clean."

"Well, that's disturbing." I stare at him. No wonder he's in knots. "Why didn't you tell me?"

"I wasn't sure you'd believe me. But, Mom, it's not me. I'm not the Pooper. I swear."

"Of course you're not the Pooper, Teddy!" *Of course he's not.* Right? It's only when he lets me touch him on the cheek without pulling away that I know how upset he is and how relieved I am that all I'm sensing is a genuine frustration at being falsely accused, not the fear of being caught.

I throw the car into reverse. "Let's go home."

"Really?"

"Really. Fuck the orthodontist."

Teddy beams, like I've just commuted his death sentence, then flops back against the seat and headrest, totally relieved. I call Michael's office from the car to cancel the appointment, then drive home, promising Teddy a special burrito for lunch as he runs up to his room, taking the stairs two at a time. But when I check the mail, I see the manila envelope and its return address — Morningside Montessori.

Inside, Grace has attached a handwritten note — *Just so we're clear* — and clipped it to a housing-in-exchange-for-tuition contract. A *contract*? Paperwork that spells out the exchange of three weeks' room and board for a month's tuition with a neatly folded and self-addressed-stamped envelope for me to return it. It all seems overly formal for a school that prides itself on having no administrative handbook and no code of ethics — basically, no rules for parents, children, or teachers. I'm taken aback. This feels like a setup. And a threat. Who is this woman and why is she suddenly so aggressively organized and professional?

I can't believe it's taken me this long to do an extensive, detailed Internet search on Grace — whose nondistinct last name —

Brown — appears on the top of her pre-printed school notepaper. After all, I'd long extolled the virtues of "researching" the people in your life for Well/er (*"Prepping for your parent-teacher conference: Why not know more about the people grading your child?" "Will you trust your doctor more if you know where he/she went to medical school?" "Ruling out the unknown: how having a mental dossier about others can lower generalized anxiety"*). But for some reason, I'd ignored her strangeness and her half answers the first time we talked — the oversharing about her eating disorder and obsessive personality; her nonanswer about whether or not she has children; her odd insistence that Charlotte was a therapy dog. Even last week after Nick told me that she and his father, Mr. Noah, were involved in an obviously secret relationship, I didn't immediately start my background check. But now it's time. Who is this person helping to run the school, cutting weird deals and sending "contracts" in the mail?

Despite over an hour of my online research efforts, the best I come up with is a few old posts on Pinterest, Instagram, Facebook, Twitter, and LinkedIn. Old ones. From a few years ago. Which produce an incomplete composite of who she is: someone with a strong interest in vegetarian cooking (with an emphasis on beets and cauliflower), an affiliation with an oboe chamber music group and a feminist drum circle, and expressed "likes" for a local female-owned craft brewery and The Container Store.

That's it? Is the person making my son's life a daily hell really a social media nonparticipant, occupying a black hole of personal information so that no one can know who she really is? Or is the biggest clue the most obvious of all: Doesn't the fact that she has almost no footprint online mean she has something to hide?

When I return from around the corner with Teddy's burrito, he comes into the kitchen and sits at the counter on the one big stool to eat the way he always did when he was little. I'm glad to see that despite the stress he's under, he still has an appetite, evidenced by how he's ripped the foil away and already has rice on his chin and sour cream on his lips. I could not possibly love him more. I think of my parents, how much they used to love to watch him eat when he was a baby and toddler — chicken, pasta, soup, cereal — how he actually smacked his lips when he chewed, how he intensely enjoyed every meal, how he rarely made a mess. He must have changed back into his pajamas while I was out, like he's taking a sick day, which in a way he is, so I rub his back gently, making slow circles on the plaid flannel, and kiss him lightly on the head. His hair is coarser than it used to be, not the corn silk I remember, but I run my fingers through it anyway, thrilled that he lets me. Then I lean against the counter with my arms under the dog in the sling and watch him eat.

He swivels toward me, wipes his chin. "Have you told Dad?"

I shrug, then sigh. "Not yet." I usually try to keep stressful things away from Gary, always fearing that his reaction to them — or his overreaction to them — will make them worse. How many times over the years did I regret telling him about minor rifts that Teddy or I was having with friends or neighbors, which would then blow up in his mind to major feuds and, ultimately, to differences that for him were irreconcilable? His loyalty to us has always been absolute and he has always been our fiercest defender, though sometimes it felt like overkill.

"Are you *going* to tell Dad?"

"Going to tell Dad what?" Suddenly Gary is in the kitchen, in his WIT fleece vest and black work clothes. "Late arrival today," he says, explaining his unexpected presence when we thought he was already at work. He looks from Teddy to me to figure out what secret we're keeping, then sits on the counter next to the sink. Clearly he's not going anywhere until we tell him.

So we do. I start and then Teddy talks over me and I talk over him, until we've told the whole story about the Secret Pooper — including the latest and the worst part, about how poor Teddy is living in fear of being wrongly accused. The more we talk, the more nervous I get that Gary is going to explode. This is exactly the kind of thing that normally makes him crazy with rage. Only for some reason, now he seems totally contained.

I stare at him. "What are you thinking?"

"Well, I'm furious of course. Aren't you?"

I nod, then bury my hands inside the sling and fill my hands with the dog's fur. "Beyond." I'm also relieved that he knows, and clearly Teddy is, too. Something in Teddy's face has already relaxed, gone back to normal. He picks up his burrito again and takes another huge bite. "I'm sorry we didn't tell you," I say to Gary, gently. "I didn't mean to keep it from you. I just didn't want you to get upset."

"And make things worse," he offers generously. "Who could blame you?"

"Thanks for understanding."

He nods calmly, then watches as Teddy puts his plate in the sink and practically skips off to the living room to watch *Sponge-Bob SquarePants.* "So," he says, jumping down off the counter and holding his hand out like an invitation. "Shall we go?"

Before I know it he has texted work to tell them he won't be in until early afternoon, and we're in the car, driving to Morningside Montessori. When I suggest we call ahead to make sure Grace and Mr. Noah can see us, he shakes his head no. He doesn't want them to know we're coming. He wants this to be a surprise attack.

When we arrive, we park in the temporary zone, punch in the security code at the front door — #thechild* — then head straight for the main office. We see Grace through the glass, dropping a swollen tea bag into a countertop composting container shaped like a miniature curbside city trash can. Before she can stir in her agave, we are through that door, too, and at the sign-in counter.

Gary waves in an exaggerated Broadway pantomime of a customer trying to get attention in a crowded department store. If

327

there were an old-fashioned metal bell on the counter, he would slap it for service. Grace turns and blanches at the sight of us. Her eyes dart around the office, trying to gauge how she can possibly escape, given that no one is there to save her, but before she can come up with anything to say, Gary is pointing to her office. "We need a word. Now, please."

She stammers, starts to say that she has class, that we should have made an appointment, that her day is very very busy, but Gary isn't interested. "Tell that to the lawyer I'll call if you don't stop harassing my son." He points at his phone, but he is holding it upside down and backward. It might as well be a toy.

She hisses, then turns toward Mr. Noah's office. She unlocks the door with a key she wears on a lanyard around her neck and lets us both in first, and we take seats across from the antique oak desk piled high with books and potted plants.

Last time we were here — two years ago — it was because Ms. Marjory had complained not about Teddy but about Gary, who had gotten agitated during our parent-teacher conference when he realized that Teddy's handwriting was so illegible it wasn't clear that he actually knew how to write. The excuses she gave — that many boys have a delayed ability to properly grasp a pencil, that she and the other teachers were focusing on other more important skills Teddy needed to develop instead of on his handwriting — all true — only made Gary more incensed. "Seriously? What could possibly be more important than handwriting?" he'd said. "Who cares about the art and customs of Peru if he can barely write his name!"

I don't remember if that's when Ms. Marjory stood and asked us to leave and then started to cry, or if she started to cry first and then asked us to leave, but either way, we were asked to leave our parent-teacher conference, a first for me, and something completely inconceivable. Gary initially refused to go, ignored me gently tugging at his sleeve to try to contain things before they got worse. Escalation is always a possibility. Even though the teacher was in tears, there had been no swearing, no name-calling, no threats of legal action from our side of the table. It was still relatively civilized. But then she had to go and call the main office from a little ancient-looking intercom system on the wall, and tell them that she was having a problem with two parents in the upper school science room.

The custodian, Ms. JoJo, almost as tall as Gary, was dispatched, and when she arrived she somewhat apologetically asked us if we would come downstairs with her. We followed without incident and were deposited in Mr. Noah's office, where we were told, in no uncertain terms, that Morningside Montessori was a place of peace, and that if we couldn't conduct ourselves calmly and with respect for staff, we would have to find another place for Teddy.

I remember apologizing immediately and profusely, assuring Mr. Noah that it would never happen again, that we were just upset because we wanted the best for Teddy, and wanting the best for him included him being able to master certain basic life skills, like handwriting, as old-fashioned and uptight as that might seem. I was vaguely aware of Gary's rising anger as I fell on the sword, but he said nothing until we got to the car, where he told me how appalled and hurt he was that I'd sold him out. Worse than that, he said, was that I'd sold Teddy out. "There I am fighting for him and you totally caved. How could you have such divided loyalty? Whose side are you on?!"

I don't make that same mistake today. I'm 100 percent Team Teddy. I don't say a word of disagreement when Gary calmly but clearly tells Grace that Teddy is not the Secret Pooper, and that any further implication that he is — the mere whiff of suspicion during the day at school — will bring the hammer down in the form of legal action. "And who wants that?"

"No one," Grace says, as if reading a hostage script.

"So we're clear," Gary closes.

"Quite clear."

"You'll leave our son alone."

I glare at her over the dog's head, jutting out of the sling, reveling in defying her don't-bring-the-dog-to-school rule. "He's not the Pooper."

Grace glares back. "If you say so."

Gary bristles at her tone. "Unless you want Judy and me to call the other middle school parents, tell them what's going on and see what they think."

I nod. "Maybe a meeting at the school would be good. Coffee and doughnuts. Chairs in a circle. A Facebook group and a social media hashtag. To give us a way to air our concerns and share information."

Gary nods now, too. "Maybe bring in a shrink to explain what's going on. Invite the board."

But that won't be necessary. Grace now looks stricken. She's heard us. She'll leave

Teddy alone.

After I drop Gary at work, I drive over to visit Glenn. How is it possible that almost a week has gone by since my last visit? With no recent doctor appointments and an email over the weekend that said she was set and didn't need any groceries, we'd taken that tiny bit of breathing room and accidentally gotten totally consumed by our own lives again. She hasn't even seen my braces, and she has no idea what's been going on with Gary and with Teddy, so I'm actually excited to fill her in, though I'm always afraid it's tone deaf for me to prattle on about the mundane details of my daily life when she's living in a parallel universe of illness. Aren't there more important things to talk about than orthodontia and private school politics?

But when I get to her house and let myself in with her key and head upstairs to her room, she looks so tired and thin that I'm too shocked to speak.

"I know," she says, tiny from her bed against all the pillows. "I look terrible."

"No you don't." I play with the car keys still in my hands.

"I love that you're lying to me. Even though you promised you never would."

"I'm not lying," I lie again.

"You are — otherwise you'd look at me."

I raise my eyes up. "Did I promise you that?"

"No. I was just trying to see if you were paying attention."

My eyes fill with tears and I sit down on the edge of the bed. "I'm paying attention."

She reaches for my hand and squeezes it. "I know you are."

We sit quietly for a few minutes, neither of us wanting to talk about the most obvious topic — the fact that she is truly in decline now; that her condition will not improve, or reverse itself, or stop. Until it stops. Even though I've known since the beginning that this terrible part was looming, I'm still shocked. Realizing that we've arrived at this final stage comes as a total body blow.

"We have to talk about this. We have to make a plan." I can barely get the words out because I don't want to talk about this and I don't want to make a fucking plan.

"I know, but not now."

I'm about to push her and say, *When? If not now, then when?* But before I can get my lips to move she deftly changes the subject.

"What's bothering you besides me?"

I close my eyes. I want to say something;

333

instead, I start to sob — a controlled heaving. But the last thing Glenn needs is for me to fall apart, so I quickly pull myself together and tell her that somebody's been pooping at the school. On the floor in front of the middle school bathroom. I wipe my eyes and nose and take a deep breath. "They think it's Teddy. And he's getting so stressed about it that he's starting to worry that he's turning into Gary. Which he's not, but still."

"Fuckers," Glenn manages to whisper.

I tell her about earlier, how we put the fear of God into Grace, how I think that took care of it. "But something's not adding up," I say, sitting up now. "How, with a classroom full of kids down the hall, does this Secret Pooper — that's my nickname for him — manage to defecate onto the floor essentially *on command* — then leave as quickly and as quietly as he arrived? It seems impossible." I look at her bedside table, all the pills lined up, all the half-finished glasses of water.

She rolls her eyes, readjusts the pillow behind her head. "You need to set up a remote camera. Catch them in the act."

"Isn't that illegal?"

She closes her eyes. "Who cares. It's your kid."

"So if the Pooper isn't pooping in real time," I say, thinking out loud, "it means they're doing it elsewhere and staging the scene at school. I think I saw something like this on *Dateline* once, only it wasn't poop but some other kind of DNA, and it wasn't a pooper, it was a killer."

"Maybe they're transporting it. Doing it at home when they have time, and then bringing it to school."

I stare at her. "In what?"

"In some kind of container. Plastic. Glass. Anything."

I shiver at the premeditation of such an outlandish theory. Especially at the notion that someone — a kid — could be troubled or angry enough to do something this intentionally devious. The more I think about it, the less I believe it's a student. "I think it's a teacher."

Glenn shrugs, then closes her eyes. I can see that she's had enough for today. I cover her with the blanket, clear away the glasses, and return with fresh water so she can take her pills. I watch as she struggles to sit up, swallow each mouthful of water, and breathe when she's finished.

"I wish I didn't have to leave," I say. "And the next few days are going to be crazy with Inhabitancy."

"It's okay. I've got someone coming at the end of the week."

"A night nurse?" Which is one of the things I know we'll have to talk about — increasing from the web of daily friend-helpers to professional overnight home health aides.

"No. Daisy." Her niece. "She'll stay for the duration."

My stomach drops. "Already?"

She takes my hand. "It's time."

But it's not time. I can't stop thinking about that all the way home. It's not time. Glenn is only sixty, just ten years older than me. She should be walking laps around the reservoir with Lucy and Charlotte and me while I convince her to try Tinder to give love another chance. She should be coming over for dinner, yelling at Gary to chill when she arrives almost an hour late even though she lives only ten minutes away. She should be here to see Teddy go to high school and college and fall in love. We should have years ahead of us, not weeks.

Dusk is already falling as I make my way along the narrow tree-lined streets between her house and ours the way I have so many times before; weaving in between parked cars and bikes and parents with strollers, all heading home after a long day; the maples already bare and naked, having dropped their leaves weeks ago in piles still waiting to be raked. But this doesn't feel like all those other times because it's not. It's the beginning of another end. Before I know it, before I'm ready, Glenn will be gone, too, and to avoid the pain of memory, I'll avoid this route, this way home, this reminder of this day and this moment leading up to this loss. The streets already seem unrecognizable. Soon they will feel as foreign to me as a moonscape. Grief obliterates the present, forcing you to relive the past and dread the future.

It takes me a few seconds to realize that I've passed my street by several sets of lights, and when I do, I remember that I need to stop and pick up something for dinner — something soft enough for me to eat with my braces, something that Teddy likes, too — so I just keep driving. When I get to Trader Joe's I park in the lot, grab a hand basket on the way in, and avert my eyes to avoid my reflection in the automatic doors the way I always do.

I can't remember when I stopped looking at myself, when my face and body, once narrow and all sharp angles and dark shadows in tight pants and short skirts, filled and rounded with age; when I became unrecognizable to myself and invisible in the world. For years I've secretly loved the anonymity, the invisibility, the freedom to move around without the annoyance of comments, of worrying about what I look like and what it means. Most of the time, no one even notices that I'm there. I'm just a shapeless blur, floating down a sidewalk or into a store, with a child beside me or a dog in front of me. A few months ago I left my hair salon wearing a clear plastic shower cap over my head because I didn't want the bad weather to ruin my blowout. The girl at the front desk laughed as I stepped out into the rain, shocked that I would walk all the way home like that. But I couldn't have cared less. Because I knew it didn't matter, that not a single person would look at me. And not a single one did.

Today is no different. I scan the supermarket aisles in search of avocados, nuts, and bananas. I stop and close my eyes when I get to the frozen Indian food, trying to remember what I'm wearing today, like a party trick. Is it pants? A skirt and Uggs? A sweater or a zip-up fleece? Except for the dog hanging from me, I have no clue what I have on, what I look like. A strange thrill runs through me — *I've escaped myself for another day* — until I open my eyes and force myself to look down: baby-pink flared cropped cords, a black long-sleeve scoop-neck thermal, flip-flops, even though it's far too cold for them. I don't even remember getting dressed today.

In line, I wait for the cashier in the store's signature Hawaiian shirt to chat up the young woman ahead of me. Every time he picks up one of her items to scan he comments on it — he loves the Brie; the garlic naan is awesome; who could get enough of these new chocolate-covered frozen bananas. The comments continue as he bags up her groceries, smiling and joking and coming out from behind his little station to personally hand her both bags. Maximum customer service. "Nice to see you. Have a great day."

It's my turn now. Once she's gone he returns to his register, reaches into my basket, which I've helpfully started to empty myself to save him time, though he doesn't seem to notice. He doesn't say a word. He's all business. Except for a quick glance at the clock and at the line behind me, he doesn't look up. Even the dog doesn't get his attention. We're completely invisible.

I could let it go. But today, for some reason, it bothers me that he doesn't see me. It bothers me that I'm here but not here. I flash my braces at him and ask what he thinks of the boxes of frozen *saag paneer* and butter chicken that I've so carefully selected because they will be soft enough for my adult braces, while also the only frozen food my husband and son will agree to eat, but he ignores me. I'm just a weird mom-lady holding up his line. When he reaches for the bananas, I grab his hand midway. "You had opinions about all her items," I say, pointing toward the parking lot, even though the young woman is already long gone. "Why don't you have anything to say about mine? Cat got your tongue?"

He looks down at his hand, which I'm still grabbing, and then up at my face. I realize I've said the quiet part out loud, in the same angry, creepy, grieving animal growl that came out in Vermont at Sari's — and that I've scared him. Before I can explain, or apologize, the dog starts barking. The cashier reaches for the bell above his head with his free hand. Before the ringing stops and the manager arrives to see what the problem is, I've dropped the basket and run back to my car while everyone in the store and everyone in the parking lot is looking at me. Finally I have their full attention.

FAMILY-STYLE

We're having dinner the night before the big night — the Spotlight performance — and I've made a big pot of chili, all meat, no beans, to try to make up for unwittingly forcing the People Puppets to eat vegan the weekend when we went to Vermont. Sitting around the table, passing salad and chips and small bowls of sour cream and shredded cheese and guacamole, talking about school — the kids and the teachers — and the news — I marvel at the scene in front of me. It's like we're a big noisy weird family, the kind I always wished for but didn't come from. Teddy is sitting next to Nick, talking and laughing. Even the dog, who is roaming free under the table and around all our legs, sniffing for scraps, seems unusually relaxed. Of course, I need to ruin it all.

"So tell us about the Spotlight!" I ask the People Puppets. We haven't been together in weeks: I need details.

"What about it?" Nick says.

"Anything!" I say.

Phoebe laughs nervously and so does Nick. "It's a surprise!" they both blurt at the exact same time.

"Really? Is this a new thing? Embargoing news about the performance program?"

"I'm not sure," Nick says. "It's our first year doing this, but Grace says it's traditional to keep the parents in the dark until the big night. The collaborative work the kids do with the visiting artists is supposed to be kind of a sacred surprise."

Grace. "*A sacred surprise.* That sure sounds ominous!"

"Does it?" Nick asks.

"It's always this way, Mom," Teddy says, nodding at Nick. "We prepare in secret for the big reveal when the parents come."

Gary nods, too. "Didn't they do this for Zirkus Schmirkus, our first Inhabitancy at Morningside, Judy? Teddy wouldn't tell us if he would be swinging from a trapeze or getting shot out of a cannon. It was all hush-hush. As it turned out it was neither: just some somersaults and minor acrobatics on colored mats."

"I was only eight!" Teddy says defensively, but he is smiling, beaming actually, in the center of the big table of food and people.

He's already helped himself to seconds and elbowing Nick to see if he wants more, too.

"I know!" I say. "Which is why we were trying to find out if we should be terrified before the show or not!"

"Yeah, well, we're excited," Phoebe says. "I think you'll really enjoy it."

I'm not ready to give up yet. "So there's nothing — not a single little hint or tidbit — you can give us?"

"Well." Nick shrugs, finally cracking under the pressure. "There are six skits — one for each of the grouped grades: preschool, kindergarten, first through third, third through sixth, and the middle school."

I'm chewing and counting in my head. "So that's five."

I feel a kick under the table and assume it's Gary, signaling me to shut up already, but he's totally preoccupied with his food. That's when I notice Phoebe glaring at Nick.

"Did I say something wrong?" I say as innocently as possible.

"No! No! No!"

I've stopped chewing and I am now watching Nick's and Phoebe's facial expressions like a tennis match. I put my napkin down. "Okay, guys. Come clean. What are you hiding?"

"Okay, we're busted," Phoebe says, with a huge eye-roll and a big laugh. "It's supposed to be a surprise."

"The sixth skit is going to be a solo, a special 'Spotlight after the Spotlight.' Just Phoebe and me, no kids."

"Oh! Cool!" I'm relieved but still not convinced anything they're saying is true.

"We just wanted to do something special. You know, since this is our first Inhabitancy. We want to make it as special and as entertaining as possible for everyone. Including you. Especially you! We're so grateful that you opened up your home to us and that you shared so much about yourself — about why you wear the dog, all the feelings and life experience behind it. You didn't have to be so honest. Especially during such a difficult time." Nick's voice cracks. He tears up.

"*Especially* during such a difficult time," Phoebe echoes.

She takes Nick's hand and holds it tight until he collects himself. He smiles at her, puts his forehead against hers and closes his eyes, then picks his spoon back up and inhales the rest of what's in his chili bowl.

"We were happy to have you," Gary says. "And we barely even saw you!"

I'm still trying to figure out what they

mean by "especially during such a difficult time" — whether they know about the tuition credit we're getting, or if they were indeed at the reservoir the day I accidentally stumbled upon Gary and his girlfriend, in which case they know far more than they're saying — when Nick leans forward with his glass raised:

"At first we felt like we made new friends, but now we feel like we have a new extended family," Nick says. "Another set of parents, but younger than our real ones, and a cool half sibling. We love this guy," he says, patting Teddy on the back.

Teddy looks up and smiles with teeth. "Really?"

"Of course. You're the coolest kid in the school."

"No I'm not." He blushes, but his eyes say *tell me more.*

"Are you kidding? When you played the guitar the other day during music, didn't you see how all the kids were in awe?" Nick turns to Gary and then to me. "They were in awe." Then he turns back to Teddy. "I wish I could play like that."

"And, not to mention the dog," Phoebe adds, "who is clearly the glue that keeps this whole family together."

We all clink glasses and smile and wipe

our eyes and pet Charlotte, who is running around, wagging her tail and whoring for attention, checking in with each of us with paws and barks. I feel like such an asshole. Here I was, as always, untrusting and suspicious, ready to suspect two young puppets of something creepy and criminal, when all they wanted to do was connect with us.

I pick up the dog and pet her as she settles onto my lap. "Well, we'll all be there with bells on."

"Even Glennie?" Teddy asks, his face wide open with hope.

I swallow hard and force a smile. "I'm not sure she's up to it right now."

"But Charlotte's coming, right?" Phoebe asks.

"Charlotte is definitely coming," I say. Teddy rolls his eyes but lets Charlotte lick his fingers when he reaches out to pet her.

Nick and Phoebe beam. "Excellent!"

Later that night, after Teddy goes up to his room to make Glenn a get-well card and the People Puppets are back in the basement, Gary and I finish the dishes, scraping and rinsing and loading plates and glasses and silverware onto the racks of the dishwasher. Usually I rearrange the plates to line up evenly on the left side — straightening them from how Gary throws them in there, seemingly without any rhyme or reason, but tonight I don't. Why bother controlling something so meaningless when everything else seems to be spinning out into the universe?

"Well, that was fun," Gary says as I shut the faucet off and bury my hands inside a dish towel. "But I'm sad. I feel like the People Puppets just got here and now they're leaving. Time really flies."

I keep my nervous hands hidden inside the towel.

"Do you think we'll actually see them after they leave or was that all just bullshit?"

I shrug. "It's probably bullshit, but I wish it weren't."

"You do?"

I shrug again. "Sure I do. I miss having a family."

He stares at me. "But you have a family, Judy. Teddy and me. We're your family."

"I know, but —"

"Okay, Judy. What's going on?"

I shrug. "What do you mean?"

"You're upset, so you might as well tell me what's wrong so we can go to sleep. We do have to sleep in the same room tonight, but don't worry," he says more sharply now, "you'll have the place to yourself soon enough. Just a few more nights of pretending to be married and things will go back to normal. Whatever that means."

I want to tell him about the reservoir — how the mob came after me and the dog, how humiliating it was to be publicly shamed for wearing her, to have something so innocent called so into question with such a malevolent take — but then I'd have to tell him about seeing him there. Seeing him there with the woman he was with, the woman who is probably his girlfriend. I don't want to go there. I don't want to hear about how he might be in love, how we're going to have to figure out a way for him to move out and move in with her.

But for once I push myself to speak. "I saw you last week. At the reservoir," I whisper. I put the towel down. My hands are shaking. "I saw you talking and laughing with someone, a woman, and then I saw you kissing that woman." I take a deep breath and let it out slowly, one last pause before ripping off the rest of the Band-Aid. "You looked happy. The way you used to look." I stare at him, at his big green eyes and his sharp jawline and silvering hair, trying to see him the way she does, the way I used to. "That's what I want for you. You deserve it. I think we should do whatever it takes to make that possible."

He nods slowly, processing. "Are you saying you want me to move out?"

I think of Glenn. "I'm saying that life is short. I'm saying that if you have another chance at happiness, you should take it."

I bring fresh blueberry muffins from Flour, Glenn's favorite bakery, and a few single-serving containers of her favorite full-fat grass-fed locally sourced maple-flavored yogurt. I also bring the card that Teddy made the night before and slipped to me in the car on the way to school — a bulging envelope barely taped shut because he'd put a small LEGO figurine inside to go along with the card. "That's the Cancer Monster," he'd said when I took the envelope from him at drop-off before he left the car. "To scare away her sickness."

"Oh, Teddy."

"Tell her I hope she feels better but I understand if she can't come to Spotlight."

I nod. And for what feels like the twenty millionth time this week, my eyes blur with tears.

"It's okay, Mom," he says, patting my arm, just like he used to when each of my parents was sick. "It's okay."

When I get to Glenn's house I let myself in with my key, then walk through the quiet of the living room, full of floor-to-ceiling bookshelves, walls filled with framed art and photographs of past husbands and authors she worked with. A clock somewhere, maybe in the kitchen, ticks. I listen to it mark time, counting the days and hours and minutes and seconds left, measurements of a life shutting down and coming to an end.

Upstairs, Glenn has no appetite, so I put the card on the nightstand and let Charlotte out of her sling, lift her and Lucy onto the bed, and then find a spot for myself. "I brought you something," I say, opening my tote bag. "It's an activity. Something we can do together."

The old Glenn would swear at me, tell me we've never needed an "activity" to do together — like playing cards or knitting or even playing Scrabble — "isn't *talking* the activity?" she would always say. But today I get no such back talk as I pull out coloring books and crayons. I give her one — *Mindful Mantras and Mandalas* — and take *Creative Coloring Meditations* for myself. Flipping through my book and cracking open the big box of Crayolas with the built-in sharpener makes me think that coloring in a giant geometric design is the most perfect and peaceful thing to do in this sad and awful moment: we will literally fill the emptiness with color.

"Sari Epstein sent me these," I say. "After I invited myself to her house and we accepted the free gift of Gary's spot and I defiled her property and fled under cover of darkness. Instead of publicly shaming me on Instagram or Facebook or sending me a furious email, she refunded my retreat fee and sent me a package full of her coloring books. I mean, who does that?"

Glenn closes her eyes. "A total bitch."

We both laugh to the point of tears.

"I'm such an asshole," I say. "And it was her note that really got me. It said, *I'm sorry you're in pain. May you be released from it soon.* How did she know that?"

This time we don't laugh.

"I *am* in pain," I say. "I'm sad about everything."

Glenn takes my hand.

"I wish this weren't happening. I wish you weren't sick."

"I won't be sick much longer."

For a second I think she's telling me that she's getting better, that a scan I didn't know about has come back showing unexpected improvement and recovery. But then

I realize what she's really saying. That it won't be much longer.

I put the crayons — a fistful of blues and pinks and greens and reds — down. I watch Glenn, with both dogs asleep next to her on the bed, close her eyes.

"It looks like I'll probably be leaving soon, a little earlier than we thought, so like you said the other day, we need to make our plans."

I start to cry. I don't want to make plans. I don't want her to go. I don't want her to leave early.

"I'm not ready," I sob.

"I know. But I am."

The plans we make are short and simple; the basics. I know the drill, the order of what's needed at the end:

We will call for a hospital bed to be delivered; we will call a home hospice service to visit and start their services; a palliative "comfort kit," with liquid morphine, will be stored in the refrigerator. I'll print out and tape her DNR — Do Not Resuscitate order — to the refrigerator so there won't be any misunderstanding should someone — Daisy, me, Glenn herself — panic and call 911. Gary and I will come by daily, but it will be Daisy, technically her cousin's daughter, who will come down from Portland, Maine, and be on call for the duration and then pack up the house and settle things after Glenn is gone.

"But you'll take Lucy," she says, an urgent reminder.

"Of course I will." I show her the pictures on my phone that I've already taken of Lucy's cabinet in the kitchen: the food she eats, the treats she likes, all the supplies — her crate, her bed, her leash, her brush, her toys. "I'll bring everything with me so that our house feels like home."

We look at the dogs, lying next to each other, similar enough in their coloring and shape and size to almost look related. I picture myself walking Lucy on a leash while still carrying Charlotte, just for a few days, until I give up the sling for good.

"Gary doesn't mind?"

"Of course not. He'd do anything for you."

"He'd do anything for you, too."

"I know. But maybe it's time we let each other go." I think, but don't say, that maybe he'd be happier with the girlfriend whose name I don't even know.

"He doesn't love her."

I turn to her. "He told you?"

She nods. "He came yesterday, by himself."

"He didn't tell me."

"He doesn't tell you a lot of things." I stare at her as she closes her eyes. "He doesn't want to leave. He's not ready yet. And he doesn't think Teddy is ready, either." She takes my hand and holds it. "I told you long ago that I was happy to be wrong about you and Gary, and I *was* wrong. Loss has made you afraid of life, but you have to stay open. Porous. You have to let all the available light — all the tiny shards of joy — still flow through you." She closes her eyes. "Who knows what beauty the rest of the way will bring."

Glenn leans her head back, lets out a long slow sigh. "I wish I'd had children. I wish I hadn't lost two husbands. I wish . . ." Her voice trails off until it is just breath. There is a long silence when we say nothing, when the enormity of where we are and how surreal it is to know that she will soon be gone hangs in the air — taken from the world any day as if by the rapture, with those of us left behind gaping in grief. "I wish," she whispers, reaching out for Lucy, "I could see how all of this turns out."

SPOTLIGHT

We dress, Gary and I, in our casual best —
he in the khakis and button-down chambray
shirt he hates, which is what he's forced to
wear to work now after a new Dockers
Dude dress code was announced — I in an
obligatory black Eileen Fisher pantsuit,
either from 2006 or 2016, impossible to
date, since each piece is so minimal it can't
possibly ever be in style or out of style.

Teddy has stayed at school, where he'll be
forced to change into whatever costume
they've decided to dress the kids in for
whatever skits they're putting on. I'm done
asking. After last night when I shamed
myself with my questions, digging around
for a crime before it happened, I'm trying
to go with the flow. To let go of my vine of
anxiety and fear and just let things happen.

It isn't going well. My decision to let go
has not left me awash in a sense of calm.
Internally I'm full of fear and dread, certain

that the seeming quiet from Grace — and the fact that there has not been a third pooping incident yet — is a sense of false calm. Don't bad things happen in threes? Aren't we due for the Secret Pooper to make his appearance again — and, if so, what better time than tonight, when there will be a captive audience of parents to shock and repulse?

Or maybe not. Maybe the Pooper, instead of wanting attention through a big public act, is looking to continue his little campaign of terror in private, waiting to strike again while the iron is cold. Maybe, while I've been expecting some kind of defecatory event tonight for maximum effect, the slow reveal will continue, day after day, week after week, creating a sustained level of discomfort and unease for people worried about the situation. Which, for some reason, appears to just be us. How is it possible that we're the only parents who've complained? Why haven't other parents heard the news from their kids and demanded a meeting, a morning coffee with stale doughnuts and bloated bagels, or an early evening after-dinner meeting with boxed wine and Costco cookies, to discuss the situation?

When I share my fears about tonight with Gary, he's certain that our meeting the other day with Grace took care of it. "We put the fear of God into her," he says, smug in the knowledge that he has protected Teddy, and us, from harm, and wholly unconcerned that some creepy kind of unmasking is about to take place. "Plus, it's Spotlight!" he says, as if Spotlight is the sacred ritual of an ancient religion, a magical time when nothing can go wrong and nothing bad can happen, like Christmas.

To calm my nerves after I'm dressed, I brush the dog, then brush myself with a lint brush, something I almost always forget to do. But I remind myself I'm going to be among people tonight, humans, other parents, and I need to not look crazy. Once I put the dog in the sling and we get into the car, Gary behind the wheel, I text Daisy to check in on Glenn. Something about her response — She's sleeping deeply — or perhaps just my concern gnawing away at me since yesterday, makes me ask Gary if there's time to stop there on our way.

"Of course there's time," he lies.

When we get there, a few blocks from our house, he live-parks while I run in. I smile at Daisy, who I haven't seen for years, as she stands holding Lucy near the bed, and then bend down to get closer to Glenn.

"We're off to Spotlight. To see the People

Puppets," I whisper. "I wish you could come. I'll give you a full report tomorrow." I put my hand on hers as gently as I can and feel her holding something in it: it's the LEGO Cancer Monster. My eyes fill and my throat seizes. Her lips move and she's smiling, but no words come out. I think she's trying to say *Teddy.*

I stand there, not wanting to move. Why do life's most terrible moments always collide with its most mundane ones? The night my mother died was one of Teddy's first rock-school concerts; I had no choice but to miss that joyful milestone — it was my mother. Tonight I have to be there for Teddy in case the Secret Pooper shows up — even though I have a terrible feeling that I may never see Glenn, my best friend, my only friend, again.

Daisy makes a few minute adjustments of the blankets and pillows, then puts Lucy down on the bed. We both watch as the dog, slowly, gently, finds a spot somewhere off Glenn's left knee — close but not touching it — as if knowing that the time for physical contact is past — that she is already beyond the tactile sense of the living and into another dimension, the mysterious and unknown one where transitioning, from life to death, takes place. Daisy takes my hand

and leads me away from the bed and slowly to the bedroom door. If she didn't, I don't think I would ever leave.

"A hospice nurse is coming tonight," she whispers. "She's on her way."

I nod with relief. "You'll call me?" I beg, hugging Charlotte in the sling, slipping my arms inside of it to get a fuller embrace and thereby undoing all the work I just did with the lint brush. I know I should be trying to comfort Daisy, who looks calm but must be terrified, her long blond hair up in a neat ponytail and her impossibly young face pale without makeup, but all I can do is reassure her that I'll be back soon, the second the show is over, which I hope is soon enough.

By the time we get to the school — the front of which is festooned with hand-painted banners promoting the night's big event — we are almost, but not quite, late. Gary searches the parking lot, swearing under his breath, every time what looks like it could be a space is taken up by a tiny hybrid or a group of bicycles. Normally he would say "What is this, Amsterdam?" but tonight he just parks half the car up on a curb, the hood pushed under a bank of shrubs, and calls it a day. "Let's go," he says. And we do.

He runs, and I follow with the dog, fast-walking into the building. He glances back at me once, negotiating the girth of the sling, and I know he's thinking he wishes just once we could go somewhere, just the two of us, without my impediment. I'm sure he's also thinking: *I wish she weren't so weird.* It's one thing when I navigate the world on my own, making my own messes, as I did at the reservoir, and then being forced to clean them up, but when we're together, he has to confront, yet again, the embarrassing fact that he has a wife who wears a dog in public. If we weren't so late to the performance, I'd worry that the huge distance Gary is trying to create between us is to make it look like we're not together — which we kind of aren't, of course — and while most people at the school know us and know Teddy — this is our fifth year — there are enough outsiders attending that maybe he thinks he'll be spared at least a few judgmental glances.

Finally he stops and waits for me. "Maybe you should get a therapy dog vest already and use a leash," he says in a loud whisper, and I know now that he is embarrassed by me. "Is it too much to ask that you get rid of that thing?" He points to the sling.

I stop, look down at myself. The sling *is*

kind of unsightly, as am I, wearing it, and though I'm full of self-loathing I pretend to take only slight umbrage at his remarks. "Really, Gary? On a night when ridiculously dressed People Puppets are going to grace the stage, are you seriously embarrassed to be seen with *me*?"

He stops, too. "Yes. Yes I am."

"Wow." This time I'm not playacting. My cheeks are hot with shame. And yet: I don't blame him.

He looks around at the empty hallway, then heads for the stairs to the middle school. He's trying to find us a place where we'll have a little privacy, since, if we stay here, someone is likely to come out of the multipurpose room to use the bathroom or make a phone call. I follow him, in the opposite direction of where we should be going — we're missing the early part of the show — the skits with the little kids — the preschool and kindergarten and elementary grades — which isn't an entirely bad thing — ill-timed marital fights have made couples miss far better things — but still I'm feeling a strange sadness creep over me: we should be sitting and watching our son and his earnest classmates perform while trying to temporarily ignore the fact that our friend is dying, not acting out the denouement of our marriage.

There's something about the hallway's echo and the dog's snout poking out of the sling that makes me want to do something big and dramatic and unexpected. Like take the dog off, lay her down on the cold linoleum floor, and walk to Glenn's, leaving Gary to deal with the dog and the rest of the evening. But that would accomplish nothing, and I'd miss Teddy's skit — miss seeing him in whatever sad and ridiculous and ill-fitting costume he'll be wearing; miss being able to compare his adolescent awkwardness tonight to the unself-conscious effusiveness of his past performances, back when he was still young enough to enjoy new experiences and loved being part of group activities, as long as they weren't about academics. So I follow Gary just inside the door to the middle school, where he's waiting for me.

"I mean, look at you, lumbering around with that thing!" he says, tiptoeing down the hallway and past a bank of open cubbies, full of sneakers and rain boots and artwork yet to be brought home. I shush him, knowing he's going to get loud, and I don't want our conversation, which could quickly escalate, to be overheard by anyone. The last thing we need is to call attention to ourselves. But Gary is just getting started. "And what did you mean by 'We should do whatever it takes to make my happiness possible'?" He shakes his head, hurt and disgusted. "What if I said, 'Hey, Judy, seeing you with some dude at the reservoir didn't make me jealous — it just made me realize how much I want you to go live your own life so I can live mine.'"

Great. Perfect timing and location for this. We're finally going to have that conversation, and I guess there's just no way to stop it from happening here, and now, probably the worst place it possibly could happen. Instead of escalating, I try to calm him. "Gary. Of course I care. It's just that —"

"You don't care. *It's fine, it's fine!*" he mimics. *"Go be with your girlfriend! Take your chance when it comes along! No problem!"*

"But I want you to be happy! I don't want to stand in your way of being happy! I thought that's what you wanted! Isn't that what you said in therapy?"

He ignores me. "All while you walk around with that fucking dog like it's normal!"

"I know it's not normal!"

"Then why do you do it? You've been wearing it for months now, Judy. When is it going to end?"

We are both whisper-screaming now, our

364

throats scraping the words out; our bodies half bent at the waist; pointing at each other with every word we say. Were it not for the dog's sudden restlessness inside the sling — in fact, she's actively trying to get out, something she almost never does — we'd continue arguing. But I have no choice except to let her out. I bend down on the floor and help her out of the sling — trying, but failing, to grab ahold of her harness or her collar before she gets away from me, running down the hallway and barking maniacally now. Gary and I both chase after her, stopping at the end of the hallway when we see that she's skidded to a stop in front of a pile of what looks to be, from a somewhat safe distance, a pile of fresh poop.

We stare at each other. The reality of what we've stumbled upon — the third instance of the Secret Pooper, just as I'd predicted — shocks us. So much so, that we actually grab, and hold on to, each other by the elbow. Do we call someone? Take a photo of it in case photographic evidence is needed later? Or wait until someone happens by and can tell us what to do? That third option becomes a reality when, from the other end of the dark hallway, Grace materializes. Her face is pinched with dread as she realizes what we've found.

"Oh no," she whispers.

I stare at her until she fidgets with discomfort. "You're the Secret Pooper," I say. Suddenly it's all clear.

There are tears in her eyes, and it looks like it's all she can do to remain upright. She lets out a sharp breath, as if in that single exhale all the past few months of her insane behavior will now be expunged. I turn to Gary, my eyes wild with outrage. "I knew it. I *knew* it was her."

She shakes her head. "It's not me."

"Oh *rea*lly," I say, full of spite, the adrenaline of defending Teddy and the anxiety about Glenn coursing through my veins. "Then who is it?"

"It's Noah."

I roll my eyes at Gary. "Sure. Blame your man-baby boyfriend."

She covers her face with her hands, then whispers, through her fingers, something I can barely hear. I make her repeat it. "Frontotemporal degeneration. Early onset dementia." Gary and I look at each other in horror, then grab each other by the elbow again.

She tells us that it started about a year ago, that she thought then that she could cover for him, protect him. She thought the

366

symptoms would be mild enough to manage, and at first they were — forgetfulness, saying the wrong word or not being able to think of the right word, the childishness — the effusiveness, the messy eating. But then it got worse. "That's when the pooping started. I kept waiting for the right moment to tell the board, but I wanted to spare him the indignity of having his career end this way."

"But making someone else look guilty was fine." Gary tugs on my arm. *Judy.* I ignore him and pull away. "It's an incredibly sad situation but you tried to make it look like it was Teddy, an innocent teenager who's been living in fear of being falsely accused of this! That's unforgivable!" Another tug on my sleeve. *Judy.* "I'm sorry he's ill, Grace, but you can't go around casting suspicion on kids, on good boys who have been made to feel like criminals. I hope Teddy isn't scarred for life. I hope you haven't caused him to develop an anxiety disorder from all this stress!" Another tug, then finally Gary holds up his phone. It's Teddy:

Aren't you guys coming?

With Charlotte back in the sling, we leave

Grace in the hallway and race into the multipurpose room, where Teddy's class is just now approaching the makeshift stage. Gary and I stand against a wall, behind rows of folding chairs and yoga mats and tumbling pads. We watch as the small group of gangly awkward teenagers, dressed as sheep, all follow a shepherd — played by several People Puppets under a big fat man's suit with devil horns over an orange wig. The sheep stop following the devil-shepherd the minute they pass a sign that suddenly appears on a People Puppet signpost:

THIS WAY TO LOVE.

Parents clap, whistle, and cheer as the sheep break out of their slow-crawl toward hate and reverse course, joining together in a joyous embrace of unity and acceptance — this is, after all, Morningside Montessori, and it wouldn't be Spotlight without Mr. Noah turning up the music and coming out to join the teens in dance to mark the end of Inhabitancy. Gary and I exchange glances — knowing what we now do about him, we can't help but feel gutted at his childlike ebullience, his blissful ignorance, the last dance of his career as head of school. The whole world is ending tonight, and we are helpless to change it.

It's then that the sheep clear out and the lights go down. When they go back on again, slowly, and dimly, there are only two People Puppets — Nick and Phoebe — for the finale they promised. They're presenting as two sheeted figures: a woman and a dog. The Puppet-Woman is sitting on the floor, crying, holding her heart as she waves goodbye and blows farewell kisses to invisible people, bereft until she looks down at the Puppet-Dog, who crawls over to her and puts its head in her lap. And then, through the magic of yards and yards of fabric and some kind of pulley system, the smaller Puppet-Dog — Phoebe — is hoisted up into a sling that the Puppet-Woman slips over her head and around her neck. Suddenly, the big sad papier-mâché face is gone, replaced by a giant papier-mâché happy face. A sense of beatific bliss, created through warm yellow lighting, bathes the stage: the once-sad Puppet-Woman is now wearing a Puppet-Dog, and she is saved.

It takes a few seconds for me to realize that they are acting out my life. That they, spies in our house for three weeks, have been preparing to make a public mockery of my story, of my most private pain.

Before I can turn to Gary and say *Let's*

leave, the room explodes in applause. I feel people's eyes on me, on the sling, on Charlotte, on Gary; it's clear to everyone who the People Puppets modeled their closing act on — me, standing there, wearing a dog. I'm so embarrassed I can barely breathe.

I wish the floor would open up or that I could disappear into the crowd the way Teddy did a few weeks ago when I came to talk about my writing, but for once the ground I'm standing on feels solid and real. It is not going anywhere, and neither am I. I glance at Gary, expecting to read shame on his face, too, but his eyes are soft, and full of love and understanding and compassion. "I'm sorry," he mouths, and we lean against each other, holding each other up, I realize, the way we always do, while everyone turns back to the stage. Then all the People Puppets and all the children, the little ones and the big ones, including Mr. Noah, who looks like one of them, return to take a noisy group bow. Nick puts his arm around Mr. Noah and hugs him, and then Phoebe, still dressed as a dog, hugs Nick. Grace finds them and joins the hug. Nick searches the crowd of onstage sheep-kids to find Teddy, and suddenly he is next to him, absorbed into the hug, too. Nick starts to cry, his body shaking in its giant white sheet: his father's brain is dying, and all he can do is weep and let himself be held together by love.

I reach for Gary's hand and hold it. Our eyes lock. I feel all the available light — all the life — all the tiny shards of joy and sadness and grief and love — flow through me, the chimera of the past finally giving way to the reality of the present: we are who we are; we are doing our best; it will all work out. It is a choice — to accept, to believe, to remain — and I am choosing all of it now. It's then that my phone vibrates in my pocket. I'm certain it's Daisy, calling to tell me that Glenn has left us, that the world as we've known it is gone again. But I'm not ready to leave it yet. I stay, where we are right now, in this place, in this moment, for as long as I can.

Thanksgiving

After we bury Glenn and bring Lucy home to live with us, we decide, as a way to distract ourselves from our sadness, to host Thanksgiving. Since we have no friends anymore, except Nick and Phoebe, I go out on a ridiculous limb and invite Michael Wasserman and David Levy and their three kids. I'm shocked that they say yes to such an unexpected and last-minute invitation, and when they do it feels like the only possible happy ending to the past few months, if not years: full circle from destruction to reconstruction, from never socializing to hosting a crowded table, with Mr. Noah and Grace, with new friends and puppet friends, and Teddy the center of attention for all the younger kids. What could be more hopeful than that?

The People Puppets have not left yet. It seemed unnecessary to make them clear out now that Mr. Noah's medical condition is finally public and Nick and Grace have started the painful process of finding an assisted living facility for him. And besides, it's nice to have the house full of people and dogs, full of talking and laughing and barking, full of life, after so much loss. So for now they're staying in the basement, and Gary and I are staying upstairs.

Instead of giving up my sling for a therapy vest for Charlotte and putting both dogs on leashes, Gary has started wearing Lucy instead. He says it's reduced his anxiety more than any drug he's ever taken — even pot, which he has markedly cut back on out of respect and caution for Teddy. The sling seems to be good for Lucy, helping her process the loss of Glenn and the move to a new home. Nick now wears Moochie, a rat-terrier rescue that I helped him pick out a few days after Spotlight. For what he'll be going through, I knew he'd need a dog to wear, too.

At night, in bed, Gary and I watch the dogs play before they fall asleep on their chew toys, and if we're not too tired we ask each other couple-versions of Sari Epstein's Noble Journey prompts. ("Describe your earliest memory of our relationship." "Tell me three things you miss about who you used to be, and three things you don't miss." "What happened today that you're grateful for?") We are trying to start somewhere. When Teddy comes in to say good night we sometimes manage, while pretending to ignore him, to trick him into telling us something, anything, about his day. We are always shocked and secretly ecstatic when the trick works and he shares a moment, a thought, a snippet of conversation from his life. Maybe he wants it to work. Maybe, like us, he's just a tiny bit happier now, and connecting is starting to feel good again.

I keep a notebook in my sling now. I pretend it's to jot down article ideas for Well/er, but really it's for me. A way to bring myself back from the dead. In the mornings after drop-off, I go to Shepherd for coffee and sit at a table by the window. When I think about Glenn and my parents, gone and missed; about Gary, still struggling but now giving Nick and Teddy bass lessons and practicing for a local club's open mic night; and about Teddy and Nick and Phoebe making dinner from the meal-box delivery service that Gary agreed to order, I open my notebook to a clean page. Sometimes I write or draw something in it and sometimes I don't. But I think *There's a Dog in Your Sling* is a working title that Glenn would like if she were still here. Which of course she kind of still is.

It is almost winter. The days are short and cold and the light is sharp. In the afternoons, and on the weekends, before dark, in a pack of people and dog slings, and with all the birds on our heads, too, we walk the reservoir. We don't know the future. We have no answers about where we will be in a month, or in a year, or in a decade; where the money will come from and how it will all play out; when and if, someday, one of us, Gary or I, will decide to take off the sling of our marriage and leave early. But for now there is safety in numbers. We are holding each other together with love. And for now that is not just enough. It is everything.

ACKNOWLEDGMENTS

Many thanks to close friends, pep talkers, faith keepers, cheerleaders, and early readers: Alice Hoffman, Ann Leary, Julie Klam, Jillian Medoff, Wendy Law-Yone, Paul Fedorko, Beth Teitell, Hilary Ilick, Pamela Painter, Janet Dale, Gesine Bullock-Prado, Katie Rosman, Lori Galvin, Lynn Bikofsky, Brendan Dealy, Ben Dealy, Erin Braddock Pearson, Kimberly Mikesh, Barbara Hall Gordon, Ashley Van Buren, Lisa Takeuchi Cullen, Reagan Arthur, Sandy Pool, Marianne Szegedy-Maszak, Julie Grau, Sue Miller, Joan Wickersham, Zoe Anderson, Donna Apostol Heimlich, Bill Mueller, Laura Rossi, and Rory Evans. I could not have done this again after so long without so much support.

Nor could I have done it without the gift of time and space. Huge thanks to friends who gave me keys to their beautiful and peaceful empty houses and apartments to use as writing retreats: Elisa D'Andrea and Glen Weinstein, Judy and John Bright, Sue Miller and Doug Bauer, and Jennifer Weiner. Thanks also to the Corporation of Yaddo where part of this novel was written.

Extra special thanks to Ivan Held for remaining "undaunted" (his word) and leading me to Stephanie Kipp Rostan at Levine Greenberg Rostan, who then led me to Megan Lynch at Ecco, and to Jill Gillet at WME — who all took a chance on me after so many dormant years. A dream well worth waiting for. Thanks to Ecco's stellar publishing team, including Dan Halpern, Miriam Parker, Sara Birmingham, Meghan Deans, Dale Rohrbaugh, Allison Saltzman, Sonya Cheuse, Rachel Kaplan, Ashlyn Edwards, Shelly Perron, and to Anne Bentley for a fabulous cover illustration. And to Sarah Bedingfield, Elizabeth Fisher, Melissa Rowland, Mick Coccia, and Cristela Henriquez at LGR for all their hard work on my behalf.

My parents didn't live long enough to see it, but they would have loved nothing more than this second chance.

ABOUT THE AUTHOR

Laura Zigman is the author of *Animal Husbandry* (which was made into the movie *Someone Like You,* starring Hugh Jackman and Ashley Judd), *Dating Big Bird, Piece of Work,* and *Her.* She has been a contributor to the *New York Times,* the *Washington Post,* and the Huffington Post, produced a popular online series of animated videos called Annoying Conversations, and was the recipient of a Yaddo residency. She lives in Cambridge, Massachusetts, with her husband, son, and deeply human Sheltie.

The employees of Thorndike Press hope you have enjoyed this Large Print book. All our Thorndike, Wheeler, and Kennebec Large Print titles are designed for easy reading, and all our books are made to last. Other Thorndike Press Large Print books are available at your library, through selected bookstores, or directly from us.

For information about titles, please call:
(800) 223-1244

or visit our website at:
gale.com/thorndike

To share your comments, please write:
Publisher
Thorndike Press
10 Water St., Suite 310
Waterville, ME 04901